Austensibly
Ordinary

Also by Alyssa Goodnight

AUSTENTATIOUS

Austensibly Ordinary

Alyssa Goodnight

KENSINGTON BOOKS
www.kensingtonbooks.com

KENSINGTON BOOKS are published by

Kensington Publishing Corp.
119 West 40th Street
New York, NY 10018

All Kensington titles, imprints, and distributed lines are available at special quantity discounts for bulk purchases for sales promotion, premiums, fund-raising, educational or institutional use.

Special book excerpts or customized printings can also be created to fit specific needs. For details, write or phone the office of the Kensington Special Sales Manager: Kensington Publishing Corp., 119 West 40th Street, New York, NY 10018. Attn. Special Sales Department. Phone: 1-800-221-2647.

ISBN-13: 978-0-7582-6745-0
ISBN-10: 0-7582-6745-2

First Kensington Trade Paperback Printing: February 2013
10 9 8 7 6 5 4 3 2 1

Printed in the United States of America

For the much-sought-after, but mysteriously elusive,
Five Ladies Bakery, who catered a launch
that would have made NASA proud.

And for Janeites everywhere.

ACKNOWLEDGMENTS

For Sophie Jordan and Erin Blakemore, for reading this book on a crazy deadline and saying exactly the right things.

And for Rebecca Strauss, the best possible person to have in your corner.

Chapter 1

"What does it say about me that I'm jealous of the lives of fictional characters?"

I posed the question nonchalantly as I nudged my Scrabble tiles around on the stand.

"Given that you're a high school English teacher, referring to eighteenth- and nineteenth-century British lit, it says you're glamorizing an era before indoor plumbing and takeout," Ethan said in his calm, rational manner. He glanced up at me over the top of his tortoiseshell frames, gauging my reaction, before refocusing his concentration on his own tiles.

I smiled ruefully and supposed in some ways he had a point.

"Besides," he continued, "what do you have to complain about?"

"Not complain, exactly. More lament."

Prefacing his turn with an eye roll and playing off the "T" from my wildly impressive "TRAMP," he neatly laid down all his letters to play "INTRIGUE" on a double-word score, earning him a whopping sixty-eight points to my nine. It was doubtful I could come back from this, particularly given the slew of vowels I'd just drawn, but I tried not to let it bother me. I never won against Ethan. Besides, I didn't need the distraction, being as I was in the middle of my own pity party.

Ethan tallied his score and slid his hand into the bag of remaining tiles. "I'll bite . . . what are you *lamenting?*"

"The reality that I may as well be wearing a tracking anklet, for all the excitement going on in my life. Then again," I said, looking out into the yard at the Bradford pear tree that had stripped down to bare branches, "the FBI would never bother to issue me an anklet because I've ceased to be a 'person of interest.' Literally."

"You either deserve the anklet or you don't, Cate. Pick a side."

I wasn't particularly interested in continuing our Scrabble game, both because I was losing badly and because I was trying to make a point, so I ignored the board—and the fact that it was my turn—and focused on the pita chips I'd "borrowed" from my mom's pantry.

"Fine. I'm lamenting the fact that my life would never make the cut in publishing. I don't have any big moments—no cliffhangers, no happily-ever-after, no thrilling action sequence—just filler."

I crunched a chip loudly, feeling violently frustrated. Yep, that was me: violently frustrated and taking it out on a pita chip. My shoulders slumped.

"This isn't about *Pride and Prejudice* again, is it? Because that book is a menace."

"We've already determined that you, Mr. Chavez, are jealous of Mr. Darcy, so your opinion is moot. Besides, you're well aware that *P and P* isn't on the district reading list this year—this year's graduates are going to go off to college without ever experiencing the wit of Lizzy Bennet and the serious sex appeal of Mr. Darcy." I gazed off into the distance, hamming it up for Ethan's benefit before getting back to business. "They did substitute *Emma,* so at least we know they're not completely uncultured." Willing myself back from the tangent, I grabbed another chip and swiped it through the hummus I'd found in my own refrigerator.

"Are you planning to play your turn?"

I looked up at Ethan, exasperated at his inability to focus.

"Are you here for the Scrabble or the company? Because if

you're just here for the Scrabble, then maybe we should stick with the iPhone app and save ourselves the face-to-face." I knew I was starting to sound snippy, maybe even a little hurt, so I abruptly stopped talking.

Ethan reached for the Corona beer, sweating and forgotten, in front of him and sat back in his chair. He lifted one eyebrow in invitation for me to continue, to talk my heart out.

I stared at him, with his tousled dark hair and weekend stubble, his deep brown eyes worldly wise behind his glasses, and I instantly regretted my snappish words. Scrabble notwithstanding, I would hate it if I missed my Sunday evenings with Ethan. He was the yin to my yang—or more accurately, the squelch to my whine, and I needed that more often than I cared to admit.

I sipped my own beer with its tang of lime, puckered my lips, and prepared to make my point.

"Much as you'd probably hate to admit it, you're living the male version of my life. We both work in a high school—I teach English, you teach French and German. You live alone; I live alone, although admittedly in my mom's backyard. You haven't had a girlfriend for as long as I've known you, and you never talk about the women you're dating. I can't get further with a man than the first Saturday night date because you pick him apart over Scrabble on Sunday. Why I continue to confide in you is beyond me." I stopped, letting that all sink in.

"That's what friends do," he said, taking another pull on his beer and keeping his tone matter-of-fact. "They warn you off unsuitable men. Men have a way of impairing your judgment—I call it the Darcy Effect. Bad manners and mediocre good looks and you think he's a worthy specimen. Turns out he's more like a bug. So I dissect him."

"I'm so glad we're friends."

"If you're looking to change things up a little, friends with benefits would be acceptable to me." He grinned, a boyish, mischievous grin that convinced me he was definitely kidding. Which was a relief. Because that would be weird. So weird.

I needed to meet someone before . . .

I blinked and shook my head slightly, hoping to dislodge that train of thought.

"I need to do something," I finally said, glossing right over his provocative suggestion.

"Dare I suggest finishing the game?" He lifted an eyebrow and tilted his head, indicating my little row of vowels.

"I wouldn't if I were you," I said, sour-sweet.

"Okay, does that mean you'll pay the forfeit? I'm thinking pepperoni pizza."

"Fine. I'll trade you the pizza for an honest answer."

"That's gonna depend on the question."

I speared him with a quizzical stare. "What have you got going on in your life that has you looking so self-satisfied all the time?"

Ethan's mouth hitched up at the corner, putting the smug out on display. "That's pretty personal."

"Interesting comment coming from the man who just suggested we upgrade our Scrabble matches to include benefits."

"I meant pizza," he deadpanned.

"Evidently you're not so much a man of mystery as a man of mystery meats." I shook my head, biting back a smile, and looked away from him out over the darkened yard. Obviously Ethan was keeping his secrets close—assuming he had any that didn't involve hot cheese.

Sitting here under the brightly decorated Japanese lanterns I'd convinced my mom we should string up under the oaks, the possibilities seemed endless, the world glowing—I just needed to hold on to this feeling and find a way to have a little adventure. It couldn't be anything too risqué—one amateur videographer with a camera phone was all it took for things to get very hairy indeed. A good friend of mine had learned that the hard way. I needed a buffer, a way to keep my real, respectable, everyday life separate from a little after-hours adventure.

An alter ego would be perfect . . . sort of a secret identity. I could be the kind of girl who would wear red lipstick and a secret smile and agree to a "friends with benefits" arrangement without batting an eye. Or maybe batting them madly . . .

"Want me to order the pizza?"

My gaze whipped back to Ethan, his face fringed in shadow as he searched his phone for the number of the pizza place. I blinked rapidly, trying to get my thought processes back on track, hoping the darkened twilight hid the flush in my cheeks and the nervous whites of my eyes.

"Knock yourself out," I finally agreed.

As we waited for the pizza and I considered, and discarded, a number of "alternative" options, opportunity e-mailed an invitation.

Derring-Do and Savoir Faire . . .
presented by Pop-up Culture
Join us for an evening inspired by the films of Alfred Hitchcock.
Suspense, my dears, is key, and so the evening's menu must
remain a mystery. . . .
The cast of characters: charismatic men, intriguing women,
and glamorous, grown-up drinks.
When? Sunday, All Hallow's Eve, 9:00 P.M.–midnight
Where? Location to be revealed on confirmed reservation
Entrée? $40, suggested donation
RSVP to this e-mail address by Tuesday, October 26

Chills edged up my arms as I scrolled through each consecutive line. This was *it!* A perfect departure from my bookish, Darcy-obsessed self.

Pop-up Culture was the current business venture of my good friend/bad influence Syd Carmelo and fellow food junkies Olivia Westin and Willow Burke. It was a sort of culinary underground, hosting über-cool, invitation-only "pop-up" events all over the city. Austin was cooler than ever. I'd been on the mailing list from Day One, but had yet to make it to an event—I had either a parent conference, a family commitment . . . or a long-standing Scrabble match. I ended up getting the details with the rest of the city in the paper's Lifestyle section. Halloween was only a week away. And this time, I was going.

Not as myself, though. I was in the mood for a little "mysterious."

Maybe I'd be a Hitchcock blonde . . . with a long, slow smile and a whiff of suggestion. The blond aspect, I had covered. The rest might require a little practice. I hurried to RSVP before I could lose my nerve. Next Sunday . . . I glanced at Ethan, who was randomly arranging tiles on the Scrabble board. Sundays were currently reserved for my "friend sans benefits." I could either ask him to go with me or I could strike out on my own. Chances were we'd be done with Scrabble in plenty of time for me to transform myself into a blond bombshell.

I'd started to type in my RSVP, single lady attending, when car doors slammed in the front yard, signaling that the pizza had arrived. Pocketing my phone, I grinned to myself, smirked in Ethan's direction, and nearly skipped through the gate at the side of the house. Only to stumble across my mother, holding a large white pizza box up over her head.

"Mom!" I glanced at the pizza dude, collapsing back into his tiny car, counting the bills in his hands.

"Hi," she said, dodging carefully around me. "I took a chance—thought maybe if I sprung for the pizza you'd let me share."

"Sure," I agreed, trailing along behind her. "Where have you been?" Somewhere casual, I assumed, judging by the charcoal gray track pants and raspberry polar fleece pullover she was wearing.

"Just out," she answered, vaguely waving her free hand, seeming to encompass all the options the city had to offer for an active fiftysomething.

"Hello, Ms. Kendall," Ethan said, politely rising to his feet while surreptitiously eyeing the pizza box currently being held out of reach. He'd been a quick study, cluing in early on to the whole "recently divorced, taking my life back" attitude my mom was projecting. As far as he was concerned, "anything goes" was a bit of a watchword when it came to my mom.

My mother smiled at him. "Final score?"

Ethan glanced over at me, leaving me to answer.

"He's waiting for you to relinquish the price of my forfeit," I confessed, not even the slightest bit embarrassed. "Mom paid, so you're going to have to share," I informed him.

"Okay if we rough it and eat straight from the box?" he said, hurriedly gathering up the Scrabble board to make room for the pizza box in the center of the table. "I'm starving."

"A picnic under the stars—lovely," said my mother, smiling approvingly at Ethan before turning to me to flash the twinkle in her eye. "I'm not interrupting anything, am I?"

Honestly, I think my mom would be thrilled if I answered Ethan's teasing booty call.

The next ten minutes were blissfully quiet as we devoured gigantic greasy triangles of pizza with single-minded determination. I noticed a few bats winging gracefully overhead, but otherwise I was distracted by the opportunity burning a hole in my pocket. Suddenly I worried that a flood of people would jump at the chance to attend a Hitchcock-inspired party and edge me out with their quick-fingered RSVPs.

"Anyone need anything from the kitchen?" I yelped, standing suddenly, my legs pushing my chair away from the table. "Napkins have become necessary."

The pair of them eyed me quizzically, but declined my offer. But as I neared the French doors leading into my mom's kitchen, she called out, "Cate, I've changed my mind. Will you pour me a glass of the Cabernet on the counter?"

"Got it," I said, stepping into the dim kitchen. The desk light in the corner was on, pooling a warm glow, and preferring to keep my little secret from the pair outside, I decided to make do without additional lighting. It seemed irrational, but I couldn't help it; I wanted this one little secret for myself. My life wasn't just an open book with these two, it was an interactive free-for-all. Mom had been running interference in my life long before Dad and

Gemma had left two years ago, within three weeks of each other, leaving us only to breathe an anticlimactic sigh of relief.

Gemma was sixteen months older than me and had long, wavy auburn hair—twins we were not, but we'd had a whole *Parent Trap* dynamic going since early childhood. Photos scattered around the house told the story and hinted at the inevitable ending. Gemma always posed beside my father, in his lap, or on his shoulders. I, on the other hand, was my mom's shadow. Gemma and Dad were outgoing, outdoorsy, take-a-chance, make-it-happen types, while Mom and I were crafty, bookish rule followers, taking it on faith that magic would happen precisely when it was meant to, a personality type crafted initially by fairy tales and honed by Jane Austen.

Starting her third year of grad school in North Carolina, Gemma came home as school holidays allowed. Dad was happily entrenched in his new life as owner of a Texas Hill Country zip-line outfit, and despite being only a quick day-trip away, we rarely saw him. As for Ethan, the pair of us had hit it off around the same two-year mark, glommed onto each other, and hung like sticker burrs . . . impossible to shake. And I didn't want to shake him . . . him or my mom. I just wanted something of my own. I wanted a secret. A little desperately.

I quickly gathered up the napkins and pulled a favored wineglass down from the kitchen's open shelving. Then, with my back to the door, I made a slow effort of pouring the wine and cleaning up an imaginary spill—just in case anyone was watching. With my free hand, I texted my RSVP and credit card number and felt the thrill of derring-do ricochet through my veins.

I returned to the table, barely able to suppress a scary sort of smile—the sort where it's obvious you're hiding something particularly juicy. This subtle sneaking around felt good—liberating—but I couldn't very well flaunt it unless I wanted to risk Ethan anteing up his two cents. I was über-conscious of their mildly curious gazes, but I stayed focused on my pizza and beer until a text came in, instantly disrupting my carefully arranged calm. I hurried to pull the phone from my pocket, my blood pounding crazily through my veins, as I urgently wondered if I'd been too late.

I hadn't. Syd was simply as psyched as I was.

So thrilled you rsvp'd! Finally! Going to be awesome! Expect a call. . . .

I smiled down at the screen, my pulse slowly returning to normal, and casually sipped my beer.

Judging by the banked look in Ethan's eyes, he could tell something was up. He no doubt assumed that it was my mother's presence that kept me from blurting my secrets.

"Do you two have any plans for the evening?" my mom quizzed, staring intently at Ethan.

Mom had been gunning for Ethan ever since I'd brought him home for our first Scrabble game a year and a half ago. She assumed that eventually one of us would realize that this thing between us could be so much more than a little word game with beer. As a romance reader, she couldn't help it—he was perfect hero material. Charismatic, clever . . . debatably sexy—it had, in fact, *been* debated, with Mom talking up his finer points and me la-la-la'ing my way through.

Ethan and I caught each other's eye, simultaneously shook our heads in one quick negative, and let our gazes swivel away again.

"I've actually got a few errands to run before tomorrow. Not to mention a little work to catch up on." He stood, eyed the pizza box splayed open on the table, and looked to me with a question in his eyes.

"I got it," I told him. "Seeing as I didn't buy the pizza, I'll pay the forfeit in cleanup. Sorry to rob you of another Scrabble trouncing."

"It had its benefits," he said, winking.

I glanced at my mom, hoping she wasn't picking up on any of this.

"Thank you for dinner, Ms. Kendall. See you at school, Cate."

And then he disappeared into the shadows at the edge of the house. Minutes later, all car sounds had faded and Mom and I were alone in the dark.

"Does he have a girlfriend?"

"No, and neither do I."

Mom's laser stare bored into me. I may as well have been splayed out on the table like James Bond.

"Kidding, Mom. But Ethan is just a friend."

"He could be a friend with benefits. . . ."

I turned the laser back on her, wondering for a moment if she'd been eavesdropping earlier and merely glossed over it by paying the pizza guy.

"Where did you say you were today, Mom?" I countered.

She clammed up immediately, which, while slightly suspicious, was just fine with me at this point.

"Do you have time this week to come in after school and help me decorate the store? I'd like to get the Halloween stuff up by Thursday at the latest."

Mom owned a vintage clothing and jewelry store down on South Congress called Mirror, Mirror. It irked her that fall retail tended to be one big blur of holidays, so she determinedly decorated for just a few days surrounding every holiday. I was always conscripted to help with window displays and ladder-top duties. Halloween, as I was now well aware thanks to my invitation to a Hitchcock soiree, was only one week away.

And I needed something to wear.

I mentally rummaged through my closet, trying to think if I had anything at all with a Hitchcock blonde vibe, and I couldn't come up with any hits. I'd have to cross my fingers that there was something in the shop I could borrow—something that wouldn't raise questions I didn't particularly want to answer. I hadn't decided quite how to play this. Spies and superheroes didn't go around outing themselves, confiding their secret identities and handing out invitations to their secret lairs. Except maybe to a sidekick.

I hadn't really considered a sidekick. Ideally there'd be one trusty soul who had my back and could save me from the laser table. But seeing as this was just a little role-playing experiment, I really didn't need a sidekick. At least not yet.

"I can do that," I agreed, flashing back to reality. "I'll come by after school, but it might not be until Thursday—this week's busy." I stood and started gathering up the bottles for recycling. "I'll get this, Mom, and then I'm going to bed."

My cell phone chirped. I glanced at the display and then took my time answering once Mom and her wineglass had moved out of earshot.

"Hey, Syd," I said, closing the pizza box filled with crusts and wadded napkins.

"Hot damn! You're coming to my Hitchcock party!"

Here, finally, was someone who could share my secret. A smile quirked my lips as I finished clearing up. "You can bet I'll be renting *North by Northwest* this week—for research purposes."

"Wait, are you coming as a character?" Judging by the thrill in her voice, this was more than she could get her head around.

I flipped the switch for the lanterns, now bobbing gently in the breeze, and crossed the yard to the garage and the steps up to my apartment. "I'm shooting for seductive spy girl Eve Kendall from *North by Northwest,*" I said, having decided just moments ago myself. "And I'm coming alone, so you can bet I'll be looking for a Cary Grant sort to finish out the picture."

"Um, sweetie, if we get any men of the Cary Grant persuasion, your competition will be fierce. But good for you—way to ratchet up the sexy! Will, Oli, and I are going dressed as cat burglars à la *To Catch a Thief.* Sorta . . . ninja-sexy."

"I need something that will stamp out the 'schoolteacher by day' vibe coming off me in waves. I'm planning to visit the shop this week, so hopefully I'll find something perfect in my size." Letting myself into my little apartment, I leaned backward against the door, dropped the Scrabble box on the hall table, and scanned the room's potential as a superhero/spy lair—the sunflower yellow bowl of Dum-Dum lollipops on the coffee table was way too Doris Day. Although, come to think of it, she'd been a Hitchcock blonde. . . .

"You just need to get your blond on, and you're gonna rock this party."

My understanding of the logistics involved in that suggestion was a little vague, but as a little fizz of encouragement, it was awesome. Trouble was, with a week to second-guess myself, I couldn't vouch for my confidence next Sunday night.

"It'll definitely be an adventure," I agreed.

It was about damn time.

Chapter 2

Mirror, Mirror was in SoCo, on the edge of downtown. Mom had scored a trim little space that saw a lot of walking traffic and pulled in a mix of loyal customers and curiosity seekers. Parking was a bit of a bitch, though.

As I drove past the Trailer Park & Eatery just before the bridge over Lady Bird Lake on Thursday afternoon, I longed to detour straight to the order window of Torchy's Tacos. My stomach was already rumbling, and I was in the mood for a little spicy heat, not to mention a beer. Later. I'd told Ethan I'd meet him there at six.

After circling the block three times in search of a parking space, I was doubly in the mood for a beer. And judging from my walk up the sidewalk, it was clear that Mom had been content to wait for me before getting started. The shop window displays still held the familiar Fall Frolic montage I'd helped create a couple of weeks ago. Mannequins with sweet painted faces were layered with fun pieces in rich autumn shades of mustard, plum, olive, ruby, and slate blue. Bare tree branches were suspended from above with piano wire, hosting the curvy little birds we'd found at the craft store. In a couple of hours, the scene would be updated with Halloween colors and simple iconic shapes.

I loved Halloween. In Texas, where the heat hung on until mid to late October, Halloween was the official kick-off of fall, a mini-season bookended by festivities, with Thanksgiving on the tail end. Costumes and masquerades were Austin's bread and butter—everyone wanted to be something they weren't.

I know I did. What I clearly *didn't* know was how to deal with the obsession. Other than keeping secrets and second-guessing myself.

I gazed at my reflection in the shop windows, remembering the moments just before the bell rang for my last class of the day.

"Why do you suppose Emma Woodhouse, the belle of Highbury, decided to befriend the common little nobody, Harriet Smith?" I'd posed the question in a rather distracted state.

I stood at the front of the classroom, propped on the edge of my desk, gazing at them from behind black lacquer frames—my "teaching glasses." Suddenly self-conscious in front of all those staring senior eyes, I crossed my arms over my chest, marking my place in my own personal copy of *Emma*. I tipped my head down, seemingly absorbed in the world of Jane Austen, but actually assessing my outfit. Taupe menswear trousers, sea green ruffly blouse, and teal suede flats. Cary Grant wouldn't even give me a second look.

I looked back up at the class, startled to see a few hands had gone up during my "lost moments."

"Yes, Jordan?"

"She was trying to be charitable?"

"Perhaps," I allowed. "But I'm not sure I believe that."

"Alex?"

"She was bored." He sounded as if he could relate. I commiserated, but only slightly. *Emma* may be, at its heart, a romance, but it is so much more than that. I'd even convinced Ethan to read it and then grudgingly admit that he'd enjoyed it—at least parts of it.

"Excellent. Why do you suppose that was?" I fiddled with the ruby glass crystal that hung from a gold chain around my neck, imagining pencil skirts and push-up bras. And heels—definitely heels. Killer heels.

Alex assumed he still had the floor and answered quickly, almost defiantly. "She was stuck with her father at Hartfield after Miss Taylor left, and teatime and archery just weren't doing it for her."

I blinked at him, then narrowed my eyes slightly. I was relatively certain that Austen hadn't mentioned archery in the text, but it had definitely featured in the Gwyneth Paltrow movie adaption of the book.

"Very insightful," I congratulated with a wry twist of my lips. "She needed a hobby . . . and decided to choose vicarious romance since *movies* weren't an option." I stared hard at Alex, but couldn't detect even the slightest admission of guilt. "She didn't need to marry—she was already rich. And other *options* . . ." I tipped my head to the side, willing them to follow the words I wasn't saying, "weren't available in the early nineteenth century." They weren't exactly lining up for me in Weird City either.

The bell rang and I quickly outlined the homework. We'd continue our discussion of *Emma* tomorrow, and I'd find a way to out Alex for choosing the movie over the book.

I was in a hurry to get to Mirror, Mirror and start scrounging for a dress to vamp me up a bit, but I needed to find Ethan before I left.

I found him in The Cave, the tiny room allotted for the school's IT guru. Ethan taught French for three periods, German for two, and he filled one as our IT guy, fixer of all things PC.

"Hey, Chavez!" I called, hefting my leather tote, crammed with term papers, up higher on my shoulder. "You winning?"

He lifted his gaze a couple of inches and met mine. When he'd taken the job of IT guru, he'd rearranged the entire room to allow him to face the door, with a table of computers and network paraphernalia in between. His explanation? He doesn't like people sneaking up on him. Mine? He's a gamer with a lithe, feminine avatar, and the new desk orientation gives him time to destroy the evidence should anyone swing by for a visit. It's mostly facetious—I've never caught him in the act, and Ethan doesn't strike me as a gamer. But he definitely has secrets—this could very well be one of them.

"Kendall?"

I tilted my head to the right, wanting to see more of him than a disembodied head sitting atop a computer monitor. From the waist up he was wearing a collared shirt under a deep red cranberry sweater. He looked cute . . . sexy, even. I shifted back, suddenly preferring the disembodied head. Evidently I had a very impressionable mind—one completely irrational suggestion, and I couldn't help but imagine the what-ifs.

"Could you run some diagnostics or a virus scan—anything really—on my computer and see if you can find out why I'm not getting my e-mails? I had two voice mails today from parents asking if I'd gotten their e-mails, really hinting that I should have replied by now." I hoisted my bag farther up on my shoulder.

"You leaving?" He glanced at his watch.

"I promised Mom I'd help her with the Halloween decorations at the shop." And I needed to find a dress that would make me into a femme fatale. My thoughts buzzed with the reminder.

"Sure. I can do it after I finish up in here."

"What are you doing in here?" I asked coyly, tipping myself away from the door frame and slowly sauntering around the blockade.

I saw Ethan's finger flicker over the mouse and knew I didn't have a prayer, but I looked anyway. A puzzle with a picture of three gray kittens. Upon further inspection, it became evident that it was the AARP daily puzzle and there were only a few more pieces left to place. I turned away from the screen to stare at him.

"This is your cover? Granny puzzles? What's your screen saver? Teddy bears?"

He fought it, but eventually Ethan's grin was so wide that his dimple popped out. "I'll get your e-mail working, chica. Just as soon as the kitty gets her whiskers."

Thoroughly provoked, I swung back around the desk and headed out the door. "Don't mess with my desktop, Chavez. Physical or computer."

"You're killing me, Kendall." I glanced back, and his face looked pained.

I chuckled to myself, picturing the shirtless hardbody who now posed on my computer wallpaper. I'd switched it out on my free period, just for his benefit. Then there was the action-figure brawl playing out on my desk, with Jane Austen ninja-kicking Charles Dickens, and Shakespeare waiting his turn. Ethan was going to love that.

"Fine. Show me what you were just working on—kitties don't count—and you can have your organizational way with my desktops—both of them."

A beat of silence passed between us, and then Ethan had the grace to grin. "Your mess is safe with me, fräulein."

I nodded, content, but with the vaguely itchy feeling that he'd won. In other words, very Tina Fey.

The reflection of a car pulling out of the street parking space right behind me caught my attention. Well, damn! Three minutes' more banter with Ethan and that spot would have been mine.

In the middle of my frustrated growl, I had a vision for the November display. Paper-wrapped books! We could sit the mannequins on stacks of them, and even buy a bunch of cheapies from a garage sale and cut out or curl the pages into decorative designs. Maybe go for a sexy librarian look.

I smiled to myself. Hmm . . . sexy librarian . . . or high school teacher by day, foxy rogue by night.

I was grinning when I pulled open the shop door.

"Mom," I called. "I already have an idea for November's windows," I said.

"If it involves turkeys or pumpkins, I don't want to know," she grumped from behind the counter. Her laptop was open in front of her on the antique hotel desk she'd snapped up at the Round Top flea market.

"It doesn't," I said, stuffing my purse under the counter and looking at her askance. "Should I assume Halloween will be pumpkin-less too?"

"I'm skipping the orange this year, decorating in black and emerald green," she said defiantly, evidently expecting me to object.

"Look at you, Mom! Boycotting the official color of Halloween in a college town that fawns over its burnt orange!" I smiled, admiring her spunk. I glanced around. "Do I have carte blanche, or are you giving me directions?"

"Go crazy," she offered. "Everything is on the storeroom table."

"Everything" included a sparkly layer of glitter and a shimmering scatter of sequins and rhinestones. Mom had apparently gotten very crafty, cutting out frogs and witches' hats and bedazzling them with a vengeance. Too bad we weren't decorating for Valentine's Day. A little pucker and some glitzy crowns and these little guys could be frog princes. I smiled ruefully. Until Ethan squished them under his car tire. But heck, frogs got their holiday start at Halloween . . . I could make this work. I could cut some skinny ribbon curls and make them into extended frog tongues. Add a few Mardi Gras beads for shimmer and some black and green tissue paper for flair, and I'd be off the hook till the next holiday window display. There were even a couple of black masquerade masks—I could slip these on the mannequins to add a touch of flirtiness.

But first, I'd need to browse the shop for a little Halloween inspiration. There were two mannequins in the front window—I'd outfit them first and keep an eye out for something worthy of a Hitchcock blonde while I was at it.

I tucked a couple of stray curls behind my ear, wishing I'd bought the dainty jeweled headband I'd recently hearted on Etsy. Although maybe I should be looking at vintage cat's-eye glasses instead and practicing twisting my hair into a tasteful chignon that could tumble down with the tug of a single bobby pin. . . . I shook my head to refocus and had to deal with those curls all over again. Having my hair in my eyes for the duration of this project was going to be irritating. On my way out of the storeroom, my hip accidentally bumped the pile of decorations hanging off the edge of the table and sent a flurry of frogs spiraling away behind me. As I turned, bending down to collect the escapees, my gaze caught on a shimmer of midnight blue flirting from beneath a plastic dry-cleaning bag.

I inched forward on my knees, too excited to worry over the risks to my trousers, and, using both hands, slowly raised the bag to expose more of that gorgeous, lustrous skirt.

"What on earth are you doing?"

A zip of shock tore up my spine, and I whipped my head around, caught in the incriminating—not to mention embarrassing—position of having my hands snaked up inside the plastic wrap, very nearly hugging this seemingly irresistible dress, my fingers skimming over the sexy sheen of brocade. And I wasn't letting go.

"Nothing." I attempted nonchalance, but my mother was no fool. "Just getting a quick preview of the new stock."

Her expression shifted. Suspicion fell away, replaced by unreserved delight. "Those just came in yesterday. I thought maybe—"

"Can I have this one??" I blurted, nearly as surprised with myself as she was. The bodice of the dress was still sight unseen. I was making a fool of myself over a pretty skirt and a feeling. I don't know how I knew it, but I did. This was the dress I needed to stoke my inner femme fatale and launch my alter ego.

A curl escaped its confinement behind my ear and fell over my left eye. Desperate to hang on to the dress, I huffed out a retaliatory breath, willing it to back off. It didn't.

My mom looked at me quizzically. "Have you even seen the whole dress?"

"Um, no. I just know I want it."

The look she gave me confirmed that I sounded as ridiculous as I looked, kneeling before a mostly obscured, plastic-wrapped dress with an I'm-not-worthy attitude.

She stepped forward, stared down at me until, resigned, I unhanded the dress and scooted back on my knees. As she pulled the relevant hanger off the wardrobe rack and proceeded to unveil the rest of the dress, I stood up and tried to regain my composure, distractedly dusting off the front of my trousers.

The top was just as lust-worthy as the bottom. There was a fitted, strapless satin bodice with lingerie stitching, a wide patent leather belt, and a flirty transparent chiffon wrap that tied in the front, all of it deep, dark, lustrous midnight blue. It was perfect. I had no trouble imagining the cool and composed Eve Kendall from *North by Northwest* sashaying through train cars in this stream-lined number.

She'd always been my favorite Hitchcock blonde. Partly because we shared the same last name; partly because she was sensi-ble and savvy, not to mention sexy enough to end up with Cary Grant.

I stared at the dress and smiled. All that was left was to wonder whether I could fit into it and fill it out. And whether my mother would let me have it.

I turned to look at her, certain there was desperation in my eyes. "So, can I have it, Mom? I'll buy it from you."

Her eyebrow went up and she eyed the dress she was still holding.

"I plan to invoke the 'Thou shall not make a killing off your daughter' commandment."

"Huh. I hadn't heard of that one."

"It's lesser known." I was twitching, my eyes moving back and forth between the dress and my mom. I definitely wasn't playing it cool. Closing my eyes, I took a slow breath. Opening them again, I tried to keep the pleading desperation carefully banked.

"You can have it. But I want to know where you're going in it. A date? With Ethan?"

"No, Mom, not a date per se, and not with Ethan. Just a Hal-loween party—one of Syd's things. It's sort of a costume party. I'm going old-fashioned."

"Okay, well, it's yours. Consider it my contribution to the Cate Kendall Happily-Ever-After Fund."

Nice. "Thanks, Mom. Okay, I'm just going to leave this back here and get busy on the shop. Is Dmitri working today?" Mom considered Dmitri one of her best finds. He was a fashion major at UT who could turn a canvas tote bag and a skein of yarn into something wonderful. Mom already had him on borrowed time.

"It's Thursday. He teaches Pilates at that men's spa. You'll be on your own—at least for a little while—the computer guy is coming."

"What computer guy?"

"The Nerd Squad or the Geek Freak . . . something." She moved to a little vanity table she kept in the corner and used occasionally as a desk. As I watched, she pulled out her powder compact and a lipstick and touched everything up.

"Uh-huh." If I thought it odd that she felt compelled to refresh her makeup for the Geek Freak, I didn't mention it. I chose to make my escape riding the high of mom's largesse. And nearly barreled into someone barging in.

"Cate?" A familiar blonde blocked the door to the storeroom.

"Hey, Court!" I leaned in for a quick hug and got thumped hard on the back.

"Sorry!" She grimaced and held up the one-pound bag of Brach's Autumn Mix in explanation, and my eyes glazed over. Courtney and I shared so much good taste.

I'd been her devoted fan since the minute I discovered she carried candy in her bag. Not Altoids—that was for amateurs. This chick packed the good stuff. For pity parties she had European chocolate bars; for gossip fests, she brought Hot Tamales; and for all-night study sessions, it was licorice. I held up the bag of candy corn and Mellowcreme pumpkins.

"Significance?"

"It's Halloween!" She glanced at me askance, clearly baffled by my ignorance. I didn't even bother to explain.

"What are you doing here?" I asked instead, wondering if it was too soon to bust open the bag of candy.

"I need clothes! One of the law firms is hosting a costume party at the Driskill with a Roaring Twenties theme. I was hoping your mom had something perfect for the occasion." As the event coordinator for the Driskill Hotel in downtown Austin, Courtney was able to seamlessly mesh her two interests: party planning and ghost stories. The Driskill was certifiably haunted, with the history to prove it, but much to her chagrin and utter frustration, Courtney had yet to see a ghost.

"Hello, Courtney," Mom said, leaning in for a cheek press and a squeeze. No doubt Courtney had gotten a whiff of Cover Girl pressed powder. Luckily Mom hadn't bussed her cheek, or it would have been necessary for her to refresh her lipstick all over again. For the Geek Freak. "I'm sure there's something here that would be perfect for your party—just look around. I'll make you a deal," she offered with a wink and a smile.

When Mom was gone, I couldn't wait any longer and ripped a hole in the bag of Autumn Mix. I reached for an orange pumpkin and sank my teeth into the sugar rush. "I'm here for a dress too," I confided. "For Syd's Hitchcock event on Halloween!"

"Ooh! I wanted to go to that, and would have too, if not for this party. Which reminds me, I need to find a date."

"You don't have to work the party?"

She reached for a candy corn with a chocolate bottom. "Don't think so. At least not too much. The catering company is completely professional—I've worked with them in the past and been very impressed. Shouldn't be any heavy lifting."

I nodded. "What about Ethan?"

"*Your* Ethan?" She shot me a look of baffled disbelief.

"What do you mean, *my* Ethan? We're not together, nor have we ever been," I reminded her. I reached for a classic candy corn and popped it in my mouth. "We're not compatible like that."

"Uh-huh."

"He and I would never work," I insisted. "Too many quirks. Besides, he's too bossy," I finished, grabbing a handful from the bag and offering Courtney the chocolate corn. "But I am meeting him for dinner at Torchy's at six. Why don't you come? Scope out his potential. I think he could pull off a little Eliot Ness. . . ."

She stared at me for a long moment and finally said, "Okay, I'm game—for Torchy's, not for Mr. Ness just yet. It's been a while since I've seen Ethan, and I need to reassess."

"Fair enough."

Setting the bag of candy corn down on the table and sparing a glance for the rack that held my dress and the secrets of a few other dry-cleaning bags, I grabbed this year's decorating supplies and nudged Courtney out of the storeroom and back into the shop.

Courtney and I browsed the racks for clothes that could be transformed into flapper couture, and any she rejected, I pulled for the display.

"So what's going on with you?" she asked, draping a low-cut, feather-edged, ruby silk number over herself and sizing up its potential.

I thought of my recent, inspired decision to introduce my budding alter ego to a little corner of Austin and elected to fill her in. I bit my lip and swiveled my head to make sure Mom was still hunched over the counter in eager cahoots with the Geek Freak before confiding my big news.

"I'm planning a little masquerade."

Courtney shot me a quizzical look, waiting for the details.

"I'm going to Syd's Hitchcock soiree, but not as myself."

Courtney's gaze bounced up from the dress she was holding and her shoulders slumped in exasperated confusion. "I'm not getting any of this."

I grinned, relishing this moment, thrilled to be sharing my pseudo secret. "Think alter ego. I'm still working out the details."

"Wait, what?" Swiveling toward me, she lost her balance and fell sideways against a rack of clothing. We tussled for a moment to get her back upright. As it was, her hair got caught on some metallic military detailing on a black blazer.

"Basically I'm going as a modern-day femme fatale."

Courtney blinked exactly four times before she came up with "Huh."

My confidence faltered, just a little bit, in the face of my best friend's dubious stare.

"What? You don't think I can bring it?" I lifted an eyebrow and waited, an insecure wimp behind all the bravado.

Three beats of silence and she was singing like a canary.

"The idea of you as a femme fatale just doesn't click in my mind. You're so not that girl, Cate. You're a wholesome schoolteacher! You believe in happily-ever-afters, not . . . sexual conquests. You accessorize with your heart on your sleeve and an artless smile, not so much a mink stole and a revolver." Her smile, when she finally aimed it in my direction, was rueful. "Just sayin' . . ."

"You do realize that one night as a Hitchcock blonde won't tarnish my reputation. In the morning I'll still be a card-carrying 'good girl.'"

"Hmm. I suppose that's true." Courtney bit her lip, still considering.

"Think Eve Kendall in *North by Northwest*," I said, anxious that she get the sort of personality I was going for here. I wanted someone to assure me that as ideas went, this one was a zinger.

Courtney narrowed her eyes, I assume remembering the curvy, no-nonsense spy girl who was savvy enough to keep her head when alternately faced with murderous foreign spies and a flirty Cary Grant in her train compartment.

Courtney's words, when they came, quickly squelched my optimism. "It's just that you're so darn cute. When I look at you, it's not glamour I'm seeing—or even moxie. I see Hayley Mills in *The Parent Trap*. Ever since we met I've been waiting for you to break into a musical number."

"Well, you can bet I'm not going to ask you to help me get rid of the body I have stashed in the trunk of my car," I said, twisting the watch on my wrist in vague irritation. "I'm going for glamour and mystery, not bitch with issues, and I think I can pull it off. It's kind of like a dare."

"Who dared you?"

"I did." I shuttered my eyes closed, trying to imagine this conversation from her point of view. No doubt I sounded like a whack-job.

"Gotcha."

"I just need a little somethin' somethin'. My life is way too tame right now."

"Maybe you should talk to Ethan," she said pointedly, turning back to the rack.

"I don't imagine he'd be at all encouraging," I said.

"Oh, I think you'd be surprised," she said, a smug little smile playing around her lips. "Just remember, I had a little somethin' somethin' too, and it turned into a whole lotta hell."

"I remember, sweetie." It was hard to forget—the silver-tongued, adorably dimpled little shit who had turned Courtney's world upside down had left a lasting reminder that still occasionally surfaced on YouTube.

Deciding it was best to drop the subject for now, I left Courtney to the dressing room and got busy with my afternoon project, relieved to have already found the perfect dress and sweet-talked Mom without having to come completely clean.

Moving back and forth through the shop, I passed the counter often and caught little snatches of Mom's curious chat with Geek Freak Brady. I had to assume that my position in the window created some sort of acoustic anomaly, because it sounded suspiciously like she was flirting with the guy.

Once I had the mannequins outfitted in ruffly georgette tank dresses, layered necklaces, and black tissue-paper turbans glammed up with sprays of cut-out bats and some sparkle, I posed them, palms up. I placed the newly 3-D frogs in their hands, attached the other ends of the ribbon tongues to the mannequin cheeks, and stepped back. I needed more color. Sparkly green tissue-paper scarves, anyone?

Brady was just packing up his things as I moved past the counter on my way into the storeroom for more supplies.

"This is your personal line?" Mom was saying, eyeing his business card.

I shot a curious look in her direction, wondering why she was teasing the poor kid. Her voice had taken on a throaty, husky quality, and from the looks of him, his voice was changing too. Seeing him push his glasses up on his nose put me in mind of Clark Kent, and I gave him a closer look from the storeroom doorway, suddenly wondering if I had cause to be jealous.

"Yes, ma'am," he told my mom, zipping up his attaché case.

"Allison," she corrected. "I suspect I'll be calling you."

I was surprised she didn't tuck the card inside her bra.

"Anytime . . . Allison. Whatever it is, I'll work out the kinks."

Ducking back through the doorway and out of sight, I barely stifled a fit of giggles. If this was Superman, then I was Marlene Dietrich.

Eager to stay away from the counter while Mom was making time with the computer guy, I took my time gathering up supplies. And my gaze strayed once again to the rack of new arrivals, the source of my new dress. With Courtney closeted in the dressing room with countless outfits and accessories and Mom oddly occupied, I was on my own—and eager for a peek at what was hiding under the other dry-cleaning bags. I checked my watch—still forty-five minutes till we needed to meet Ethan. Plenty of time to finish up the displays after a quick little reconnaissance mission.

I beelined and riffled through the plastic on the first bag to uncover a sweet little dress of gray linen with a pleated bodice, layered cap sleeves, and flap pockets under a banded waistline. It didn't exactly scream femme fatale, more efficient, albeit stylish, secretary—or English teacher. I held it up in front of me, my mind skimming through possibilities. Paired with some sexy pumps, a cleavage-dipping pendant, and some Lolita-red lipstick, it could be perfect—very *Mad Men*. As a disguise, it wouldn't fool anyone, but it would get me in the mood for a little scandalous behavior.

I unhooked the next in line and realized my luck couldn't run forever. I could see enough through the transparent wrapping to tell that this one was a bit dowdy. Taupe and cream, it was a slim skirt and crossover blouse. It screamed society matron, but I felt compelled to take a quick peek. I was rather impressed to discover the blouse was both sleeveless and backless! Add a chunky choker and a cuff bracelet, and it was deliciously Grace Kelly gone vixen. I glimpsed a firecracker red something in the back when Mom breezed through the door, humming to herself.

We both started in surprise.

"Mrs. Robinson," I said, with a nod and a smirk.

She ignored that, eyeing my handful. "What are you doing back here? I thought you were thrilled with the blue dress."

"I am," I admitted, hooking the red mystery back on the rack, "but this new shipment is making me greedy. I've got the gimmes for all of them. It doesn't even matter that I haven't looked at some of them, never mind tried them on. I *crave* them."

"Lord." She rolled her eyes to spell out her opinion on my lunatic behavior, but then caved. "Take them home, try them on, get it out of your system. Sometimes a girl just needs to play dress-up."

"And sometimes a girl just needs to flirt with a Geek Freak," I teased, giving her a hug. It was clear Mom needed a date. If I gave it a few minutes' thought, I could probably come up with someone suitable—someone to keep Mrs. Robinson in check. I wasn't talking about sex—*good God, no*—I didn't want to walk in on anything on my way to borrow the guacamole, just a companion—someone to play Scrabble with, minus the benefits.

When Dad had left his orderly life of ones and zeros in the semiconductor sector for a chance to give canopy tours in the Hill Country, Mom had filled his absence with Mirror, Mirror, *Burn Notice*, and Zumba dancing at the local YMCA. She was an active woman with a great figure, a business in the heart of Austin Weird, and a lot to offer. The right man could be great for her. Maybe I'd ask Gemma to weigh in. . . .Then again, Ethan was closer, geographically speaking, and he probably already had an opinion on the matter. I shook my head, desperate to clear it. Right now, I was too distracted with my own issues; Mom's romance was going to have to wait. In fact, I needed to get busy and finish up the decorations. Candy corn could tide me over for only so long. Besides, I wanted to see if Courtney and Ethan could play nice together.

Chapter 3

"How do you feel about Eliot Ness?"

I'd snuck up behind Ethan as he stood perusing the Torchy's menu to pose the question.

He didn't even turn around.

"Relatively unaffected. Is this your way of announcing another ill-advised crush? Seeing as he lived in twentieth-century America and not fictional eighteenth-century Britain, I'd say definite improvement. You'll get there."

I elbowed him in the side. "I do not have a crush on Eliot Ness. But I kinda told Courtney that you might be her date for a 1920s-themed Halloween party at the Driskill."

Now he turned around. I cringed ever so slightly under his blistering stare.

"Is this about you not having a full-access pass to my life? Finding a back door? Setting me up with a friend of yours with intent to snoop?" With his arms crossed over his chest, he definitely looked mad—and a little intimidating.

"Get over yourself, Chavez. If you want to keep secrets, keep 'em!" I kicked at the gravel and heard a rock ping against the metal trailer. "Courtney needed a date for her event, and you haven't mentioned any Halloween plans, so I merely suggested you might be an option. Nobody's locked in. You have time to make up an excuse before she gets here, let her down easy."

"What do you mean, 'before she gets here'?" His eyebrow winged up in disbelief.

Justifiably on the defensive, I fired back, "I invited her. She was at the shop, and I graciously included her in our plan to eat chips and salsa at picnic tables in a parking lot. If, however," I continued, "that's too much of an imposition, we'll be happy to sit at a separate table. You could use the space for your ego."

Ethan snorted, looked out over the darkening city skyline, his lips twitching alternately in frustration and amusement, and then turned back to gaze at my stubborn expression.

"No, I insist that the two of you sit at my picnic table. Drinks on me."

I smiled, relieved. I didn't like to fight with Ethan—it rocked my world—nothing seemed right when he and I were at odds. Luckily, it didn't happen often.

"You're one of the good guys, Chavez," I said, nudging into him, haphazardly scanning the menu.

"And you, Kendall, are transparently fickle." He elbowed me back. "In the interest of staving off all other setups, you should know that I have plans for Halloween. Eliot Ness will have to find another reincarnation."

My little bubble of contentment popped audibly, and I yanked my gaze away from the taco trailer to home in on Ethan all over again. "You have plans? Why didn't you tell me you had plans? What are they?"

"He's coppin' out on Eliot Ness, isn't he?" said a chipper voice from behind us.

We both swiveled and stared at a grinning Courtney. "No big deal," she assured us. "If I don't find a date, I'll go alone and on the prowl." She winked and shifted her attention to the taco menu, not seeming the least put out.

At this point I think the guy behind the counter was fed up with all of us, so we ordered quickly. Ever the gentleman, Ethan bought the drinks and the tacos, and the three of us crunched over the gravel, slipping under the fairy-lit canopy of oaks to park ourselves at picnic tables and eat.

"Why don't *you* spend Halloween at the Driskill, Cate? Storm the place with a fake Tommy gun as the female half of Bonnie and Clyde," Ethan suggested before biting into a green chile taco.

I'd been just about to take a bite of my own barbacoa taco— Torchy's Democrat—when the question was posed, so I lowered my arms, carefully holding the overflowing taco together. "I could totally pull that off, but I too have plans," I told him sweetly.

"Are they for public consumption?" He tipped back his beer and then waited for my answer.

"Why not? I don't have any secrets." *Poker face, don't fail me now.* Normally I couldn't really claim any secrets, but recent developments had me daydreaming of secret identities, obsessing over alter egos, even lapsing into awkward thoughts of Ethan. . . . I prayed Courtney wouldn't give me away.

"Well, *that* needs to be remedied, my friend," Courtney teased, sipping the dregs of her lime-doused Corona. "Every girl should have at least one really good secret." Her cheekbones rounded in teasing amusement.

"How many do you have?" I said, remembering our little chat in Mirror, Mirror.

"Not enough," she assured me. "And it's not for lack of trying." Her grin widened into a Texas-sized smile. "Just means I need to try harder. Or in different places," she said, letting her eyes slide over and hook mine.

"What about you, Ethan?" she said, inviting him into our little girls' club. "Got any secrets?" I looked up from my taco, wondering and curious.

For one unhurried moment, he seemed to consider while Courtney and I waited him out. Then again, he could have just been stalling, messing with the pair of us.

"None that would interest the two of you," he finally answered.

I stared at him, considering, concocting potential Ethan-worthy secrets. Piggybacking on his neighbor's cable signal? Occasional Internet porn? Bootlegging the *Glee* soundtrack?

The corners of my lips edged up, and I bit back a smile. Let the poor guy keep his secrets. Mine would probably shock the pants off him.

"Cagey . . . I like that," Courtney said, flirting effortlessly. She was a natural-born charmer.

My eyes shifted back to Ethan to gauge his reaction to her. He seemed immune. It occurred to me that they probably knew each other too well, by virtue of being friends with me. I talked to one about the other, and gradually, curiosities were quenched and mysteries disappeared. They were probably beyond any possibility of future romance, and I had to admit to being just a little relieved. Also weird.

"Now that that's taken care of, tell us about Halloween," Ethan insisted, fiddling with his empty beer bottle.

"I'm going to one of Syd's events—a Hitchcock-themed party—I couldn't pass it up."

"I notice you didn't ask me to go with you," Ethan accused, smirking good-naturedly. "Got a date?"

"I would never intrude on your private life, Chavez. I'm going alone."

Ethan laughed out loud at that blatant untruth, and Courtney narrowly avoided spraying her final swallow of beer.

"By my count, that's two chicks going solo. What about you, Chavez . . . you got a date?"

Courtney's timely arrival thirty minutes ago had distracted me from that very question. I popped the rest of my taco into my mouth and waited to hear the answer.

He glanced over at me. "Afraid not," he admitted. "No secrets, and no date." This was hardly surprising.

Courtney offered up a "poor baby" smile. "Well, if your plans fall through . . . or you feel a little Eliot Ness coming on . . . swing by the Driskill," she offered, climbing off the picnic bench. Taco basket in hand, she said her good-byes.

"I need to go check that a *quinceañera* is positively perfect in every way." She batted her eyelashes and smiled angelically.

"Thanks, guys—Cate, for your help with a dress, and Ethan, for dinner. Catch you later." She waved and was gone.

Ethan and I focused on finishing our tacos and studiously avoided any further mention of Halloween plans. I was desperate to know his, but didn't want him probing further into mine.

Our awkward silence was broken by three guys in polos and jeans, still sporting their company name badges, wanting to share our table amid the after-work crowd. Ethan and I shifted down a couple of feet. My knee bumped the table's leg bracket and nudged something loose.

I leaned down to peek under the table and noticed a dark shape lying in the shadows. I reached for it, careful not to bump my head on the edge of the table and curious to examine it in the fading light.

It was old, or made to look old—vintage was king these days. And it was charming, from its worn leather cover to its pretty brass hardware. It looked like a secret door.

"What's that?" Ethan asked, eyeing my find.

My eyes, I'm sure, lit up with excitement, but almost instantly my shoulders slumped and the twinkle died. With my luck, this would be someone's Weight Watchers journal.

"Looks like some sort of journal," I said, nudging it onto the table in front of me, preferring the mystery to the reality, at least for the moment. I figured my curiosity would hold out maybe until I finished my tacos.

Some excited murmurings filled the trailer park, and glancing up, I caught a glimpse of a few renegade bats, likely having just emerged, right on cue, from beneath the Congress Avenue Bridge and winged back in our direction. Twilight lit the sky with sherbet colors and gave the little mammals a lovely backdrop for their nightly appearance. Luckily, we were well out of range of the rest of the little buggers and the great guano drop. Ethan had taken advantage of the distraction to bogart the first look at the journal. Evidently, his own curiosity was a bit of a lightweight.

"What happened to ladies first, Chavez? I hope you at least used a napkin."

He lifted both hands, displaying them palms out, then flipping them to expose the backs.

"Anything up your sleeves?" I inquired sourly. He ignored me, running curious fingers over the little key placket and knob, flipping the book onto its back for further perusal before cracking it open. I concentrated on my taco.

I glanced up when I heard the familiar "Huh." That one non-committal syllable expressed Ethan's grudging curiosity.

I swirled a tortilla chip through my little cup of queso. "What?"

"Strange. There's a flowery dedication in here that can't have been written recently, but the rest of the book is blank." He riffled through the pages all over again and then raised his eyebrows at me. "What's it doing under a trailer park picnic table?" he asked, nearly swiping the leather volume through a salsa spill on the table as he moved to hand it back to me. I snatched it away from him.

"Maybe someone had just bought it, needed a taco fix, and stashed it under the table to keep it away from a sticky-fingered companion." I speared him with a look, curling my lip ever so slightly.

Carefully wiping my hands on my napkin, I gently touched the tarnished hardware and brushed my fingers over the worn leather. It felt significant . . . substantial. As if secrets revealed inside would be held dear. I turned back the cover and read the flowery script with my bottom lip caught between my teeth.

> " . . . I dedicate to You the following Miscellanious
> Morsels, convinced that if you seriously attend to them,
> You will derive from them very important Instructions,
> with regard to your Conduct in Life."

"It looks like someone intended this as an instructional manual, but then never followed through with it." I glanced up at Ethan, who was back to concentrating on his own taco. He shrugged in response.

But I could. I could write in this diary from the perspective of my impending alter ego, recording thrilling adventures and dispensing exciting life advice to inspire the English teacher side of me. It sounded like the perfect outlet—judging by Courtney's reaction, my friends weren't ready to hear about my fantasy of "going rogue." It could be my little secret, kept safe in this little book.

"Do you think anyone's coming back for it?"

I scrunched my nose a little and ever so slightly shook my head, going for subliminal.

Ethan's lips twitched in amusement. "No way to tell. Why?" I frowned at him as he took a sip of beer.

"Can't you, for once, just be my partner in crime, Chavez?" I asked, thoroughly exasperated.

The amusement disappeared, and I couldn't interpret his long, steady gaze. Finally, he seemed to come to a decision. "Possession is nine-tenths," he reminded me. "You're in possession."

I looked down at the book, wondering if I'd glossed too quickly over the possibility that anyone would come looking for it, feeling vaguely guilty that I didn't plan on leaving it for them to find, and a little bit thrilled with my decision. I'm sure I was grinning like an idiot when I looked up again.

"So . . . do you want me to smuggle it out in my pants, or ask the taco guy for some foil so you can wrap it up to go? Because I'm all in, baby."

My laugh sounded suspiciously like a guffaw. It was the "baby" that did it . . . and the gangster voice. I stared across the table at Ethan, his face now mostly in shadow under the string of light-bulbs hung up over the lot. Imagining myself with a secret life was one thing; imagining Ethan as anything other than a clean-cut, hardworking geek was completely laughable.

"Perhaps Eliot Ness was a miscasting. You could hit the Driskill as Al Capone . . . or Pretty Boy Chavez." I grinned.

"I could . . . except, as I mentioned, I already have plans."

"Right. What did you say those were again?"

"I didn't," he reminded me. "You ready to bust that book outta here?"

Chapter 4

Thrilled with my luck in convincing Mom to let me "borrow" the entire rack of her latest finds, and exhilarated by my under-the-table score at Torchy's, I'd hurried back home with a smile on my lips. Now I was sprawled on the couch in my little Doris Day–inspired garage apartment with a butterscotch Dum-Dum tucked into the corner of my mouth. I'd changed out of my teacher clothes and couldn't decide what to do first. I was twitchy with excitement and eager to try on those dresses that oozed vintage sex appeal, but just as impatient to christen my new journal.

But I needed to get into character first. More than that, I needed a definitive alter ego—a secret identity—a Hyde to my Jekyll. My life was quite suddenly—and thrillingly—turning into a good story, and I needed to flush out a name and personality for a very important character.

I was Cate Kendall, and that name spoke volumes about me. Sensible, reliable rule follower. I wanted to be mysterious, flirtatious, and sexy. A bit of a minx . . . Cat. I smiled to myself. If I were an author, it would be the smile of the cat that got the cream, but I wasn't, and that was a little clichéd. I liked it anyway.

Now for a last name. I could pick something completely deviant from my real name, but I felt like I'd have a better connection if the new identify was a shade of myself.

Kent . . . Kettering . . . Kimball . . . *Kennedy!* The second I hit on it, I knew it was the one. Cat Kennedy hinted at a sophisticated, independent woman with an undercurrent of sex. Perfect.

I climbed off the couch, pulled the midnight blue dress down off the corner of the armoire, and stepped behind the door—as a sexy little boudoir or a phone booth, it was the best I could do.

I emerged feeling very sexy indeed—I couldn't keep my hands off me. The line of the bodice, sliding smoothly down into the trim fit of the skirt, and the crisp lustrousness of the fabric was irresistible. Then there was the transparent little shrug, tied above the waist, teasing and hinting at the curves beneath—I was in lust! I slipped into some dark heels and posed in front of the mirror. My legs looked like they were a mile long. What can I say? Clichés were clichés for good reason.

Something would need to be done about my tousled blond bob and fresh-faced makeup, but for now, this would definitely do. The Dum-Dum lollipop wasn't exactly anachronistic, but it was definitely out of character. Shooting myself a smoldering gaze in the mirror, I trapped the stick between my fingers and pulled it out of my mouth, cigarette style, casually puffing out imaginary smoke like a ten-year-old.

Definitely glamorous, but not worth the risks. I flipped the stick into the trash and waved my hand in the air in front of me like a moron, dispersing the imaginary smoke I'd conjured. Cat Kennedy was definitely not a smoker. And she only experimented with lollipop sticks.

I kicked off the heels and dropped onto the couch, reaching for the purloined book. I shook my head faintly. No, not purloined, *found, without identification.* I sat with it in my lap and tucked my feet up under me. This was the beginning . . . of something. It could be anything. I just had to decide. And I wanted it to be good. Novel-worthy. No, take that back . . . banned-book material.

Paging past the dedication, I stared at the first clean page, took a deep breath, and began to write.

Hello, I'm Cat Kennedy

I lifted my pen off the paper and stared at those words, tipping my head back and forth, feeling them out. They felt good.

and I'm about to inject a little moxie into your life. I don't plan on making an appearance just yet. The great reveal will happen at Pop-up Culture's homage to Hitchcock this Halloween. I'll be the chick channeling Eve Kendall, exuding an air of mystery in a killer dress and heels. I'll likely have made an appearance a few times before then, but only in the mirror. Call them practice runs—I want to be ready. But I'm not telling—not after Courtney's reaction—and certainly not Ethan. He definitely wouldn't approve. But I don't answer to him, and this isn't exactly his choice. I'm perfectly happy to hint at a hidden agenda and let him try to puzzle it out.

Fair warning . . . you may have second thoughts, although I doubt it, and either way I fully intend to railroad you into submission. You need to take on your twenties with more than a pair of reading glasses and a copy of Emma. You need to do this. Say good-bye to your plain-Jane life and set your sights on a little style!

Tipping the book closed, I stayed in character, keeping a mysterious smile on my face until I'd emerged from the makeshift phone booth in my jammies. Then a huge grin split my face. This was totally going to happen, and it was going to be awesome!

I spent a solid minute reveling in the possibilities before I slipped on my teacher glasses and propped myself up on the couch with a stack of term papers and a red pen. I still needed the day job to pay for the glamorous dual life I planned on leading.

By Sunday afternoon I was a wreck . . . in a good way, but still a wreck. Saturday I'd been good, grading papers and finalizing lesson plans. Mom had spent the day working the kinks out of her computer with the Geek Freaks—their boxy little green Scion had been parked in the driveway for at least three hours. I didn't even want to imagine what was wrong with it—I always just called

Ethan. I suspected he'd be happy to deal with her wonky computer if I asked him, but I dreaded the matchmaking fallout. Saturday night I'd spent rewatching *North by Northwest*, swooning over Cary Grant, awed by Eva Marie Saint's portrayal of an undercover spy, my head spinning with intrigue. Now I was jazzed to step back into the phone booth and suit up for the evening ahead, but I couldn't. I needed to focus on being Cate Kendall for a few more hours yet because Ethan would be here any minute for our weekly Scrabble match. I was prepared for a thorough trouncing and actually a little relieved to finally have an excuse for one. Not as thrilled to have to keep it to myself, but those were the breaks.

Pacing the tight quarters of my little apartment, a piña colada Dum-Dum lodged between my teeth, my gaze bounced from the armoire and away, over and over again, finally touching down on the journal I'd laid on the coffee table. Perfect. I'd while away the minutes with my alter ego and give myself a little pep talk.

A glance at the clock indicated I had about ten minutes before Ethan was due to show up, so I kicked back in my at-home jeans and propped my feet on the coffee table, wiggling my pale-polished toes in excitement.

Settling the charming little book on my lap, I traced my fingers over the detailing, once again marveling that someone had left this treasure behind. Guilt nudged at my conscience, but I tamped it down quickly. Finders, keepers. Besides, I'd already written in the book, and nobody wanted a used diary. I flipped to the one and only entry, my proof of ownership . . . and found it not quite the same as I'd left it.

Weird. How could it have all disappeared? Well, *all* of it hadn't disappeared, just most of it. A few words hadn't budged, and that was every bit as weird as the rest of them skedaddling. I stared at the page, my eyes scanning over each word in turn. It almost seemed . . . but that was impossible! And yet, I was staring at the proof. There was a message here. Oh. My. God. My world had gone Gothic!

I quickly rallied. It absolutely had not. I, unlike Courtney, did not believe in ghosts even one little bit. And the possibility of one haunting a journal stashed under a picnic table in a trailer park was ludicrous. I flipped back to the cover and tumbled the volume over on itself, looking for any clues, and found nothing I hadn't noticed before. Hmm.

The dedication got another quick perusal, put me in mind of Jane Austen, and was promptly abandoned. At that point I resumed staring at the words remaining.

at

times

the

answer

is   *hidden*

in

plain

sight

Now the left side was populated with all the little words, while the bigger ones were clustered mostly on the right, all of them pretty evenly spaced. It was like a particularly daunting game of Red Rover with words. Probably not a plausible explanation for the missing words. I blinked and looked again. With a little zigzagging, scanning top to bottom, putting it all together, it read *at times the answer is hidden in plain sight,* and that had potential written all over it. My mouth dropped open and I heard my own audible gasp of astonishment. This really was a message. A secret message to me . . . A small voice in my head whispered, "Or, more likely, the journal's previous owner," but I shushed it.

For one fleeting moment, I imagined this was a philosophical truism posed by the universe and magically appearing in the book like an image of the Virgin Mary in the rind of a cantaloupe. Good sense quickly took over and just as quickly subsided when I succumbed to the power of wishful thinking as my eyes widened in mingled excitement and disbelief. Clearly this was some sort of wonky spy gadget!

As far as I was concerned, this was as good an explanation as any, and further, it was the one I wanted right now. Beyond that superior logic, everything was nebulous, but I had a good feeling about this. Questions and possibilities flooded through my mind and left me clinging urgently to this solution.

Was this like *Charlie's Angels*? Would I be messaged instructions for secret missions via this book? Would I need to learn some karate kicks and maybe the wuxi finger hold? Was I ignoring a completely obvious explanation, letting my imagination spin away from me, altering reality to fit my daydreams? Was I hallucinating the whole thing? Mom had made grilled vegetable sandwiches for lunch—had she been experimenting with questionable outsourced mushrooms?

Okay, wait! What about the dedication—how did that fit in? Could Jane Austen be the key? Were the remaining words some sort of book cipher key that used one of Austen's novels to send a secret message? That would be freakin' awesome! But which one? And how the hell was I going to figure out how to do that?? I was a British lit major. My code-breaking skill was limited to figuring out which of my students read the assignments based on their answers in class and which chose the Dark Side. And even if this were true, who the hell was sending the code?

And let's not even forget the personal questions: Why me? It was pure coincidence that I was at Torchy's Tacos Thursday night, that I sat at that table and knocked the book from its hiding place. Was it meant for me to find? This was sounding embarrassingly ridiculous, even within the confines of my own mind, but how could I not ask these questions?? This stuff was always happening in books . . . *Alice's Adventures in Wonderland, Mary Poppins, Peter Pan* . . . And probably plenty of modern fiction as well, which I'd be up on if I weren't so enamored with classic British lit. So why couldn't it happen to me?

A squeamish little shiver ran up my spine, and I felt compelled to rain on my parade a little. Did I really *want* any of this to happen to me? Did I want the responsibility involved with quests, secrets, and missions?

It took me all of two seconds to decide.

Hell yeah, I did!

Still . . . I didn't have a lot to go on. Other than *at times the answer is hidden in plain sight.* Right. I guess I'd figure it out. Or maybe an experienced sidekick would show up with all the answers.

The sudden knock on my door was way too clichéd, but it sent my heart ricocheting around cartoon-style all the same. I slid my cagey little spy book under the couch and answered the door.

Of course it was Ethan.

I knew that. I'd been expecting him. I just hadn't been expecting him to show up at the precise moment I was itching for a sidekick. I gave him a quick once-over, getting momentarily hung up on the slope of his biceps in the short-sleeved, oil-stained Austin City Limits T-shirt he had on. Ethan could be great sidekick material if he wasn't always treating me like I needed to just grow up and get on with things. Then again, maybe this was my moment of truth, my chance to show Ethan what lurked behind my teaching glasses and teasing grin.

Friday's class discussion of *Emma* had touched on this very topic: how one person's preconceptions about another can blind them to the reality. I'd considered it an elegant little tease, hinting at the undercurrents of my own personality. I seriously doubt any of my students picked up on it.

"You all may only see a high school English teacher, but what *don't* you see? For all you know, I'm a millionaire with an altruistic love of the classics." I leaned my rear against the front of my desk facing the smirks and twitters, lifting my eyebrows in question, daring them to look closer. "An undercover narcotics officer . . . a jewel thief . . . a government operative. I could be anything with the cover of a high school English teacher, using my position on the faculty, spying for personal gain."

"Seems like the irritations would far outweigh any potential benefits," Alex murmured sardonically.

"Oh, it definitely *seems* that way. But perhaps that's what makes me the perfect candidate. Beyond reproach, above suspicion," I said, walking around the side of my desk. A mystery," I said, meeting his eyes with a smile and relishing everything the word implied.

The bell rang then, with impeccable timing, and I imagined they all trailed out wondering about me and my secret life. Deluded, I know. Still, *I* knew, and that was plenty.

With the recent developments in the found-object department, my status as a woman of mystery was now spot-on. Beyond my evening in character, I was now on the verge of something pivotal, the scope of which, for the time being, remained boundless and undefined. It made me wonder now about the man standing in front of me, ready to bandy words.

Maybe Ethan *was* the answer. Heck, maybe he had an undercurrent of his own—the Will Schuester of Travis Oaks High, minus the singing. (Or maybe not minus the singing—what the heck did *I* know?) He definitely wasn't above keeping secrets, and he was "in plain sight" on a regular basis. I'd give it some thought—I wanted a bit longer to think things through on my own first. If I pulled Ethan in now, *I'd* be relegated to the position of sidekick, and I wasn't about to put up with that.

"Cate . . . ?" By the time my eyes focused in on Ethan, I'm sure he'd seen a schizophrenic play of emotions run across my face. I smiled, smoothing them all out.

"Yes. Ready for Scrabble." I reached behind me for the box I kept on the little table just inside the door. "How about we play outside?" I didn't want to take any chances with all the secrets I now had packed into this tiny apartment.

"Sounds good," he agreed companionably. Ethan was always in a winning mood on Scrabble day. I grabbed a sweater from the hook by the door and followed him down to certain defeat.

By the time I swung back in the door, it was 7:30. Mom had made Philly cheesesteak sandwiches, and Ethan had devoured every last bit she'd forced upon him. I needed to get on with the total transformation, and it was imperative that I not forget to brush my teeth. Sautéed pepper and onion breath didn't really send out the vibe I was going for.

Dress first. Part of me was excited just to slip into my make-believe phone booth again, and the rest was totally psyched to be zipped into that dress, for real this time. It inspired confidence and took sexiness to a whole different level. The same was true of the heels, but they could wait.

I'd just finished smoothing the fabric over my curves when I heard the knock. Mom probably just wanted to double-check that Ethan and I weren't engaged . . . or better yet, engaged in something frisky. I slipped around the sofa, tying on the filmy little wrap, and pulled the door wide.

It wasn't my mother. And sidekick or not, it looked like I was going to have to come clean on a few things with Ethan.

"Whoa!"

As responses went, it was certainly gratifying.

"Did you decide to cancel your plans and tag along with Courtney tonight instead?"

"What?" I propped my fists on my hips and waited, my synapses trudging along in confusion.

"Eliot Ness, Bonnie and Clyde . . . the Driskill?" When I didn't respond, he added, "Are you packin' a flask under that skirt? Because it doesn't look like there's room—"

"No, and no. What are you doing here, Chavez?" I snapped, simultaneously wanting to share my secrets and keep them to myself.

He held up his hands to ward off further waspishness. "Just wanted to let you know that I'll be out of town next week . . . in case you're looking for me."

I dropped my arms and frowned in confusion. "The whole week? Where are you going?"

He suddenly looked vague, suspiciously vague. Ethan never

looked vague. Slippery, cagey, evasive . . . yes. "I just have some things to take care of."

"In the middle of the semester? Can't it wait until the Thanksgiving holiday?"

"No, Lady Buttinski, it can't. And why are you so concerned?"

"I'm not."

"No? Okay, well then, are you going to tell me where you're going, all vamped up?"

I crossed my arms over my chest, the corset top tightening up. Ethan flicked his gaze down and blinked twice before whipping it back up again. I waited till I had his full attention before answering. "No. I'm not," I said flatly. "You keep your secrets, I'll keep mine. And I'll see you when you get back." I smiled, trying my damnedest to convey that he was missing out on some *really* good stuff.

Ethan's jaw tightened fractionally. "Isn't that a little juvenile?"

"Quite possibly," I said. "I'm good with that." I raised an eyebrow and pressed my lips together, refusing to break even though it would be *really* nice to tell somebody about the secret messages.

Ethan held my gaze for one last excruciating moment before turning to walk back down the stairs and mysteriously disappear for one long week.

Chapter 5

The Hitchcock soiree was being held in a finished but unrented space in the Second Street district. Waffling over whether to get there early or a little late, I chose early. Better parking, and a bit of time to test out my new "by-night" personality before the crowd descended.

The split second before I slid through the glass door decorated with a full-body silhouette of Alfred Hitchcock, I had the uncomfortable feeling that someone was watching me. Holding tight to the door handle, I pivoted on my heel, glancing behind me, right and left, my newly sleek bob shifting against my cheek. I saw no one even remotely suspicious—this was Austin, after all. Nothing seemed out of place.

All at once, I felt in character . . . a Hitchcock blonde, edgy and on the run. Not to mention off the grid. As ridiculous as it was, I'd stopped to buy a burner phone just in case (in case of what, I had no idea), and I'd sat in the car until I'd memorized the number so I wouldn't have to write it down. I was positively itching to make a call.

I smiled to myself. I was totally getting caught up and it was awesome!

Slipping through the door, I nearly screamed my head off. Somehow they'd managed to rig some of those cheapy black birds that go on sale at craft stores every Halloween to attack unsuspecting partygoers as they came through the door. I was certain my hand had come up exactly like Tippi Hedren's trying to ward them off. Damn sproingy things.

Smoothing my hair in case I was sporting beak-head, I inched farther into the space, my gaze panning over the spotlit walls decorated with Hitchcock movie scenes. It was like the sets from a year's worth of high school drama productions: Mount Rushmore, a cramped city apartment building, the roof of a French villa high above a glittering party, an apartment with a desk in the foreground holding an old-timey phone and pair of sewing scissors, and a bell tower. And hanging suspended above it all were cables dangling those creepy black birds.

"Ms. Kendall has arrived!" I swiveled to see Sydney bearing down on me in a catsuit that left nothing to the imagination. "Should I call you Cate, or would you prefer Eve for tonight?" Her grin was edged out by surprise as she looked me over. "Holy crap, you're a fox! But you've still got your brainy school—"

"Don't say it," I interrupted, whipping off my glasses, which I sometimes used for night driving, not wanting to jinx what I had going here. "Tonight I want to be someone different. Not Eve or Cate. I created a whole new identity . . . just for one night." The rest of my plans weren't quite fully baked yet. "Tonight I'm Cat Kennedy, Hitchcock blonde, woman of mystery."

"And sexy as hell! If I didn't know you'd be going back to life as a schoolteacher tomorrow, I'd be coming on to you myself." She winked and commenced a full perusal all over again.

Beyond the dress, which was smokin', I'd slipped on my highest heels, slicked on my reddest lipstick, and lined my eyes with sultry black, layering on the mascara at the end. I was minus a cape, but I felt totally transformed . . . sort of like a superhero. Except without a project—a regular Mr. Incredible.

"Oli and Will are in our little makeshift kitchen, but they'll be out in a minute. You are gonna blow their minds. Hell, you're gonna blow everyone's mind. And Cary Grant, if he shows, will be in the palm of your hand."

I looked around us. Tables were scattered, draped in black, each with a movie-themed centerpiece. And in between, a trio of party-goers mingled, all of them in stark black, with maybe a sparkle or two. I might just be a standout, and that was fine with me.

Within fifteen minutes the place was packed, and I wasn't the only one in costume. One woman had shown up with her own birds attached to her head, complete with blood spots, and believe it or not, a guy in baby blue pj's and full leg cast rolled through the door in a wheelchair with a floaty Grace Kelly companion. No more than ten minutes later he stood beside me, the evening's signature drink, a limoncello, in hand, his look-alike companion nowhere in sight.

Judging by the look in his eye and the amused quirk of his lips, I got the impression that this was the Cary Grant of the evening. Tonight though, he was disguised as Jimmy Stewart and hampered by a couple feet of gauze and Mod Podge.

"You're not Grace Kelly or Tippi Hedren. . . ." He tipped his head, seeming to study me closely for clues, but I wasn't fooled. "Eva Marie Saint . . . the sexy spy who handled the inestimable Cary Grant." It wasn't a question.

"What gave me away?" I'd briefly considered shifting my voice to be throaty or breathless, but decided I didn't have the follow-through to carry that out beyond the introductions. I tried for flirty, though.

"You have an obvious backbone . . . a very attractive one. And you look dangerously capable." Damn, he was good. I sidled right into the picture he was painting.

"You have a good eye. I'm Cat Kennedy," I told him, extending my hand, daring him to expose me as a wannabe.

"Cat, hmm? Very nice. Jake Tielman." His grip was cool and smooth but for a few calluses. It gave me chills.

"You lost your wheelchair," I said, glancing down at the bandaged leg that now supported his sturdy six-foot frame. "Not an easy thing to do," I said.

"Not to worry. It's valet parked." He smiled and looked curiously at me. "I come to a lot of these Pop-up events, but you're a new development. First time?"

"It is," I confirmed, turning slightly away from him to face Oli and her tray of drinks. Amusement twinkled in her eyes—after being introduced to my evening persona, she and Will had made a point of circulating past me on a very regular basis.

"Dinner will be served shortly. Seating is open and at your discretion." Biting her lip, she aimed a subtle wink before moving on.

"Shall we?" suggested the charmer, offering his arm. What can I say—I took it.

After seating me at an empty table under Mount Rushmore, Jake Tielman retrieved his wheelchair and managed to position himself so awkwardly as to discourage anyone from joining our little party of two. I had no doubt it was intentional, and I was very impressed.

He flirted easily in the candlelight as we carved up our Cornish game hens under the watchful, beady eyes above. Even the vegetables were creepy, roasted haricot beans and root vegetables, looking enough like colorful finger and knuckle bones to be off-putting.

"New in town or Hitchcock devotee?"

"It's a little more complicated than that," I admitted. His hair was slicked back and parted with precision, clearly in character as Jimmy Stewart's *Rear Window* 'do, but I got the impression he wasn't quite so fastidious on an average day-in-the-life. We were both playing a part. Made me wonder which of us would be exposed first. And that thought led to another, which likely led to some very pink cheeks on my part.

He raised an eyebrow, but didn't press the issue or inquire over my sudden blush. "Which are you?" I asked.

"Neither. I try to surround myself with unique and imaginative people as often as possible."

"Should I feel flattered?"

"Absolutely . . . but for a different reason entirely. I gravitate toward dangerously sexy women too. Besides, I don't know anything about you."

"Is it possible you're not trying hard enough?"

He raised an eyebrow, amusement evident in the set of his lips. "Gloves are off, then; gauntlet's down. Let's get to it. You up for twenty questions?"

"Yes or no, or anything goes?"

"Oh, I'll always vote anything goes." He smiled. Great teeth, classic cheekbones, dangerous dimple. His eyes were deep, dark chocolate brown. Willy Wonka would have been jealous. The pajamas, while kitschy, didn't have the same appeal as a well-cut suit. They could have been saved for a more private showing. Then again, maybe he didn't have any use for pajamas. . . .

Cat clearly doesn't waste any time.

"Fine, but I expect you to answer the same questions," I insisted, still waffling as to whether I should fabricate an entire alternate universe for myself.

He conceded the suggestion with a slight nod and promptly posed the first question. "Single or something else?"

"Single." That, at least, was woefully true.

"Same," he concurred, with a sly grin.

"Last serious relationship?"

I had to think a minute. "Three years ago."

"Two," he countered, sipping his drink.

"Work?"

Trial by fire . . . "Austin Museum of Art." I thought it sounded sufficiently cosmopolitan and comfortably vague, and I figured "spy in training" would skew the next seventeen questions.

"Entrepreneur." *Very interesting. I just might have some follow-up questions of my own.*

"School?"

"Brown, BA in art history." I was becoming fast friends with the little white lie.

"UCLA, BS in physics, UT MBA." *Impressive.*

"Perfect. Now for the good stuff."

"Favorite Hitchcock film?"

"Charade." The irony was my little secret.

"The best Hitchcock movie Hitchcock never made?" His grin was cocky.

"Honestly?" This was a shocker—and even more ironic. *"North by Northwest*, then," I said truthfully.

"Rear Window." He grinned. "I drew the line at carting a camera in here."

"The wheelchair was a nice touch. And the tag-along Grace Kelly even better."

He leaned in, his eyes shifting left and right, clearly not trusting our self-imposed privacy. Unable to resist any sort of secret, I met him halfway. "I met her outside and convinced her to walk in with me—even got her to push the wheelchair." He winked mischievously. Made me wonder about his plans for me. And mine for him.

"Very crafty," I said, impressed, flirting ever so slightly behind the swing of my hair.

"So why not Audrey Hepburn?" He had a knowing look in his eye, which had my nerves crackling.

"Is this one of the twenty?" I said, stalling. Truthfully I think I would have had an easier time with Audrey. More wide-eyed wonder and shy ingénue. I'd likely have spent the evening lurking in the kitchen with the girls.

"Absolutely."

"I can't blame Audrey—I might not have been able to resist a sixty-year-old Cary Grant either, but I'd much prefer a younger version. So my choices were Grace Kelly or Eva Marie Saint."

"If you'd come as Grace Kelly, I might have bumped into you outside instead."

"True, but if you had, would you be talking to me right now?"

"I'd like to think so, but maybe not. Excellent decision." He raised his glass and downed the contents just as Will made the rounds with a blood-red cocktail and Syd served a portobello mushroom salad drizzled with balsamic vinaigrette and paired with a wafer-thin piece of herbed focaccia. Mine was shaped like a butcher knife, his a pair of sewing scissors—classic Hitchcock murder weapons. The Pop-up Culture chicks had achieved an impressive level of creepiness, aided considerably by their cat-burglar costumes, the heavy shadows in the room, and the element of surprise.

I carefully sipped my drink, eyeing the focaccia. I tasted pome-granate, felt the quick trail of heat from the vodka, and focused on settling the nerves in my stomach. Damn if I didn't feel like an operative, finessed, via some tech-savvy cohorts, into a critical situation to play a part and steal away before my cover was blown. But nobody was parked outside in a van, talking into my earpiece. I was playing this all on my own. I spared a quick thought for Ethan, but tamped it ruthlessly down. He would never approve.

"Reading between the lines . . . should I assume you're on the hunt for a modern-day, Austinized Cary Grant? Should *I* be flat-tered?"

A little smile tugged at the corners of my mouth, and all at once, I felt quite the vixen. Leaning my elbow on the table, I propped my chin on my hand and looked past the centerpiece, at Mr. Jake Tielman, through lowered lashes. "Hard to say. Technically you found me, but I let you drag me along. And now it's just the two of us. . . ." I slid my lips into a long, slow smile, starting to get the hang of things. Less was definitely more. Conversationally speaking.

I took my time with a slow perusal, squelching the self-consciousness as he watched. He was obviously pulling off charm-ing, seeing as I'd let myself be cornered by a cute Jimmy Stewart in old-fashioned pajamas. And I suspected there was a great deal of sexy just below the surface. It occurred to me that I needed to wrap things up or risk sending the wrong message.

"Would you say you make a worthy comparison?" I flicked one eyebrow teasingly up.

"In some ways," he granted, setting down his fork and fingering his cocktail glass.

"Any of the good ones?" I pressed, completely amused with

myself and him. I was all but oblivious to the homage going on around us. All but those damn birds.

"What are the good ones? Charm? I'd say I've got a bit of that, more if I try. Rugged, manly good looks? I'm obviously relatively secure in my mojo, or I wouldn't be out in the city in my pajamas—even if it is Austin. Charisma? I'm guessing that's the only reason you're sitting here right now. And oh yes, virility. I'd say that's a question that will have to be answered on its own."

I was full-out grinning now, I couldn't help it. He was crunching into his focaccia, looking confidently insecure, as if he knew who he was but couldn't guess if I'd drawn the same conclusion. Far from being finished playing hard to get, I figured he deserved a little thumbs-up. It was just good sportsmanship.

I tipped my head down and bit my lip. On any other night, my ingrained shyness would have been calling the shots, but tonight flirty seduction was the name of the game. "It looks as though I'm sitting in exactly the right spot," I said, edging out a wide close-lipped smile.

It wasn't long before Will and Oli sidled up in their catsuits, purveyors of Linzer cookies served facedown, the jam from the cut-out "windows" smearing bloodlike on the stark white plates, a nod to the classic Hitchcock *Rear Window*. They brought coffee too, steaming hot in old-fashioned diner cups.

We were quiet for a minute, letting the coffee and our flirtation cool off a little bit. Jake glanced at his watch—his very expensive-looking watch—glinting in the candlelight.

"It's closing in on midnight. . . . I'd offer to drive you home, but we both know the logistics of that would be crazy. It's a shame we aren't staying in adjacent rooms at the same hotel."

Seeing my eyebrow shoot up in curiosity, he quickly added, "That's the Cary talking . . . remember *To Catch a Thief?* The man could work an angle."

"He worked it better in *North by Northwest*," I countered. "He ended up sharing her train compartment."

"The man is a legend."

I sipped carefully and felt the zing of caffeine spiral through my blood, causing trouble. I tamped it down with strict instructions from a certain high school teacher who had to be in her classroom by seven-thirty A.M.

"How about," I offered slowly, "I give you my number and you can call me when you think we could work something out." Even I didn't know what I meant by that, but it felt suitably vague and surprisingly seductive. It was also possible the evening was getting to me—that I was on sensory overload and needed to get back to the Bat Cave to regroup. I reached into my purse for the little pad of paper and pen I'd intentionally planted there and dashed off the memorized burner phone number, folding the paper in half, very for-your-eyes-only.

This was the perfect moment to slip out and away, keeping to the shadows, but I'd let my emotions come into play: I wanted one of those Linzer cookies, and I wasn't leaving without one.

While Jake Tielman was eyeing my phone number, and me over the top of it, I slid a delicate cookie off the plate sitting between us on the table and indulged in a tiny bite, letting the buttery crumb dissolve on my tongue as a flurry of powdered sugar fluttered down around me. My cover was undeniably blown—it was literally impossible to be taken seriously as a femme fatale, not to mention a spy, with a dusting of powdered sugar covering your person. I used my napkin and subtly licked my lips, not wishing to get the flirtation started all over again, but evidently I wasn't thorough enough.

I was easing myself into the good-byes when Jake reached almost negligently across the table, cupped my chin in his hand, and brushed his thumb slowly and deliberately over my upper lip before letting his fingers slide away. My heart pounded and my breathing slowed, and as our eyes met, I wondered how best to respond to this seductive development.

James Bond's MO was not an option—I wasn't ready to seduce him just yet. As a woman with a secret and a flair for the dramatic, I decided to play it cool . . . *cagey* . . . and leave him wanting more.

Reaching for my bag, I got slowly to my feet, bent at the waist in my high heels and pencil skirt, licked a bit of moisture onto my lips, and slid a marginally wet kiss across his cheek. Hampered by the wheelchair, he was slow in scrambling to his feet, and I was three steps on my way to the door, calling back over my shoulder, "You have my number."

I skipped half the way to my car, thrilled with the evening's success—even the powdered sugar had led to a whopper of a cliffhanger. I couldn't wait to "go rogue" all over again. And I was definitely going to need a theme song.

My phone didn't ring until I'd switched back to normal and was settled in on the couch, ready to delve into the mysteries of the Trailer Park Journal all over again. My real phone, that is, not the burner. I'd hidden the burner at the bottom of the bowl of Dum-Dum lollipops on my coffee table. I figured it was Ethan asking for a favor or wanting to remind me not to leave too many Internet browsers open on my classroom computer. But a tiny little girlish part of me wondered impossibly if, just maybe, it was Jake Tielman, itching to say good night. It wasn't either one of them. Syd had dialed me up, wanting to know why I'd left in such a hurry.

"You didn't get sick, did you? Tell me that's not what happened. Was it having to eat poultry with those creepy-ass birds draped from the ceiling? For the record, I voted against that."

"No, Syd," I assured her, my eyes falling closed on a wave of tiredness, "it wasn't food or décor-related, but those creepy-ass birds didn't make it easy. I left because it was almost midnight, and I need to work tomorrow."

"Yeah, okay, I get that," she said. "So what'd you think? How'd we do on the homage?"

"Stellar, Syd. Honestly. It was creepy, and sexy, and super stylish. I loved how only half the guests came in character—it made things quirky and interesting. Even more than they already were. Seriously, it was awesome. Was there anyone there from *The Chronicle*?"

"I think maybe one dude, and then a food writer for the *Statesman*."

"It's gonna be a great write-up," I said, hoping to wrap things up.

"And what about you, showing up in that dress?! Hot damn, Cate . . . or should I say, Cat? What happened with the guy? The two of you were very private over in the corner by yourselves."

"We flirted shamelessly. I'm sure you and your minions got an eyeful. But I came home alone. He went home with my phone number. We'll see."

"This is going to be really good for you, Cate. I feel it."

"Could I ask a favor?" I begged.

"Name it."

"Could you not mention the alter ego to anyone?" Specifically Ethan, but honestly, I didn't want the gossip getting around, particularly back to the high school. It would be so much worse this time around. Being a teacher with a juicy secret was a little bit thrilling. Having the secret get out . . . not so much. My face was clenched, waiting for her response.

"It's in the vault, baby! Oh! Gotta go—apparently I'm supposed to be helping clean up."

Letting out an all-encompassing sigh, I dropped the phone and focused on my quirky and interesting journal. I tapped the end of my pen on the cover in a quick, nervous tattoo. Far from being turned off by the inexplicable element of the journal, I was in awe. Nervous awe. The world was full of weird and unexplainable phenomena—who was I to question it? I'd never understood the city's annual Spam festival either, but I wasn't out there investigating SPAMARAMA. For all I knew, the end pages could be concealing a computer chip with a transmitter—but that was kind of creepy, and right now I was full up on creepy.

Clearly, someone was sending me messages. The trouble was that now I wasn't sure what to write. This could be important stuff. What if . . . what if I didn't use the right words? What if the journal couldn't work its magic because it couldn't parse my stream-of-consciousness jots into something useful? Crap. Well, I was just going to have to wing it and hope for the best. I was too tired for much more than that anyway.

Rolling my shoulders and then stretching my neck, I feinted once and then let her rip.

So . . . I did it. I played the part. Tonight I <u>was</u> a flirting femme fatale, and I rocked it. But I'm not sure I accomplished anything other than giving my phone number to an eligible entrepreneur. I'm not sure how this is supposed to work. The message in the journal, I gotta admit, was unexpected, and I'm not sure I totally clued in on its underlying meaning. Unless it was hyping the book's "bonus features." I'm new at this. . . . I figured I'd be on my own with the dress, just having a sexy little adventure, but a chance at secret agent status is a little bit of perfection.

Obviously, I have some questions, namely, who's calling the shots, and what's at stake? Am I like a spy? Some sort of operative testing out developmental spy gadgetry? How did you find me? The Trailer Park was an interesting choice, but you took a risk—Ethan was there (and Courtney too, earlier). So can I tell anyone, or is this strictly need-to-know?? Adding an element of mystery to my open-book lifestyle might be nice for a change. While I might eventually like to confide in Ethan, as far as I'm concerned, he hasn't earned it yet. He's being very close-mouthed about something. . . . I just haven't figured out what it is yet. So secret is fine with me.

What's next? I'm up for anything and everything, just so long as it's legal (that's slightly negotiable) and I can do it after school. I assume all communications will go through the journal. I'll check in tomorrow. Bye, Charlie! (I promise I won't do that again.)

I tipped the journal closed again, freshly irritable over Ethan's surprise news. An entire week?? I'd need to have this secret identity thing down by the end of it . . . at least the secret part.

With a sudden flash of curiosity, I whipped the book back open again, wondering if my message had been read and answered.

It hadn't. But in fairness, I had asked a lot of questions. And probably my success as a virgin operative needed to be vetted somehow. I could wait.

Chapter 6

Utterly dependable, Ethan had worked his IT magic, getting my e-mail back online. I had to admit, dependability was an attractive quality in a man; overprotectiveness, not so much. I sat at my desk on my lunch break, reading through the e-mails that had just popped up in my in-box. There were three from concerned parents, one wishing to confirm that her child would not be reading any books that might have even brushed up against the possibility of getting banned.

I paused with a forkful of salad halfway to my lips and inhaled slowly, tipping my eyelids down, channeling inner calm. I did not want to get sucked into an e-mail smackdown. I could not educate these parents on my own, and neither the school officials nor the school board would thank me for trying. I typed back a brief response that I hoped would set her closed mind at ease that her child's mind would, at least on my watch, remain uncorrupted by controversial literature.

There was also a staff meeting reminder for tomorrow afternoon, which I confirmed was on my desk calendar and typed into my phone, a request for volunteers to sponsor a Model UN team (no thank you), and an invitation to a leadership conference hosted by the local arm of the teachers union (pass—two years in a row was more than I could take).

Courtney's e-mail I saved for last, figuring it would put a smile on my face to carry me through the afternoon. A can of Orange Crush from the school vending machine could only do so much.

> *C—*
> *The party was sparkly and glamorous and carried on long past my bedtime. Maybe I had stars in my eyes . . . or maybe I just can't spot 'em like I used to. I spent the evening—well, the moments I wasn't putting out mini-flares—flirting with a gorgeous Robert Pattinson type at the bar. We had quite the little seduction going. Until a second Rob Pattinson type sidled up and stole him away from me.*
> *I do realize I never had him, but it felt like I did. After that, I was done. I went home, defeated and alone. I think I've sworn off men—for now. I could be talked back in by the right guy, but honestly, I'm not convinced he even exists. I've decided to wait for Mr. Darcy to saunter into the Driskill and sweep me off my feet with a single haughty stare. You can be proud of yourself for corrupting me.*
> *And since I need to start hanging around the Driskill a little more, to improve my odds, what do you say to an after-hours ghost hunt? Don't think about it— unfurrow your brow before you get wrinkles—just say yes. We'll use my office as a command center, I'll see if we can get into room 525, and we'll test out my new ghost-hunting gear. Sound good? Tuesday at seven fifteen? First rule of ghost hunting is "Don't hunt alone."*
> *Wear comfy clothes and quiet shoes. See you then,*
> *C*

Her new ghost-hunting gear? I could only imagine. Reading between the lines, I should prepare to look and act ridiculous and hope that no one I know sees me. Seeing as I didn't have any plans for Tuesday night, it looked like I was free for a little ghost hunting. At the very least it was the perfect excuse to dress like a ninja. With luck it might tide me over.

I didn't really have a good feel for when I'd next be going rogue, and I didn't know what to make of the cryptic message I'd found in the journal this morning:

an unexpected development can change everything

This one was every bit as vague as the last one. They were like fortune cookie fortunes, open for interpretation no matter who cracked them.

As far as I was concerned, I'd had one "unexpected development" after another: the alter ego, the journal, Ethan's mysterious week-long disappearance, Jake Tielman. . . . I wondered if and when I'd hear from *him*. Crap! I'd forgotten to retrieve the burner phone from the Dum-Dum bowl! He'd just have to leave a message. Which meant he'd have to listen to the attempt I'd made at being mysterious and alluring in the space of a five-second greeting. I'd recorded it so many times I had it memorized:

[Slightly breathy] "Hi, this is Cat. I'm having entirely too much fun to answer my phone. Leave me a message and maybe I'll invite you along."

I said it out loud into my empty classroom and suddenly wondered if it was too much. I cringed slightly, almost wishing I had it to do over. But then I rallied. No, this was good . . . this was exactly the sort of image I wanted to portray. A feisty femme . . . we could forget the fatale. Courtney was right—I didn't have it in me. I'd be the Sandra Bullock of spies.

With any luck he wouldn't go looking for me at my made-up museum job, because that had the potential to get a little awkward. I'd just have to wait, seeing as I had deliberately left without getting his number. Or I could Google him.

Goose bumps crowded up my arms as I checked the clock: ten minutes till next period. I opened up an Internet window and typed "Jake Tielman Austin." The top five results referenced entrepreneur, philanthropist, sports enthusiast Jake Tielman. There was even an image, culled from the *Statesman* online, of the man I'd flirted with last night. I minimized the window, thoughts and questions flitting through my already slightly frazzled brain. Did I want to look? Could I resist the opportunity? I felt like I was running an unauthorized background check, but wasn't this what people did these days? Technology had corrupted us—we had too much information available to us, and it was impossible to know what to do with it. Was he Googling me?

With a flash of sudden insight, it occurred to me that I was impervious to the Google search. Cat Kennedy was a front woman for my little fantasy turned cover op. Nothing he found would lead him back to me.

It wasn't possible that he *was* the op, was it? Had I unintentionally gotten close to the target? My heart was pounding out an erratic beat. I'd really liked him too . . . but I wasn't about to sleep with him solely to get information. Hell. This stream-of-consciousness thing I had going was making things sound more and more ridiculous by the minute. And it was beyond obvious that I'd been watching way too many spy programs.

I focused on my salad, quickly scarfing it down before twenty kids trooped in, hoping to convince me that they'd read the assigned pages. And then I remembered . . .

I'd planned to do a quick search for the quote on the frontispiece of the journal, just in case something interesting came up. Key words, key words . . . I gently tapped the keys, searching my memory. "Miscellaneous morsels" stood out in my mind, seeing as it had made me think of Toll House chocolate chip cookies. I typed the words into the search box.

Jane Austen's name came up in the first four results. Weird. The next two offered up morsel-infused recipes. I clicked on the second of the four, scanned the contents, and blinked several times in mind-boggling disbelief. Taking a deep breath and hoping I still had a few moments to myself, I reread the words carefully.

To Miss Jane Anna Elizabeth Austen

My Dear Neice

Though you are at this period not many degrees removed from Infancy, Yet trusting that you will in time be older, and that through the care of your excellent Parents, You will one day or another be able to read written hand, I dedicate to You the following Miscellanious Morsels, convinced that if you seriously attend to them, You will derive from them very important Instructions, with regard to your Conduct in Life.—If such my hopes should hereafter be realized, never shall I regret the Days and Nights that have been spent in composing these Treatises for your Benefit. I am, my dear Neice

Your very Affectionate Aunt
June 2d. 1793

The dedication in the journal was only an excerpt of this longer passage. Rather apropos. Even so, it made no sense to me. Did this mean that whoever was sending me these vague little instructions was an avid Jane Austen fan? Was the quote merely a diversionary tactic, to throw suspicion off the book's real purpose? Was I, in high school speak, just trippin'? It was impossible to tell. The undeniable facts were: I'd found a journal (outside a taco truck), which was inscribed with a quote from über-author Jane Austen; and somehow, some way, the journal was communicating with me. Making suggestions, giving advice. Seemingly irrelevant advice.

At that moment, my students traipsed into the classroom, thumping down their backpacks, sliding into their seats, delving into their backpacks for composition books and pens. I couldn't think about this right now. I needed to mentally switch gears and decode a different, relatively clear-cut morsel of Ms. Austen's writing for a bunch of jaded seniors.

Trying to teach with a conundrum swirling around in my head was exhausting, and by the time the bell rang, I'd had enough. Rather than sit for one more helpless minute in my classroom, I packed my leather satchel full of papers and trudged home, determined to get some answers from the journal, the universe, or the covert ops team running point from a utility van parked down the street from my house, lurking amid the leftover Halloween decorations.

I hadn't made it to the grocery store for more than a week, so I popped in at Mom's house first. She wasn't home, but she'd left the house looking oddly rumpled. Pillows were askew in the living room, as if she'd spun them away from her like Frisbees. The kitchen sink held two forks, the tines of both coated with chocolate frosting. The cake itself, displayed on Mom's favorite fancy glass cake stand, had a Jekyll and Hyde thing going on. One side was beautifully frosted in a smooth buttercream, and the other looked like a raccoon had mauled it and then left without using Saran Wrap. What the hell?

Clearly Mom was dealing with some sort of crisis of her own. She must have come home for lunch and had a little meltdown. I seriously hoped she hadn't been eating with two forks at once . . . although the evidence was pretty damning. I'd come down later and try to feel her out. Right now I was headed to the Bat Cave, and I needed sustenance. Pulling open the fridge, I grabbed a package of bagels and some feta cheese. Then a tomato off the counter and a twist of homegrown basil from the pot on the windowsill, and I was all set. Wine I had. Taking one more look around the place, I shook my head in bewilderment and pulled the door shut behind me.

Dinner could wait. I needed to get the crowd of thoughts out and on paper so I could have a moment of peace. This time feeling a little unsure of myself, as if someone was watching and waiting, I hurried through the writing.

Typically I'm every bit as patient as a situation demands (okay, not always), but nothing about this situation is typical. And honestly, I need some answers. I'm trying to be accommodating and ready for anything, but as a form of communication, this is far from perfect. Rather than provide any useful information, you seem intent on playing some sort of game. If you're keeping score, I have no doubt I'm losing abominably, but you're not playing fair. We'd be far more evenly matched if you'd consent to tell me something—anything—useful. I don't think I'm making unreasonable demands. When a girl discovers an inanimate object talking back to her, she's well within her rights to toss the offending object at the first opportunity. But I am striving to have an open mind. Try not to take advantage, or you might find your communiqué in the compost bin.

That entry had felt particularly empowering. I decided to reward my indomitable spirit with a little TV before succumbing to the never-ending paper trail of high school English. I cued up *Glee* on my DVR, quick-prepped my dinner, and made an effort to relax.

Forty-five minutes later, buzzing through both the commercials and my glass of wine, I felt lighter, happier, and slightly bummed that real life never presented spontaneous song-and-dance numbers. Honestly, if people could pull together on occasion for an impromptu flash mob, the world's problems probably wouldn't seem so insurmountable. Maybe in a few years I could run for mayor of Austin on that platform.

Before settling in with my red pen, I decided to check the journal for a response.

a perfect match demands an open mind

Dislike. I was unimpressed with everything about this response, with the possible exception of its promptness. I flipped back to the previous little pearls of wisdom and read them in sequential order, looking for a clue, a pattern, a reason not to pursue a little Chinese water torture in the toilet tank in an attempt to short out all further communications.

at times the answer is hidden in plain sight
an unexpected development can change everything
a perfect match demands an open mind

Okay, brainstorming . . . they all seemed to be hinting at something, leading me to draw a conclusion that so far had eluded me. The answer, a development, a perfect match. Perfect match didn't sound very national security . . . unless it was referring to counterfeit currency, a priceless artifact, or a faked retinal scan. Perfect match sounded more online dating or custom paint colors.

I heard a car door slam in the driveway and remembered the mess I'd encountered in the house. With my mind wandering the way it was, it occurred to me once again that Mom could use a date. There'd been no one since the divorce, and judging by Mom's awkward flirting with the Geek Freak, her embarrassing tendency to hint at the possibility of romance between Ethan and me, not to mention today's cake binge with double forks, it was definitely time for Mom to get back out there. I'd work on that.

As a matter of fact, there was a world history teacher at school—a handsome retired air force captain, Mr. Carr—who would probably welcome the opportunity to spend time with a pretty whirlwind like my mom. I could invite him for dinner, making sure to specify that I'd like him to meet my *mom*. No sense giving the man the wrong impression.

I glanced again at the little excerpts. Somewhat coincidentally, they all seemed to make sense within the general theme of a romance . . . an unanticipated romance begun in an unpredictable fashion in an unexpected place. Or perhaps not so coincidentally. I'd imagined secret missions, code names, and privileged information, but was I instead facing a grown-up game of M.A.S.H.? Was I meant to be the facilitator? Miss Match herself? And if so, when was I going to get the details, the dossiers? Who the hell was I supposed to be matching up?

I supposed I could use my mom as a guinea pig. Naturally without telling her. And maybe Ethan. That could get interesting. He'd be a tough sell. I could do this—I'd probably be really good at it given my Jane Austen obsession. I'd be clever, cagey, keeping my interference subtle, letting the couple imagine they'd found each other all on their own. Like Jane herself, crafting swoony romances for her heroes and heroines. I could imagine that there would be a certain satisfaction in that. And there was no reason that I couldn't keep my Cat Kennedy persona, wielding my charms on a romance of my own . . . assuming Mr. Tielman ever decided to call me back. And if he didn't, well then, I'd go on the prowl again and relish every minute.

Unwrapping a tangerine Dum-Dum, I slid the journal under the couch, grabbed the remaining bagels and feta, and skipped down the steps to quiz my mom.

She was standing at the kitchen sink, eating a bowl of cake crumbs and slivers when I walked in. The cake had been carved back into shape, and the couch cushions were once again in position.

"Hey, Mom. I borrowed a couple of things." I held them up, eyeing her, wondering if an explanation for the strange happenings afoot would be forthcoming. From this angle she seemed to have smudges under her eyes. *Please, God, don't let her be crying.*

"Hey, sweetie." She sounded tired. "Piece of cake? It had a little accident, but I've mostly cleaned it up." She turned briefly toward me, and in the light of the kitchen, her cheeks looked flushed. Or else she was blushing. Weird. I wasn't sure I wanted to know what had gone on here today. Maybe a particularly wild hot flash?

I stashed the food in the refrigerator, considered getting myself a piece of cake, remembered the state it had been in earlier, and decided against it. "Um, no thanks. How were things at the shop today?"

"A little slow . . . Mondays always are."

"So you came home for lunch?"

Looking startled, she turned toward me.

"Dmitri was working today," she said, sounding defensive. "And I had a . . . chocolate craving. Hence the state of the cake."

Uh-huh. Maybe if she was a chocolate vampire.

"How's your computer working these days?" I asked, wondering if the Geek Freak had managed to work out the kinks, as it were.

She choked a little, put her hand up to her lips, and murmured, "Fine. Good."

Clearly something was up, and she wasn't interested in letting me in on her little secret. Just as well; she wasn't getting in on mine either. I'd just hint around about Mr. Carr. . . .

"Mom, how'd you like to meet one of the teachers I work with? I could bring him home for dinner, Wednesday maybe . . . You could make your famous lasagna and have him eating out of your hand. . . ."

"Why in the hell would I want your date eating out of *my* hand? Lasagna is not finger food."

Obviously my wording had been faulty. "No, Mom, he's not my date. I'd like to introduce the two of you because I think you'd hit it off."

Mom put down the bowl of cake carnage and turned to look at me, the flush gone.

"Hit it off? In what sense?" she inquired sardonically. "Intellectually? Spiritually? Emotionally? Or sexually? I'd like to know going in."

I goggled at her. Sexually? Who was this woman? In our house, "sex" had always meant male or female and not anything going on betwixt the two.

"Um . . . hard to say. Maybe you could play a little Yahtzee and see where it goes from there."

She speared me with a warning glare. "I don't need to be set up, Cate. I'm doing just fine on my own."

"Got it," I said, not willing, at this moment, to argue the point. If she'd been hoping to hide the evidence of her "just fine" existence, she needed to do a lot better. "I'll set it up—we'll have fun." I started casually backing out the door. "Thanks for dinner, Mom. I've got to go grade some papers. Sweet dreams."

I pulled the door shut and leaned my head against it. Whether or not the journal was offering up matchmaking advice, I clearly needed to do *something*. Strolling along the little breezeway connecting Mom's house and mine, I asked myself, *What would Jane Austen do?*

Mom needed a stable, dependable fellow with enough imagination to surprise her every now and then . . . perhaps a Mr. Weston. Rodney Carr would be perfect. If I could convince him to come *and* get Mom to nix the sex talk. I suddenly wished Ethan hadn't disappeared—he could have rounded out our little dinner party and helped smooth over all the awkward moments. He was particularly good at that. Hell, he was good at a lot of things.

I trudged up the steps to face the "irritations" involved in maintaining my English teacher "cover," feeling slightly better about them in that context.

"She makes a mean lasagna," I cajoled. I'd been very careful in phrasing my invitation to Mr. Carr, trying through subliminal mentions of my mom to ensure he knew what exactly was on the table, i.e., lasagna and Yahtzee. Mom's no-sex criterion had not been precisely spelled out—I figured she could cover that end of things. "And who can say no to Yahtzee?"

"Does your mother know you're asking me to dinner?" he asked cautiously. It was ten minutes till the staff meeting, and he was making short work of a Granny Smith apple while drafting essay questions with a pencil and yellow legal pad. Old-school.

"Of course," I assured him, waving my hand dismissively. "She loves to meet new people. And you two have a lot in common. *You* teach European history, *she* wants to go to Europe; *you* were in the armed forces, *she* admires men in uniform." I didn't know too much more about the man, other than he was a great teacher and a good role model. "You probably love a challenge . . . and she can provide it." The last words were spoken through my teeth, and I felt compelled to end on a more convincing argument. "Along with homemade lasagna, garlic bread, and dessert." I flashed a smile.

He smiled back, and new wrinkles creased his face. But they were just surface wrinkles; they didn't go deep. I could sense he was hesitant, and failure looked imminent. But then he said the magic words, "How can I resist?" and I breathed a sigh of relief. Evidently the man did like a challenge.

"Excellent. We'll see you Wednesday at seven."

Now all I needed was for Mom to bring it.

I'd definitely dressed like a ninja. In envisioning Operation Let's Get This Over With, an evening of ghost hunting with Courtney, I'd gone dark. In black ballet slippers (they did have little rhinestones on the tips—maybe ghosts liked sparkles), black trousers, a sleeveless blouse patterned mostly in black, and a black cardigan (with a bit more sparkle), I looked more like an apathetic cat burglar than an indifferent ghost hunter. This was called taking one for the team. I felt painfully nondescript waltzing through the imposing front doors of the Driskill amid the golden glow of ambiance.

Courtney had changed from her work clothes into cargo pants (lots of pockets), a black T-shirt, and a trim little olive jacket with still more pockets. She looked ready to be dropped behind enemy lines, and judging by the equipment spread out over her desk, perhaps she was.

My cell rang before I could get the rundown.

"Hey, chica," Sydney said. "You don't know how hard I'm fighting the urge to make one of those claws-out cat sounds after your dramatic entrance Sunday night."

"I appreciate your self-control." Courtney's head whipped up and her forehead wrinkled in question, but with no explanation forthcoming, she lost interest and turned back to her hunter paraphernalia.

"What are your plans for tonight? Or are they need-to-know?"

"You wouldn't believe me if I told you," I said, eyeing Courtney as she flicked on an ergonomically shaped black box that had obvious flashing and clicking capabilities. If nothing else, it would at least *seem* like we were doing something.

"Well, damn. I thought maybe I could convince Catwoman to come out and play."

Sydney had a knack for bringing out my bad-girl impulse, a fact we'd discovered approximately fifteen minutes after getting paired up at the Central Market Cooking School . . . long before she'd become part of the culinary underground and I'd started spending every Sunday afternoon playing Scrabble. Between her pixie cut, tank tops, and shoulder tattoos and my towheaded tousle and Anthropologie obsession, we'd been an unusual pair. But something had definitely clicked between us, and we'd been asked to leave for instigating a food fight in the middle of class. It had been a simple miscommunication, involving some newly pitted olives and some skinny little breadsticks. We'd spent the next two hours giggling over coffee in the café beneath the cooking school.

"Sorry," I said, secretly relieved I wouldn't be spending the evening getting dragged along Sixth Street in Syd's bouncy, mischievous wake. I eyed the goggles Courtney had laid out on the desk—two pair. It seemed likely that I'd shortly be second-guessing that assessment.

"How about you give me a hint of your plans for the evening as a consolation prize?"

"It involves goggles," I said, hoping her imagination could run with that.

"Ooh, tough one," she said. "Sounds intriguing—you're off the hook. Wish me luck . . . I'm on the prowl." Then she did make the feral cat sound and was gone.

I pocketed my phone, staring at the results of Courtney's continued preparations. "Are you telling me that we are going to have to walk around a five-star hotel in downtown Austin wearing goggles?"

She held up a finger. "You're going to need to leave your cell here. We don't want anything interfering with the hunt—the ring, the vibrations, the frequency—who knows what spooks these ghosts." I pulled the phone from my pocket, dropped it into my purse on the floor beside her desk, and held up my hands, palms-out and innocent.

"Don't sweat the goggles, Cate. I need to go whole enchilada." She dropped into her desk chair, looking a little defeated. "You'd think the most haunted hotel in Texas would have a ghostly little welcome wagon. Nope. It's been *months,* and nothing. So I'm pulling out the big guns."

Having a sudden vision of the Ghostbusters crossing the streams and making a gigantic, slimy mess, I asked, "What exactly are the big guns?"

She grinned widely, placed her hands on the arms of her chair, and stood, the better to wow me, I'm sure. She laid her hand softly, confidently on the black box. "This is Casper, the Friendly Ghost Finder."

"Seriously?" I asked, wondering how I could have imagined I wasn't having any adventures with my life.

"I want to see dead people," she deadpanned. "And this will help me do it. I saw Casper on an infomercial, and the testimonials were really encouraging."

Oh, well in that case . . .

"What is it supposed to do, and how is it supposed to do it? And *why* do we need goggles?"

"It has the dual capability to sense temperature gradients and changes in an area's electromagnetic field, which doubles our ghost-sensing probability." She flipped the switch and a bright green screen flickered on, the numbers on the screen settling to near zero with an occasional flicker. The temperature gauge winked on at the high end of a color spectrum, a sign that Court's office, at least, was not a hotbed of supernatural activity. "The goggles are just a precaution. Lost souls have been known to hold grudges and get ugly. I'd like to be prepared."

I stared at her, wondering what had happened to the straight-shootin' Texas co-ed I'd met at the UT swim center. Evidently Austin had taken its toll, and she was determined to drag me along for the ride, awkwardness be damned. Just as long as I didn't see anyone I knew as I skulked through the opulent halls of the Driskill with Courtney and Casper . . . in goggles.

"Fine," I agreed, just wanting to get this over with.

"Okay," she said, grinning and pulling her hair into a quick ponytail. "I didn't get permission to go into room 525—still working on that—and the other two high-profile rooms are booked, so we're going to have to stay on the two main floors, taking readings near the grand staircase, the elevators, the bar, and maybe the bathrooms."

In other words, we'd be skulking through the busiest areas of the hotel.

"But it's a Tuesday." She shrugged. "So it's not likely we'll run into the usual crowds. Although . . . there is a cocktail party going on in the bar. Maybe we'll save it for last. Ready?" she said, clearly psyched. "I'll give you the lowdown on the rumored hauntings in each area as we get close."

She slipped Casper's strap over her head and let it fall across her chest so that the black box settled on her right hip. She pulled two flashlights from her desk drawer, slipped one in her jacket pocket, and handed me the other. It hung limply in my hand. Next came an expensive-looking camera with a protruding lens, which she tried to pawn off on me. "I thought you could take the pictures."

"Unless it's point-and-shoot, you don't want me in charge of getting documented proof," I warned her.

"Good point." She lifted Casper's strap over her head. "I'll take the photos, you can operate the ghost tracker." I eyed it distastefully before eventually accepting the inevitable. Ironically, I was now thrilled to have the goggles—they'd seriously lower any chance I had of being recognized. Why I hadn't thought to wear a better disguise to this little party, especially given my current obsession with spies and alter egos, was beyond me.

Courtney loaded another pocket with a sharpened pencil and a notepad. Next she lifted a miniature tape recorder to her lips and pressed the Record button.

"November second, 2010." She glanced at her watch. "Seven forty-six. The Driskill Hotel, Austin, Texas. The Lower Floors. Hunting with Cate Kendall." I rolled my eyes, wishing I hadn't deserved a mention. Leaving the recorder running, she slipped it into a smallish pocket on her chest, with the microphone exposed and ready.

My patience was hanging by a thread. "Hey, Court, I don't have a lot of time here, so could we speed things up a little? Some of us have to be up by six."

"Okay," she agreed, patting down her pockets, obviously concerned she might be forgetting something. I was only conscious of needing to leave my pride behind. She reached for my hand, and rather baffled, I offered it up. She leaned over to read from a sheet of paper on her desk.

"Saint Michael the Archangel, defend us in battle. Be our protection against the wickedness and snares of the devil—"

While I was loath to interrupt a prayer against the devil himself, I didn't think I could take much more of this. Knowing Court's quirky mentality, I should have seen this coming, but honestly I hadn't wanted to give this any more thought than I had to, and besides, I had a little situation at home. When she squeezed my hand on the "amen," I squeezed back—what else could I do? And then I hustled her out of the room before she could hold a séance and call forth a little evening entertainment.

We started with the enormous painting of Colonel Driskill, the hotel's first owner, overlooking the landing between the lobby and the mezzanine. Rumor had it that guests could occasionally smell cigar smoke lingering near the portrait, so Courtney and I led with our noses, sniffing like bunny rabbits until my lungs and pride were simultaneously exhausted. I glanced to Casper for a second opinion and was forced to give Courtney the bad news. "I got nothing." One last glance at Colonel Driskill almost had me believing he was smirking at us and our measly attempt. We pressed onward.

"How'd your masquerade as a femme fatale go?" Courtney smirked.

I blinked at her. If she could see herself at this moment, in full ghost-hunting garb, she might think twice about that teasing little smirk.

"It was like I was born for the role."

"Sweep the wand," she bossed, and I dutifully swept it out in front of me as I climbed the steps to the mezzanine. Every now and then I'd glance at the box, ostensibly checking for a reading.

"Did your sex appeal intimidate or entice?" she quizzed. Before I could answer, she pivoted on the top stair and led us back down to sweep the other side of the split staircase. I rolled my eyes safely behind my goggles.

"I attracted at least one man's attention," I said, preening a little. "A Cary Grant in Jimmy Stewart disguise."

"Is that like a wolf in sheep's clothing?" she said, her blond ponytail swinging in an arc.

"In the best possible way," I confirmed.

"So . . . ?"

"So, I flirted, and he flirted," I said, sweeping, "and when the party was almost over, I gave him my number and a sorta sexy kiss on the cheek and disappeared into the night."

Courtney turned to look at me, surprise in her eyes. She then grabbed Casper's wand and began sweeping it over my person.

I swatted her hand away, glancing around me in embarrassment.

"Sorry," she said, clearly not. "I thought maybe I could get a read on you if you were possessed, because that doesn't sound like the sweet little schoolteacher I know."

"Very funny," I said, feigning amusement. "Well, the joke's on you, because I switched up my accessories. No heart on the sleeve for me . . . only a little cleavage and a lot of leg."

"How va-va-va-voom of you!" she said, laughing. "I'm gonna have to look at you differently now." She glanced over her shoulder at me. "Well, maybe when you're not wearing goggles."

Skulking through the art deco lobby of the Driskill wearing goggles was a lesson in embarrassment. I had to keep reminding myself that I couldn't possibly be recognized, but there was a good chance that was simply wishful thinking. So I moved as stealthily as possible over the marble floors, dodging between the Grecian columns and lurking behind potted palms, sweeping Casper's sensor wand casually out in front of me. Our target: the ghost of a four-year-old girl, a Texas senator's daughter who'd fallen to her death down the grand staircase in 1887 while bouncing a ball. Creep-y!

We couldn't detect even a hint of her in the lobby or along the sweeping grand staircase up to the mezzanine. The two of us were not similarly inconspicuous. Alone I could have kept things discreet, but with Courtney following close behind me, camera at the ready, murmuring meaningless updates into the voice recorder, we were likely to be posted to YouTube within the hour. At the very least, we were entertaining the surplus of bellhops at the Brazos Street entrance. Every time the doors were pulled open for a hotel guest they'd all crane their necks for another peek at the geeks.

"Thank you for insisting on the goggles," I said, sotto voce, as Courtney came close.

"This isn't my first rodeo," she told me with a sassy little tip of her head. "Oops!" She glanced down at her recorder, overcompensating because of the goggles. "Probably should have switched off the recorder for that. Oh well. Okay, so the senator's daughter doesn't want to play with us tonight, but there's one more place we can look for her. Ladies' bathroom near the bar. Wanna risk it?"

"Sure," I agreed. Whatever it took to get this over with.

"We might find Colonel Driskill in there too, so get ready!"

I blinked, wondering what the colonel might be doing in there, and my eyelashes brushed against the plastic. I swept my arm out in gallant fashion and waited for her to take the lead. I'd quiz the colonel himself if he decided to show.

So far we'd detected a "cold spot" beneath an air-conditioning vent and increased electromagnetic frequency outside the engineering room, I assume from whatever machines were stashed behind the door. The ghosts were, predictably, playing hard to get, but Court didn't seem to mind. She was content just to be on the hunt.

I'd never stepped foot in the hotel's bar, and having spent the last quarter of an hour surrounded by so much opulence, I couldn't resist sneaking a peek. I tipped my head around the corner and gawked at all that Texas good-ole-boy décor glowing burnt orange under the copper-plated ceilings. The cocktail party was in full swing, mostly guys in suits, their ties loosened ever so slightly, trying to look relaxed and casual and failing miserably. At least they had access to a full bar. The ghost hunt might be a whole lot more tolerable if I had a drink in my hand. Maybe next time I could convince Courtney to let us wear flasks. Then again, maybe there wouldn't be a next time. Wishful thinking.

As I started to turn back to the main hall, my eye caught a familiar profile, and I turned back, suddenly, avidly curious. Despite the suit and the stubble on his jaw, which seriously upped his sexy quotient amid the rest of the mingling suits, the man was unmistakable. I'd walked away from him on Sunday night, crossing my fingers that he'd call me. He hadn't. And now, here I was, standing not fifty feet from him, not as Cat Kennedy, sultry charmer, but as Cate Kendall, ghost-hunting sidekick. *Shit!* And worse still, he'd just leaned down to whisper in the ear of the only woman in the vicinity, causing a blush to crowd into her cheekbones as she crossed her legs and let her skirt ride up her thighs another unseemly inch. *Shit, shit!*

I whipped back around the corner before Courtney came looking for me—two chicks in goggles would likely result in a domino effect of further goggling, and then my cover would be blown, my secret identity no longer secret.

I leaned against the wall, needing just a minute to assess the situation.

"What's the matter?" Courtney said matter-of-factly, sidling up beside me. She'd likely been scoping out the upper reaches of the lobby ceiling for ghostly avoiders.

"Taking a quick break," I lied.

She pressed the Stop button on the voice recorder. "Want to go sit at the bar for a minute and strategize? I'll buy you a drink," she offered, starting to pack things away.

"No thanks!" I said jauntily, pushing myself off the wall. "I'm ready to push on." I definitely didn't want to go in there and come face-to-face with Jake Tielman and his little friend, particularly as a ninja geek. And I definitely did not want to explain to Court that this was the star who'd played opposite my femme fatale. Particularly given that he was flagrantly flirting with someone else. I would just have to make do without the drink that sounded really, really good right now.

She looked at me sideways, convinced there was more to the story, but unconvinced it was better than the paranormal possibilities. I smiled, channeling the gung-ho best friend, and Court tamped down on her curiosity and refocused on the hunt.

As we trekked off to the bathroom, I tamped down on my emotions (and frustrated lust) and tried to make an unbiased assessment. While it was true we'd flirted shamelessly and I'd very deliberately given him my number, no promises had been made, and any expectations I'd harbored of a romantic entanglement between us were my own. Besides, I wouldn't be surprised if The Skirt was the most interesting person at that cocktail party . . . other than Jake. I couldn't fault him for good taste. Cary Grant would have done the same. For all I knew, they were keeping a running tally of everyone in the room with visible nose hair or ear fuzz. Or he could have been letting her know she had a poppy seed between her front teeth. . . .

"I don't know any summoning chants, or we could try one of those," Courtney said as we reached the door to the ladies' room.

"Nothing useable in Harry Potter?" I murmured grouchily. Aloud I spitballed, "Don't we want to observe them in their natural habitat, roaming and haunting unfettered? If we summon them, they're bound to be irritated. I mean, wouldn't you be?" Evidently I had some talent with a shovel.

The ladies' room was a fortress of beige marble and brass fixtures, and I couldn't imagine any ghost wanting to spend their time there. But I dutifully stepped into each closeted stall, swept the wand around each immaculate toilet, and then finished up with the vanity sinks. No cold spots, no EMF, and zero confidence that there was anything lurking here to find.

"One more spot," Courtney begged.

"Where to?" I asked, trying valiantly to be supportive and tightening my grip on my patience. I gritted my teeth.

"The elevators. It's possible the senator's daughter could be lurking in one, or P. J. Lawless, the phantom railway ticket taker who lived at the Driskill for thirty-one years."

Seeing my surprised expression, she seemed pleased. "I'll loan you my reference manual, *Haunted Texas*, and you can brush up on all the ghosts for next time," she said, grinning. Naïve was actually cute on her.

As we padded over the hotel's plush but gaudy star-spangled carpet on our way to the elevators, I crossed my fingers and hoped desperately that the cocktail party had either dispersed or was still going strong . . . and that Jake hadn't slipped away with The Skirt to take a little ride upstairs. My steps faltered slightly, but I rallied. I had the goggles, and I'd keep my head down. And marvel that I'd taken on two semi-secret identities in the space of a week.

When the elevator doors slid open, Courtney strode in, uninhibited by a dark-haired dude in a navy sport coat and worn jeans giving her the eye. I stepped in more gingerly, smiling apologetically. Mostly I was just sorry for myself. The etched glass mirrors inlaid in mahogany paneling were having a field day with the pair of us, bouncing our goggled reflections into infinity. I turned to face the elevator doors, noticed the button was pressed for the third floor, and then tipped my head up. I met the eyes of our hostage and looked away.

"In the southernmost elevator, riding up from the mezzanine," Courtney said, speaking quietly into her recorder. I cringed ever so slightly, then glanced at Casper, relieved he was still keeping quiet, and shifted my gaze to the ceiling, letting my eyes dart about aimlessly. I had no idea what Courtney was doing. And I didn't even want to know about Sportcoat.

"Sorry to intrude, but are you ladies ghost-hunting?" Sportcoat just couldn't resist.

I let my eyes shutter closed and braced myself for Courtney's answer.

"First time," she admitted. "And no luck yet. We were hoping to catch a glimpse of P. J. Lawless here in the elevator."

My eyes fluttered open, I couldn't help it, and through the mirror I watched him check his watch.

"It's 8:52. A little late for the trains to run. I've read that Mr. Lawless appears on schedule with the old train timetable and that he doesn't like a crowded elevator." He grinned and revealed a dimple in his chin.

Holy heck! Who is this guy??

As I watched, he lifted his arm to reveal a book he was holding. I couldn't make out the title in the mirror.

"I haven't read that one yet," Courtney said softly, her gaze focused and intent.

"It's fascinating."

"Have you ever actually seen a ghost?" she probed.

"I think so. I've definitely measured readings that could corroborate that claim."

He gestured toward me, well, Casper, but continued to chat with Courtney. "Have you picked up any anomalies?"

"Not yet," she said. "The only cold spot we found was near the air-conditioning vent."

The two of them shared an amused chuckle, and my eyebrows tipped down as I squinted into the mirror at the pair behind me. These two ghost-hunting goobers were flirting with each other in a haunted elevator. What was next, the ladies' bathroom, local ghosty hotspot? Aha. Perhaps the colonel was looking for love. . . .

"Any EVP?" Sportcoat said, gesturing toward the voice recorder that she was holding propped on her shoulder, no doubt recording this whole mind-boggling exchange.

"What's EVP?" I couldn't tell if she was faking ignorance or not. I wouldn't have put it past her.

Putting out his hand, he said, "I'm Micah, by the way."

"Courtney," she answered. "And that's Cate." *The third wheel on the ghost-hunting-mobile, evidently.*

He glanced once more up at the ceiling. "I don't think the ghosts are wandering tonight. Would you like to have a cup of cof-

fee in the hotel café? I'd be happy to share my amateurish expertise." His gaze and invitation included both of us, but it was clear
that I was expendable, and I couldn't have been more thrilled.

Not so thrilled about Courtney getting involved with a ghost
hunter, particularly one who actually admitted to *seeing* ghosts, but
what was I supposed to do?

It was only later that I recognized this as my own personal "bat
signal."

For now, I took it as the perfect opportunity to disappear.

Chapter 7

Naturally, I had to turn in my goggles on my way out of the Driskill, and not wishing to be caught off guard (ghosts were the least of my concern), I used the little mirror Courtney had mounted on the wall behind her filing cabinets to finger fluff and comb my hair and to reapply some lipstick to my otherwise pasty face.

I walked nervously through the sumptuous lobby, heading for the Sixth Street exit, and the second I felt the cool night air brush over me, my relief was palpable. I barely noticed the man beside me holding open the adjacent door for a woman whose head was turned away. By the time it registered with my slightly addled brain that he looked vaguely familiar, I was standing on the sidewalk looking in at him as he glanced back over his shoulder at me. Evidently it went both ways.

I'd figure it out sooner or later. But right now I was blissfully oblivious, relishing the feel of early November on my skin, and wanting nothing more than to drop into bed with a good book . . . and maybe a little fantasy about Jake Tielman. Because I'd decided to pretend I'd never spotted him flirting in a hotel bar—Cat certainly hadn't. And if he ever did decide to call her, they'd pick up precisely where they'd left off.

* * *

After a thoroughly itchy Wednesday, I decided that if Jake Tielman didn't call me by Friday morning, I'd call him. There was no reason for me to wait for him to make the first move—I was a modern woman . . . who dressed like a vintage vixen thanks to the little hoard of dresses I'd borrowed from the shop. I was desperate to wear the rest of them, but I needed an occasion . . . an *affair*. And a backyard dinner party wasn't precisely what I had in mind.

By the time Mr. Carr had progressed from the front door to the back that night, I was already mentally lambasting Ethan for disappearing for an entire week. He would have been very useful. As it happened, though, we didn't need him. After a shy start, Rodney and Mom hit it off swimmingly, discovering a mutual love of *Burn Notice*, baking, and bird-watching over the course of a rather spirited discussion.

"The yogurt, I don't get." Rodney was referring to Michael Westen's snack of choice on the show. "The man never eats anything else. You don't build a body like that with yogurt."

"Maybe he's just maintaining at this point." My gaze swiveled over to Mom. "At least he has a healthy body weight, unlike Fiona!"

"She could stand a little meat on her bones, but seeing as she's only eating from the same yogurt-stocked fridge, she must be maintaining too." I hid a smile, wondering how Mom would respond.

She pursed her lips, but the edges quirked up in a grudging smile.

"Well then I suppose they all need to celebrate the next spate of vigilante justice with a trip to Golden Corral."

"Maybe we should collaborate on an episode script and send it in," Rodney suggested, I assume, facetiously.

"Maybe we should." Mom's eyes turned bright with excitement as she eagerly blurted her idea. "Maybe Michael and Fiona get into a tricky little pickle and his mother gets them out," she said casually, deliberately not looking in my direction. "A little more romance couldn't hurt either. And fewer girls prancing around in bikinis."

Rodney chuckled. "The project has been tabled due to creative differences."

Eventually, the red wine lulled a bit of the awkwardness into cozy camaraderie, and I left them chatting amiably over slices of Italian crème cake as I stepped inside to make coffee. Through the window they were adorable, Mom's eyelashes sweeping down onto cheeks rounded in amusement, and Rodney's animated expressions keeping them both entertained. This had gone entirely better than I'd expected. Jane Austen would be downright proud of me; these two were my Mr. and Mrs. Weston, a perfect match to set as an example.

I was confident I could claim more matchmaking savvy than Emma Woodhouse, seeing as I'd only pair two individuals who had a chance of success. This being the twenty-first century and not the nineteenth, I could concede I had a few advantages, my magical matchmaking journal being only one of them.

I carried the coffee cups out to the patio on a tray, my expression marginally smug. The pair of them had been chuckling companionably and now let their amusement fade out on a sigh. We each took long, contemplative sips and listened to the night sounds lurking in the dark.

Rodney was the first to break the silence.

"When Cate showed up in my classroom with an invitation to dinner, I recognized it for what it was: a setup. But I figured it couldn't hurt. Worst case, I'd get a plate of homemade lasagna and Cate would owe me a favor." That earned him a hearty laugh all around, and I winged my eyebrow up teasingly. "Turns out the lasagna wasn't even the best part." I glanced over at my mom, whose eyes were shining under the soft, warm glow of the lanterns. "The *cake* was incredible!" I cut my eyes back to Rodney. *WTF?* "I would love to get your recipe, Allison." He shifted his concentration back to his plate and forked up another bite.

Obviously there were a few kinks to work out, but it was a start. At least Mom wasn't shooing him out of the yard.

"I'm high-tech now," she told him coyly. "I can print you up a copy and you can take it home with you."

"Or we could go green together and you could e-mail it," he teased.

The start of a beautiful friendship, I thought wryly.

Between the high-spirited exuberance and the daredevil flirting, Yahtzee was a bit of an ordeal. By the end, it felt as if the dice were careening around in my head. But I smiled warmly as Mom and I walked Rodney out to his car. He'd readily accepted an offer of leftovers and was toting a stack of Tupperware containers.

"Thank you ladies for the invitation," he said, "I enjoyed it. Next time I'll cook . . . *and* bake," he offered. The words hung in the night air, shimmering with possibility. I was the first to grab onto them.

"What about next week?" I blurted into the silence, quickly wondering if my suggestion had come off as a pushy imposition. "You could come back here . . . we could barbecue. . . ." Ethan would be back to shoulder a bit of the chaperoning. "I'm sure Mom would share her kitchen." I nudged her playfully with my elbow, and at long last, she took the bait.

"Absolutely. Maybe you could teach me a few tricks," she said, a little twinkle in her eye—heck, maybe they were stars.

"Well, I'd certainly enjoy trying. But don't bet on it. I have a feeling you already know your way around." My smile chipped away a little as I tried to follow the trend of the conversation. Were we still talking about baking strategies? I couldn't tell for certain, but right now it didn't matter. The wheels were officially in motion. When Gemma flew home for Thanksgiving, it was entirely possible that we'd be having Beer-butt Turkey à la Rodney.

Gemma, who had recently broken up with her boyfriend. She might be looking for a little holiday romance. As Rodney drove off in his shiny beige Chevy truck, I began to plan another bit of matchmaking. It was addicting!

While I still couldn't pinpoint the particulars about the found journal, it didn't stop me from pouring out secrets, strategies, problems, and solutions all in one info dump. I had questions; I needed answers, and with Ethan out of town—where the hell *was* he?—the journal was having to pull its weight as a sidekick.

Okay, so I took your advice—well, I assume I took your advice; the absence of actual instructions made things pretty ambiguous. If your MO is crafty, cagey matchmaking, then I'm officially on board. My virgin attempt sparked a little something between Mom and Mr. Carr, leading me to believe that I may just be good at this. In fact, I'm currently brainstorming possible pair-ups for Syd, Court, and even Gemma, but the men aren't exactly lining up! Between the teachers at school, my girlfriends, and their girlfriends, there's pretty much a dearth of good guys, other than Ethan, who's a regular fixture but a bit of a dating anomaly. Still, I could ask him for help . . . maybe he can produce a couple of friends willing to be guinea pigs, but I'll likely have to endure a lecture.

He's really rather devious, luring my secrets out of me over Sunday-afternoon Scrabble games, while presenting his poker face—poker person-ality—to the world. What the hell is he hiding?? I could smoke him out. . . . Huh. That's an interesting proposition (me to me). My tour as a superspy was cut waaay too short, and I still have the wardrobe. But I'll need to be prepared for the fact that I may discover something I don't want to know. Am I ready for that? I think I am. I still have a couple of days before Ethan gets back to perform a preliminary search—after that, I'll have to be very crafty. I might even have to demand to be taken back to his apartment.

That leaves Jake Tielman as the elephant in the journal. Why hasn't he called me? I dressed up, I played the game—apparently I wasn't quite as desirable as I imagined. He was at the Driskill, very likely flirting, but maybe that's his MO: a no-holds-barred, anything-goes flirt-a-rama, just once, no repeat customers. God, I hope not. I really, rather desperately, hope not. This must be the superhero effect: Once you've tasted the thrill of adventure, it's all you can think about.

It was a little while before I had the spare moments to gaze into the journal in search of pilfered words of wisdom. And by then, my life had shifted all over again.

I decided to use my free period to skulk around Ethan's class-room for any possible clues. I'd just lowered myself into his desk chair when "Kung Fu Fighting" chimed out of the phone I'd laid on his blotter. I'd picked that ringtone specifically for Ethan's calls, and having it go off at the precise moment I'd started my snooping seemed more than a coincidence—it seemed diabolically ironic. My heart ricocheted around my chest like a panicked animal, and I had to remind myself that this was a natural time for him to call—he'd know I was free to talk. I reached for the phone.

"The prodigal friend. What can I do for you? Order a meat-lover's pizza in preparation for your return?" It came out a little bitchy, which seemed rather two-faced given that I was both peeved that he was gone and using the opportunity to sweep his classroom for clues.

"That would be truly appreciated." Ethan's voice was like a tickle in my ear. It made me feel even guiltier, sitting in the dark-ness, my free hand casually mussing the neat organization of his desk. "But I have a bigger favor to ask."

I held perfectly still. "Do tell," I said, casually, doing my damnedest to squelch the nerves that were running rampant over my body, sending out goose bumps and cold sweats. Clearly I wasn't cut out for espionage.

"I'm the best man at a wedding on Saturday, and I need an es-cort—a *date*," he quickly amended in a louder voice.

I opened my mouth to answer, not entirely sure what I planned to say, and was saved the effort.

"And that's not all," he warned. "I'd also consider it a big favor if you'd let me drag you to the rehearsal dinner too. I'd owe you," he clarified.

My lips curled into that cat-with-the-cream grin, and I knew what to say. Because having Ethan in my debt was not something to take lightly, and in fact it was an opportunity impossible to pass up. And seeing as I hadn't any other plans, it was a no-brainer.

"I'm in," I told him, suddenly feeling inexplicably gutsy. This would be the perfect opportunity to foist Cat on Ethan in a little trial by fire. He could either be my sidekick or my nemesis—it was his choice. But I planned on coming out the winner.

"You're a lifesaver, Cate. I'll pick you up Friday at seven."

"I'll be ready," I assured him. He had no idea.

"So what are you doing on your free period?"

He also had no idea how very loaded that question was.

I tried for offhanded. "Just a few little tasks that I've been putting off." I switched the two pens I'd just stashed in the pencil cup back to their specified place, figuring I'd prefer not to get caught over messing with Ethan's head.

"Okay, well. Good luck with that, and I'll see you Friday." And just like that, the tickle was gone.

The search turned up absolutely nothing. Not only were his desk drawers locked and his desk calendar blank for every month through the rest of the year (I checked), his desktop could have belonged to anyone. Well, anyone with a compulsion for neatness and secret keeping. I nudged the mouse, hoping for a quick look at his computer, and a little box appeared on the screen. Above it swirled a series of characters from a language I didn't recognize.

I rolled my eyes. Either Ethan was learning another language, or he was making one up. I turned toward the keyboard, intending to type in "geek" and leave it for Ethan to find, but when I pressed the keys, more swirly, unidentifiable characters showed up. The man had programmed his computer to translate the English alphabet into some mystery language. I held down the Delete key until all the characters disappeared from the input box. Then I carefully typed "Got secrets?" I had no idea if it would still be there when Ethan got back. Or if it would translate correctly. Or if he'd dust the keyboard for my fingerprints in addition to his general dusting. It didn't matter. I could think of a believable excuse for being in his classroom, sitting in his chair, and typing at his keyboard. I'd work on it.

The second interesting call of the day came in around the time a museum curator—or whatever it was I imagined I might do at the Museum of Art when I let the little white lie slip—might have lunch. It came during fourth-period English at Travis Oaks High

School, during a discussion of *Emma. On my burner phone!* Which I had pulled from amid the lollipop jumble on my way out the door that morning. I ignored it while my pulse jumped in my throat and my voice caught on a question to the class.

"If we could chat with Jane Austen over tea at Starbucks, what do you think she'd say about Emma Woodhouse? Do you think Jane herself subscribed to the idea of matchmaking?"

These questions had more than a literary component; I was still trying to get a feel for the Jane Austen influence on the journal. Outside opinions couldn't hurt.

Piper Vane raised her hand and then answered. "I don't know what she'd say to Emma—maybe 'listen to your future husband and mind your own business'—but I definitely think Jane had the itch. Could be she was just like Emma, but with enough sense to manipulate fictional characters instead of real people."

As usual the bulk of the class made a show of solidarity, slowly nodding in ponderous agreement, letting their chins jut forward so as to suggest that there was really nothing more to be said. I wasn't in the mood to draw anyone out.

"I agree, Piper. Ms. Austen was an observer of human nature who couldn't resist the challenge of throwing people together and carefully nuancing the outcome by her own design. Behaving in such a way in real life could be disastrous. But there is always the chance that it could work out beautifully."

I was counting on it.

"Anyone else?"

"If I were chatting at Starbucks with Jane Austen," drawled Alex, a pencil tucked behind his ear, "I would have suggested she add a character or two with the balls to go up against Emma to make it interesting. Everything was too easy for her. Mr. Elton put up a little fight, but it's not much of a fight if you spend half the time telling your opponent you're in love with her." He quirked an eyebrow in my direction. "I'd also suggest she skip the tea and go for the espresso."

"Good point, Alex," I said, glossing over the "balls" mention. "Mr. Knightley was the intended foil for Emma, but I'm not sure he really rose to the occasion as he might have. I think a little more spirited opposition from that quarter would have made him a more interesting character, and perhaps *Emma* an even more interesting book." I speared him with a look, still not entirely certain he hadn't chosen Gwyneth Paltrow over the printed word. He gave up nothing.

And for the time being he was safe.

I didn't get a chance to check my messages until the last bell rang and I dropped into my chair with a bottle of Orange Crush from the vending machine. Every part of me felt fluttery and excited. I let my eyes slide shut at the sound of his voice, remembering.

"This call is for Cat Kennedy. This is Jake Tielman. We met at the Hitchcock shindig on Halloween, where I was an over-the-top Jimmy Stewart. I wanted to let you know that the cast is off, I've gone cold turkey off the hair gel and ditched the pajamas. I'm hoping I can convince you to be my date to a wedding this Saturday. Good friend, gotta go—we can pretend we're spies if that sweetens the deal any. I still haven't gotten to finish out the twenty questions you promised me. So please call me. This line is secure." He added the last almost as an afterthought.

I smiled to myself, appreciating the *North by Northwest* reference and licking the taste of gummy orange slices off my lips for five long, luxurious, imaginative seconds before my eyes flashed open in sudden awareness. *I can't go.* I'd waited long, urgent hours for this call. I'd second-guessed, made excuses, and even begun to formulate a backup plan. And now he'd called, and I'd let his voice, full of playful confidence and flirty innuendo distract me. But I couldn't go. I was going to a wedding with Ethan. And I could guarantee we wouldn't be pretending to be spies.

Seriously, what were the odds of me being asked to two weddings at the very last minute by two separate guys?? They were insane is what they were.

Damn, I was tired of being thwarted.

But it didn't stop there. It was just one of those days. The journal had it in for me too.

absence may In fact produce a very desirable effect

I stared for several long uncertain moments, wondering how to take this one. With every new little snippet of advice, I went haring off on a mental scavenger hunt, trying to find the link that would bridge the clues and help me decode the secret message. It was my fault, clearly, for having entirely too much imagination and no one to keep me in check, but that didn't ease the situation any.

This one could be referring to my recent snooping session into Ethan's private life, or it could be playing off the clichéd sentiment about absent hearts, hinting at my growing obsession with Jake. With that interpretation, it was even possible the reference was giving me a heads-up for next week's barbecue night with Mr. Carr and my mom. Suddenly I was tired and not particularly in the mood to puzzle it out.

I'd called the mysterious Mr. Tielman back after a fifteen-minute pity party and gotten his voice mail. I'd carefully declined, casually hinting at my other plans and a desire to meet again. I relished the feeling of playing hard to get, but I didn't want to overdo it. I suppose if nothing else, I could attend Syd's next event and hope to run into him there. Although . . . Syd and her crew were pretty unpredictable. Our next meeting could very well involve dining family style in the middle of an organic farm field, which didn't exactly scream vintage vixen. I needed the man to call me again—for a night I *hadn't* agreed to step in as a token wedding date.

I was starting to have a bit of trouble trying to keep track of all the little subplots in my own life. It was almost as if I was in the middle of an Austen novel, and while exhausting, it truly couldn't have been more thrilling.

I'd made a deal with Mom: She wouldn't object to an evening of lasagna and Yahtzee with a strange man her daughter had hand-picked for her if I'd come back to the store this week and switch out the Halloween window displays for something appropriately autumnal. Judging by the number of times Mom had managed to work Rodney into the conversation since the "meet-cute," she'd gotten a twofer.

Ideally I would have gotten this all done on Thursday, seeing as I'd committed to a two-night extravaganza with Ethan starting Friday, but Dmitri taught Pilates on Thursdays, as I'd recently been reminded. And I wanted to feel him out on the topic of Syd. Falling victim to a slew of social stereotypes, I'd initially assumed he was gay, but after a quick little storeroom chat, I stood (flabbergastedly) corrected. It went something like this:

Dmitri: You think I'm gay, don't you?

Me: Not . . . necessarily. Although I've had an occasional suspicion.

Dmitri: Because of the fashion major, because I look like a J.Crew catalog model, or because I do Pilates?

Me: All of it?

Dmitri: I've got good news for you, Cate. Not only am I not gay, I'm the whole package, exactly what women want: a sexy, sensitive guy with rock-hard abs and an obsession with clothes. *And* I'm available.

Me: Are you flirting with me?

Dmitri: God, no.

I thought maybe I could get him on the guest list of the next Pop-up Culture event and then step back and bask in another match well made.

So on Thursday, I borrowed a bunch of outdated textbooks and classroom copies of past years' required reading, dragged them home with me, and hunkered down in front of the television with Mom to watch a *Burn Notice* marathon. She'd taken the script-writing suggestion seriously and kept making mental notes to herself. Audible mental notes.

"Sam could stand to ease up on the beers a bit and work on buffing himself up. It's pretty obvious that his Hawaiian shirt is hiding a little potbelly. Or maybe it's not so little," she'd opined, sliding her scissors skillfully along a roll of kraft paper.

I refrained from commenting.

"He may be charming and a sexy salt-and-pepper, but a woman needs more than that."

I cut my eyes around at her. "A sexy 'salt-and-pepper'? Is that a new term?"

Mom's lips twitched. "I think my lunch bunch made it up. They tend to be rather feisty."

"What do they call 'women of a certain age'?"

"Cougars," she said, giggling. I rolled my eyes and turned back to finish taping the end flaps on the book I'd just finished wrapping.

"Well, Rodney's all that and a bag of chips, which he can eat because he doesn't have a potbelly."

"Not yet," she admitted, clearly not optimistic about his chances to "maintain."

"Well, Dad didn't have a potbelly when you decided to split up, and he's in even better shape now."

"Your father likes to impress the chippies, always did. I give him full points for staying fit and attractive at his age. Sex wasn't our problem, sweetheart. We did just fine in that department."

I slid my finished book onto the stack and hopped up, looking for a quick escape. "I'm just gonna get a snack. You want anything?"

"I wouldn't say no to a Milky Way Midnight," she said, her attention already refocused on the diversionary explosion on TV.

I blamed Gemma for this. Her little bomb drop had liberated Mom a little too much. When my sister had decided to enroll in grad school in microbiology, Mom had informed her that she'd either need a grant or a student loan because the money she and Dad had put away for college had run out after one degree per daughter. Gemma won three separate grants, but they weren't enough, and rather than supplement with a student loan, she decided to take a job as a phone sex operator. She spent hours every day alone in a lab and could pretty much let a phone chat run its X-rated course. Little did her call-ins know that she was wearing a Bluetooth, lab coat, and sexy spectacles and running her experiments while giving them exactly what they wanted. Or maybe they did know, and that just helped things along. I was left to deal with Mom and the sex talk.

I slipped quietly back into the living room and settled in to finish wrapping books, trying not to engage Mom in any questionable conversational gambits. It was a long night.

On Friday afternoon, I hustled out of the building after the last bell, jumped into a car overflowing with kraft-paper-wrapped books, and hightailed it down to Mirror, Mirror, parking illegally in front of the shop to unload the cascades of books. I needed to work like a fiend to give myself enough time to get dressed and ready by seven.

I requisitioned Dmitri to help me, putting him in charge of the mannequins, and did my best to have a serious conversation while squatting in the storefront window, fanning books open and folding pages into billowy loops, precise chevrons, and whatever else I could come up with.

"Have I introduced you to my friend Syd?" I asked casually. "She's the one that started up the culinary underground business—their events tend to get pretty regular write-ups in *The Chronicle*." I glanced over at him as he cinched a black patent leather belt over a mustard yellow cardigan topping a forest green wool pencil skirt.

"You've mentioned her, but we've never met." He pulled a trio of vintage brooches from his pocket and pinned them onto the cardigan in a cluster.

"I need to get you on their mailing list—their events are Weird City renowned. From the outside they have the feel of an exclusive party with a secret password to get in, but inside it's just cool people sipping signature drinks and eating gourmet food."

"How many have you been to?" he said, distracted by the effort of stretching some patterned tights from beneath the mannequin's skirt to the aubergine suede Mary Jane pumps waiting on the floor below.

Hadn't seen that coming. "Um . . . just one. But I've heard about a bunch more."

Ironically, I now had his full attention. His riot of black curls was so artfully arranged that he looked like a classical statue. In fact, that was probably what he was going for: Adonis with fashion sense. In his trim khakis and black V-neck T-shirt, he only needed to lose the chunky black frames settled on his nose. Then again, what did I know—he was the fashion major. He propped his hand on his hip. "Why just one?"

"Oh, I've just been really busy."

"Doing what?" he demanded with a sardonic tone that put me immediately on the defensive.

"Plenty! But now I've been to one, and I'm definitely going to another." I made sure to keep the sassy little "so there!" I was hearing in my head silent. "You should seriously consider being part of the city's cultural underground. Who knows who you might meet. . . ." I thought of Syd, with her smoky bedroom eyes, her athletic body and well-placed tattoos, and smiled to myself.

"Uh-huh." He turned back to the mannequin, gave her a quick once-over, and shifted his attention to the next one. "So sign me up. If it gets too pricey, you can be my sugar mama."

I glanced over the piles of books at Dmitri, who was efficiently shimmying the skirt right off the mannequin. Clearly the man was talented. If Syd could see past those Clark Kent glasses, I bet she'd be willing to comp him the night.

Suddenly it seemed as if everywhere I looked, there was an alter ego just waiting to be unmasked.

"If I'm even going to consider being your sugar mama," I drawled, "I'm going to need some Sugar Babies." And Mom still had a bowl of Halloween candy on the counter. I carefully unfolded myself from my crouch, checked my watch, and limped out of the window display with the slightly exhilarating feeling that I was moonlighting as Miss Match.

Chapter 8

When Ethan knocked, I was waiting, and I slung the door open, holding it in my grip and striking a pose in the doorway. In black loafer heels, my eyes were almost level with his, and I locked onto them. His gaze roamed all over, from my charcoal gray pencil skirt to my black button-up silk charmeuse blouse with cap sleeves and red piping, all the way down to my hose and heels, and back up again to my chandelier earrings of jet beads and Swarovski crystals. Oh, and the lips. He definitely noticed my Lolita lips. And I suspect that was all he could handle.

"What the hell, Cate?" I could tell he'd tamped down on what he really wanted to say, but he seemed genuinely puzzled. Clearly he'd been anticipating a date with a schoolteacher, not a curvy, sexy siren. I bit my lip to hide my amusement.

"I'm sorry, what's the question?"

His eyes flashed, and he put his hands out in an *isn't it obvious* gesture. I softened toward him just a little. Here he was, looking very handsome in a beautifully tailored suit, come to pick up his date for the evening, and she was almost unrecognizable.

"Remember when I said I was looking for a little more excitement in my life?"

"Yeaahh," he said, drawing the word out, probably cringing against the possibilities.

"I found some," I confided, feeling giddy over the big reveal.

"Where'd you find it?"

"This is Austin . . . it may as well be floating in the air." I was teasing him now.

He leaned forward a little, glanced over me again, and dragged his eyes back up to mine. Tension was high, and I was riding it.

"I created an alter ego . . . like Superman and Clark Kent, only I'm not a superhero. I'm more of a friendly femme fatale, flirting shamelessly. Meet Cat Kennedy," I suggested, lifting my free hand in spokesmodel fashion.

"Holy crap, Batman!" Ethan blurted, his lack of creativity surprising me. I waited, certain there was more.

"So you're just vamping up and going out? Isn't that a little reckless? What if some guy takes you up on your shameless flirting?"

"Who says one hasn't?" I countered waspishly, wishing one in particular had. "And what business is it of yours if one does? Fresh meat for Sunday Scrabble," I reminded him.

He was staring at me, wide-eyed, utterly baffled, but he quickly regrouped, running a rough hand over his face, clearly trying to form a cohesive argument.

"I haven't told you all of it yet," I said, torn between wanting to and not.

He pulled his hand away. "Do I even want to hear the rest of it?"

"You don't have a choice," I said.

His shoulders slumped slightly.

I took a deep breath. "Remember that journal I found under the table at Torchy's last week? Well, the week before you went missing?"

"Yeah," he said warily.

"It's a little wonky. And it definitely factors into this. Maybe I should tell you in the car. Otherwise, there's a good chance we'll be late, and that sort of behavior is frowned upon in a best man."

Ethan conceded the point, turning to step down the stairs of my garage apartment. When I turned from locking the door, I found his gaze heavy on me, even in the dark, and I felt self-conscious as I carefully maneuvered the steps in heels. Things were just as awkward in the car.

"So tell me about the journal," he said, eyeing my legs in the deepening twilight before shifting his gaze back to the road. I couldn't get a good read on him—was he disappointed in me? In my legs?

I stared at his profile, wondering how he was going to take this. It would probably be a tough sell, but I knew that going in . . . I could work with that. "The journal sort of has a mind of its own."

"What the hell does that mean?" He glanced over at me again, and his jaw tightened almost imperceptibly in the light of a street lamp.

"It means that when I write in it, it somehow erases the words it finds . . . superfluous. And when it's done, there's a message."

Ethan shot through a yellow light going over the Congress Ave. Bridge.

"What?! What sort of message?"

"The latest one said, 'absence may in fact produce a very desirable effect,'" I told him, cursing myself for bringing up the journal. I should have known that it would be impossible to explain. Words were simply not enough; he was going to have to see it to believe me, and even then he'd have a hard time with it.

"Cate—" he said, shooting another look at me, probably in an effort to see if I was messing with him. For once, I wasn't.

"I know. *I know!* I honestly have no idea what that means, but I do have a few theories about the whole thing." Theories I'd be a little squeamish about telling Ethan. But I would, because I'd decided I needed a sidekick. He could be my behind-the-scenes code breaker slash tech guru, should an instance arise that I needed a tech guru. He could wear all black, maybe a leather jacket. . . .

"Yeah . . . ?" he said, zapping my little fantasy bubble. "Lay 'em on me." We were already pulling into a parking spot on Brazos.

Ethan shifted into park and killed the engine, and suddenly it was very quiet . . . and awkward all over again. It felt weird, like I was sitting beside a stranger. He'd been gone—mysteriously—for an entire workweek, and in those five days, things had changed big-time. All because of a magical journal that, until now, had been my little secret.

"You need to see it for yourself, Ethan," I told him, not quite meeting his eyes. "It's impossible to explain without the journal, because without the journal it all sounds like a load of crap. I get that. But when have I not been straight with you?" Forcing myself, I lifted my gaze.

In the darkness, his eyes stared into mine, impossible to read. Whether he believed me or not, he was back, and everything already felt more normal.

"All right. Why don't we just get through this dinner, and you can show me the journal when I drop you back at home?"

"Sounds like a plan," I said, nodding.

I'd noticed when Ethan had come to pick me up that with heels I was only a couple inches shy of his six feet. And now, as we walked along the sidewalk together, it occurred to me that my eyes were just about on level with his lips.

I stumbled, my heel caught on a tree root pushing up between the concrete squares of sidewalk—something I probably would have noticed if I'd been watching where I was going instead of measuring myself against Ethan like a little kid. Ethan caught me easily, his hand gripping my arm just above my elbow.

"Thanks," I said. "I'm good." I nodded and sent him a sidelong smile, evidence of my careful concentration.

I could feel him staring back at me, but I didn't look. After a beat of silence, he conceded, but rather than let me go completely, he slid his hand down to clasp it firmly, securely around mine.

He must have had a sixth sense about me in those heels, seeing as I stumbled again, almost immediately, on a clear, flat stretch of sidewalk. Weird.

Ethan was quite the attentive escort, although I suspected he kept close to me, often with his hand on my lower back, to make sure I didn't go all Catwoman on him. It felt strangely like we were on an actual date. Very strangely.

By the time Ethan had pulled back into Mom's driveway, I was carrying my heels and desperate to get out of that pencil skirt and into some pajama pants. Judging by the speed with which he shrugged off his suit jacket and yanked off his tie, Ethan had precisely the same idea.

"I'm making hot chocolate," I told him, scuffing through the apartment on the way to my mini-kitchen. "You want some? I add lots of marshmallows."

"Sure," he agreed. His eyes were already shuttered closed as he lounged on the sofa, no doubt gearing up for our little show-and-tell-all. Too bad nothing would prepare him.

I came back to the couch carefully toting two mugs of cocoa and a bag of Pepperidge Farm Mint Milanos under my arm. Settling everything on the coffee table, I unearthed the journal from underneath the sofa. I was slurping up marshmallows and the journal was waiting patiently between us when Ethan finally opened his eyes.

"You wanna do this tonight?" I asked, offering him an out.

"I think we'd better," he said, looking me over. "You're easier to talk to like this."

"You mean in flannel?" I teased.

"Yep," he said, reaching for his cocoa. "So tell me again about the journal, and I'll see if I can make sense of what you're saying this time."

I pulled my legs up onto the couch, sitting cross-legged, and suggested, "Why don't you take a look for yourself, and then I'll answer your questions till we're on the same page?"

So he looked. He looked at the inside, glanced at the dedication, paged through and pored over the four pages with messages, and even riffled through the blank pages till the end. Then he closed the book and examined it all over again from the outside. As a silent observer, it didn't appear that his efforts produced any additional findings over and above the original perusal in the Trailer Park. He looked up at me.

"No joke, right?"

I stared at him from under lowered lids. "Well, it's not funny, is it?"

"Judging from past experience with you, that doesn't exactly eliminate it as a possibility."

I plastered on a snarky little smile before confirming, "No joke."

"Anybody know you found this journal?"

"Nobody but you."

"Where have you been keeping it?"

"Under the couch."

He shot me a look, but didn't comment.

"Okay, let's see it in action." He held the book out to me, and I took it cautiously.

"What do you mean?"

"I mean, let's write in it and wait for words to disappear and the secret message to emerge." By the sound of his voice, he wasn't taking this completely seriously, so I wasn't about to reveal any of my conspiracy theories. At least not yet. Maybe I'd wait to hear his theories before telling him mine. But clearly he was going to have to see the little transformation for himself.

"Fine. Do you want to do it, or shall I?"

"Why don't you do it? You're already pen pals." He tipped his head back against the couch and smirked. I considered popping him with one of the pillows, but rose above it. I did, however, spoon the rest of the marshmallows out of his mug and into mine before settling in to write. In pen.

I get that you're calling the shots—erasing words, offering up clues, refusing to answer any questions or supply any more information than you deem necessary—but I'm still clueless, so I've been forced to call in backup. Ethan was with me when I found the journal, and we've been friends for a long time. I trust him, and he's clever, good with words and puzzles. He is not, however, as open-minded as I am, and is not likely to go haring off on a mystery adventure without more information. And even then, it would be a stretch. He's humoring me now, despite really believing this is all one big practical joke. Either that, or else I'm out of my mind.

So this time, it's for posterity. We need to convince him between the two of us (whoever you are) that, logical explanation or not, this is really happening. Let me down now, and something nasty just might happen to you.

Well, it wasn't much, but I couldn't very well write any private things because Ethan would obviously want to read the before as well as the after.

"Okay," I said, nudging his thigh with my foot. "The hard part's done. Now we wait." I leaned over to retrieve my cocoa, holding the journal open between us. We'd have to go through this entire procedure all over again if Ethan didn't get a peek at my entry before it got hacked to bits.

Ethan leaned forward, took the open journal, and then propped his elbows on his knees to read over my token entry. Just after his muffled snort of amusement, he turned his face toward me, eyebrows raised and lips quirked. "I'm flattered."

I shrugged. "Just greasing the skids, my friend. Now you're in a much more accommodating frame of mind." I sipped my cocoa and smiled to myself.

"That remains to be seen. So now what?"

"Now we wait."

"How long do we have to wait?" He glanced at his watch, which likely read the same as the clock on the wall beside the kitchen: ten-thirty.

"No idea. I write in the journal and then stuff it under the couch and check it when I get a chance."

"What kind of experiment is that?" He reached for his mug, started to take a sip, immediately noticed the missing marshmallows, and glanced over at me in exasperation. Worth it.

"It isn't one," I confirmed. "I brought you in as a sidekick—this is your area of expertise. I'm the front woman; you're the details man."

He ran a heavy hand through his hair and ignored me for several moments. I assumed he was coming up with a strategy. I waited. It didn't take long.

"Okay." He turned toward me on the couch. "Let's start with this: We're going to tip the journal closed and open it right back up again."

"I'm all in," I assured him, not moving from my lounge position.

"Ready?" He held the journal out in front of him like some sort of offering, used his finger to save the page, and then closed and opened it again in the space of a single second.

"No change," he told me. That didn't surprise me.

"Okay," he suggested quickly. "We'll close it completely, count to five, and *then* open it."

I stayed quiet, content to just watch.

Predictably, that didn't provide the expected results either. This little trial-and-error-fest went on for a little while, and I couldn't tell if Ethan's mounting frustration was with the journal or with me. Foreseeing an imminent need to tack on a few ego-boosting sentences to the original entry, I decided to step into the fray.

"What if we just give it a little privacy to work its magic and check it again in fifteen minutes?"

Ethan tossed the journal onto the coffee table and collapsed back onto the sofa. "Fine. This can be the absentee experiment. We don't talk, we don't move, we just wait." So decreeing, he crossed his arms over his chest and closed his eyes. I snapped mine shut too, thinking of several other things I would be jotting into that journal should a follow-up experiment prove necessary.

I blinked my eyes back open, squinting against the light. At some point I'd shifted onto my side and stretched my legs out onto Ethan's lap. He had his head turned away from me, but his hands were settled comfortably on my knee and ankle . . . awkward! Sitting up slightly, I peeked at Ethan's watch. It was almost midnight!

I attempted to slide my legs out of his grasp, but he only

gripped them harder. So I went with Plan B: Reaching for the journal, I lay back on the couch, closed my eyes, and smacked it hard against the coffee table. We "came awake" at the same time, and I pretended not to notice as Ethan slipped his hands from my legs and rubbed his face into semiconsciousness.

"I suspect it's been more than fifteen minutes," I offered, vaguely chagrined. This had, after all, been my idea.

"Little bit," he said, after glancing at his watch. "It's been almost an hour and a half. I guess we'll check in with the journal." He reached for it as it hung half-on and half-off the table. Unwilling to surrender first dibs, I scrambled up and leaned in next to him as he turned back the cover and paged through the first few inconclusive "communiqués." Just before turning the page to finalize this latest experiment gone awry, we glanced at each other, cognizant that this was somewhat of a moment of truth. And then he flipped it.

puzzle it out between you

"Aha!" I announced. "There it is, in black and white. Proof."

Ethan turned carefully and raised an eyebrow. "Unless you only faked being asleep. You didn't drug my cocoa, did you?" I elbowed him, hard.

"If I'd drugged your cocoa I'd have thought of something considerably more imaginative to do with the time and opportunity," I assured him. It was gratifying to see the uncertainty in his gaze, no matter how short-lived.

Shifting his attention back to the book, Ethan stared at it a long moment, either trying to determine a strategy of attack or desperately wishing he could chuck it into the trash can and pretend we'd never had this conversation. I decided to take the opportunity to warm up my long-cooled hot chocolate—I knew from experience that Ethan did not partner well in brainstorming; he preferred to work alone.

Ten seconds was all the time it took the man to start banging the journal on the coffee table.

I hurried back to the couch and grabbed it back from him, snapping, "I don't think corporal punishment is the way to get it to talk."

The minute it changed hands, something slipped from the binding and fell to the floor with a muffled thud before bouncing under the couch. A quick glance flashed between us before I was on my knees, clutching the journal to my chest while leaning over to peer under the couch. Luckily I quickly found the escapee, which meant that I could ignore the crew of dust bunny squatters hanging out under there. It was a key. And I could only assume it was the key to the journal, although what it had been doing tucked into the spine was just one more mystery to add to the growing list. I held it up for Ethan's inspection, casually pulling off a dusty little hanger-on.

He shot me a dubious look and asked, "That key doesn't fit the journal, does it? The key plate doesn't even look functional."

I shrugged and proceeded to make an attempt. As I slid the key into the evidently more-than-decorative keyhole, something strange happened. Stranger than the things that had already been happening for more than a week now. Feeling a bit out of my depth, I came off my knees on the floor and jumped onto the couch next to Ethan so I could divvy up the weird, wild stuff.

The journal was growing in my hands. It wasn't a trim little purse volume anymore—by the time it finished, it was the thickness of an encyclopedia, and my fingers were trembling, cradling the book, as I turned to peer up into Ethan's face. He was blinking rapidly, his mouth set in a grim line. With tacit approval from me, he relieved me of the weighty tome and flipped it for a hasty examination before settling it on his lap and tipping it open.

I inched closer and our collective gasps came out side by side just as my finger shot out, homing in on one word . . . "Austen."

My heart, already galumphing audibly along, was now joined by odd whistling, fangirl sounds emanating from my throat. I was a regular one-man band. But *Oh my God!*

The first page—the dedication page that mentioned the morsels— was magically (because really there was no other word to describe what had just happened) wordier now, and it hinted that my Jane Austen suspicions hadn't been completely off track. In fact, if we were to take the newly expanded dedication at face value, then Jane had, in fact, believed *this very journal*, and its bonus features, to be the perfect Austenesque gift for her niece.

I sat quietly, if twitchily, and read the new and improved version, which matched the online version I'd read earlier in the week, marveling that something once belonging to Jane Austen had found its (marginally ignominious) way into my hands via a picnic table at a trailer park in Austin, Texas. And I'd saved it, making me something of a hero.

June 2d. 1793

1793 . . . It was true . . . it *had* to be true! I turned triumphantly to Ethan, but his face was still scrunched in ponderous thought. Too bad—my patience quota for the evening had shriveled to nothing the second Jane Austen had come into play. But I couldn't very well turn the page until he was ready. . . .

"Don't even dare suggest that I slipped you a hallucinogen, Chavez," I warned.

He smirked and turned toward me, now fully awake with his eyes lit by curiosity.

"Fair enough," he said. "I didn't drink enough of the cocoa anyway."

I punched him on the arm. "So??" I grabbed a pillow and wrapped my arms around it, hugging it tightly. "You go first. What are you thinking?"

I held my breath, waiting, hoping desperately that he was going to step up to the occasion.

"I would love to write this off, but as much as it pains me to say it, this round goes to the journal. I have no idea what the hell just happened—or what we're dealing with here."

I grinned at his casual use of first person plural, but my expression quickly morphed into shock as he tipped the book closed.

"In fact, let's try this again," he suggested. He took hold of the key, very obviously on the verge of removing it, and I lunged to stop him.

"Veto!" I said.

"What?" he said, obviously confused by my outburst.

"This isn't *Mythbusters*, Chavez. We don't need to understand the nitty-gritty of how it works right this second. Some of us just want to revel in the fact that it does and keep reading. Sound like a plan?" I kept my hand snug over his, conscious suddenly that we were, in effect, cozied up on my couch after midnight, pretty much holding hands. And reading Jane Austen. I bit back a smile and waited for Ethan's answer.

"Fine," he said, waving his free arm expansively. "We'll read." He tipped the tome open again, flipped past the facing page, and attempted to skip over the dedication. I laid my hand steadily on the open page, shuddering just slightly over the feel of the brittle pages and the deep-seated knowledge that the one and only Jane Austen had penned the words.

"And the possibility that Jane Austen once owned this journal . . . ?" I inquired, pressing him to acknowledge the full scope of the situation.

"Well, I'm sure there were other, lesser known women named Jane Austen. It could have belonged to one of them."

"Uh-huh," I said brusquely. "And what about the magic?"

"To my knowledge, Jane Austen has never been credited with any magical abilities. The weird workings of this book could be purely coincidental." He shrugged. "Or," he opined with a grin, "maybe one of those other Austens I just mentioned was a witch and she put a hex on this journal so that anyone who wrote in it—"

I promptly removed my hand from the page in question and relinquished my grip on the pillow to let it fly toward Ethan's face.

"Don't talk. Just don't talk," I insisted, desperately hoping I hadn't been hexed. "You've been demoted to page-turning lackey."

He nodded agreeably and turned the page, and we both began to read.

There is to be a dance, and in as much as that is delightful all on its own merit, I have a better reason to be fidgety, for afterwards, I shall be <u>out</u>! I confess to being both nervous and excited at once. I am to have a new gown and am truly hoping for something lovely. Simply the thought of it will help me to happily endure the days—and moments—in between. Mother will surely endeavor to make use of these golden opportunities to warn me against future folly while at the same time urging me to embrace all that is good and true. But I will endure with high spirits, for I intend to remain, for as long as possible, pleased with the World in general and everyone in it, Mother included.

I was fairly salivating, reading the giddy exuberance of a young girl—a young *Austen*—about to make her debut into society. My shoulder brushed against Ethan's as I eagerly reached to turn the page. He put up a hand to block my attempt, turned to look at me, eyebrow raised, and said, "Control yourself, Cate," before slowly turning the page.

The next entry was even better. . . .

I find myself in quite a conundrum. Despite having written to you, Aunt Jane, and discovered that, by some strange magic, you are able to advise me through the pages of this very journal, I cannot claim even a vague understanding of how you are able to do so. And while you must know the esteem in which I hold your good advice and opinions, I admit that I can no longer consider this a private journal in the traditional sense, knowing that every careful word is on display. I can, however, delight in using it just as you intended, to record the little dilemmas that life presents, expecting, in response, your prompt and sound advice. I expect I will need it more than you know, because I have decided to follow in your footsteps, Aunt Jane, and dedicate myself to my writing, and I fear that Mother will take very vocal exception to this, a very much unintended path. With lifelong admiration and newfound awe, I remain your loving niece, Anna.

I waited until I'd reached the end of the page before triumphantly pronouncing, "I knew it! It's exactly as I suspected: Jane Austen herself, the literary treasure, not the witch," I specified, cutting my eyes around at Ethan, "is giving the advice. She's the one trimming off the excess words, *editing* the entries, and leaving behind little snippets of, well, ambiguity." A little of the fizz went out of my discovery.

"That's not completely conclusive," he said, "And how is a dead woman—not even a witch—managing that?"

"I don't know *how* she's doing it, but neither do I know how Wi-Fi works, and I don't question it every time I use it to get on the Internet. Besides, she's Jane freakin' Austen; give the woman some props."

"You have got a serious fangirl crush on her." Ethan smirked.

"Bet your ass I do," I said. "So let's get back to it, shall we?"

"Okay, hold up. You can pore over the secret diary entries of Jane Austen's niece later. Let's try to keep things big picture for right now, okay?"

"Okay, fine," I agreed, longingly wishing Ethan shared my fangirl crush.

"Good. So the snippets are, evidently, gone. The entries are here in their entirety—I'm assuming from everyone who's owned the journal since Jane Austen Junior. So . . ." He flipped forward, gripping hunks of pages and pushing past them, quickly nearing the end of the book.

I realized, almost too late, what was about to happen and fairly threw myself onto the book and effectively onto Ethan's lap in my urgency that he not read the entries I'd written. I couldn't remember exactly which bits I'd put in writing and which still floated through the ether, weaving in and out of my consciousness as the occasion demanded. It didn't matter—private was private.

"What are you doing?" I demanded, one eyebrow raised, trying for casual and failing miserably.

"Right now? I'm wondering if 'fangirl crush' is actually code for 'huge turn-on.'" I could hear the amusement in his voice as he let go of the book to cross his arms over his chest, playing right into my hands. I snapped the journal closed and pushed off his (surprisingly muscular!) thigh back into a sitting position.

"Interesting question. I've never put it to the test," I said, lifting my own eyebrow. I settled the big book back on my lap and studiously avoided looking at him as I admitted, "I don't want you to read my entries."

A noise escaped him, part laugh and part huff of disbelief.

"They're private," I insisted, shyly smoothing my fingers over the worn leather of the journal and the delicate curves of the key protruding almost defiantly from the tarnished little key plate.

I suspected him of exaggerated eye rolling and didn't bother to confirm. "So I'm never gonna get to see them?" He seemed resigned. "What about the excerpts? Do I get to see them?"

"Absolutely," I agreed. "Seeing as they're the only clues we've got."

"So what's it gonna be? If you want my help tonight, you need to pull out the key and show me what's left. Or I can go home and leave you to pore over the details of every previous journal owner's private life, and we can deal with the rest later."

My gaze darted from the journal up to his face as my brain teeter-tottered between the options. It was excruciating. My answer, however, was inevitable.

"You can go." I offered him a rueful smile of apology, but knowing me as he did, I'm pretty sure he was expecting me to side with Jane.

"Works for me," he said, rising slowly, sleepily from the couch. "Knock yourself out. Just don't stay up too late. I've still got you on the hook for a date tomorrow night." Two steps to the door and he turned back. "Should I be expecting Cate or Cat?" he asked, and it was impossible to read his expression.

"Which do you prefer?" I parried, smugly expecting him to go conservative.

Standing in my doorway, slightly rumpled in his evening attire and shadowed with the beginnings of tomorrow's stubble, his dark eyes seemed as sharp as mine were bleary.

"Surprise me," he suggested. "See you at seven." And then he turned and was gone.

Chapter 9

I stayed up way too late, and rather inevitably, I dreamt of Mr. Darcy. Normally, that would have produced a lovely, swoony sort of morning, but oddly enough, I woke up a little bit peevish. Darcy had been a bit standoffish, lording it over someone or other in that arrogant manner of his that every true fan knew was simply misunderstood. But I wasn't in the mood, seeing as I was full up on "misunderstood" at the moment.

Fully intending to stay in my pajamas today until it was time to get ready for my "date" with Ethan, I shuffled into the kitchen to fix myself a cup of hazelnut coffee, lugging the super-sized journal along with me. I had papers to grade, but I wanted a few more minutes of heartfelt, romantic prose before delving in to run-on sentences, absurd analogies, and dubious connections. Rather than keep reading where I'd left off early this morning, I paged quickly to the entries following those belonging to Jane Austen's lucky niece.

Jane Elizabeth had loaned the journal to a close friend who, due to dire financial circumstances, had found it necessary to find work as a governess. And then found it unavoidable to fall head over heels in love. But not with the chiseled cheekbones of the master—nothing so clichéd. She'd fallen in love with the music master. I felt like pinching myself, this was so good. Folding myself onto the couch with my coffee, I slipped into the past all over again.

The situation I find myself in is awkward in the extreme. Now I need not only deal with a thoroughly unwise and unrequited romance, but with the impossible, albeit well-meant, suggestion that I seek advice on the matter from this very journal, on loan from Jane. But how difficult to reveal the feelings that I have long locked away in secret, or in whispered confidence with Jane herself! For even the barest possibility of a happy resolution, I will. I cannot confess to understanding Jane's fantastical explanations . . . but with faith and trust in my friend, I will here record my unwieldy dilemma.

I am governess to the children of Hambleton: two boys, James and Andrew, and a girl, Harriet. By most standards, they are well-behaved children, high-spirited, good-humored, and intelligent. They are not musically inclined. However, their mother Lady T believes that with enough tutelage they will be, and so has engaged a Music Master to instruct the children three afternoons a week. And this decision, I believe, will be the death of me.

You see, Dear Journal, I have fallen quite irreparably in love with Mr. Edgerton. He would never be described as handsome, with his intense but distracted gaze, his harsh features, and the spectacles that are as often torn off in agitation as they are settled on his face. But I find him as beautiful as the nocturnes he plays in solitude, forever seeping under the door of the music room. He is elegant, and ever a gentleman, but I suspect he would not even recognize me if we met on a walk about the grounds. I am invisible, and consequently yearn to make myself seen. To make him really see me, see my admiration and even my affection. I fear that if subjected to much more of his polite dismissal, I will shatter, or worse, step defiantly beyond the boundaries of propriety and surely be shamed or dismissed.

I truly hope for some sort of guidance, Dear Journal, for I fear my sanity is fragile.

I let out a deep sigh and felt it catch in my throat. If this was a historical romance novel, it wouldn't be long before this music master became a servant to his desires, tossing off his spectacles and laying this feisty governess over the top of a piano, resulting in a glorious duet. And judging from the next entry, that wasn't far off. And as telling as it was, I couldn't help but wish I had a sneak peek at the little snippet of advice culled from this impassioned entry. I read on.

It seems I shouldn't have doubted either you, Dear Journal, or Jane Elizabeth, for the transformation occurred precisely as described. The mystical nature of it all puts me in mind of the gypsy fortune-tellers that sometimes camp in the woodlands surrounding Hambleton. Cross their palm with a piece of silver, and they will read the future in the lines of yours. But this was no vague prediction, but rather precise instructions, sufficiently specific as to eliminate the weighing of decisions and the uncertainties of a decision made misguidedly alone.

I wish to confide that I've begun. The slow and steady erosion of Mr. Edgerton's blissful solitude is progressing nicely. Sunday, gifted with a bit of time to myself, I stepped quietly into the music room and inquired as to whether I might sit with my needlework and listen. Between the blinking and the staring, you'd think I'd asked if I could sit on the top of the piano as he played! But he agreed. Today, when the children went out riding, I sought him out a second time and sweetly inquired as to whether he might spare a few moments to take on a new pupil. How amusing it was that I needed to specify that I referred to myself! I know I am flustering him and should probably be feeling a bit contrite, but wicked or not, I find instead I'm feeling rather triumphant!

I could guess how the advice read this time, because by the next entry, things had progressed significantly, and the sassy little minx had made it on top of the piano!

Tipping my head back against the couch cushions, I marveled at this . . . *firecracker* trapped in the body of a governess. She may as well have been me a hundred plus years ago, except that I was more of a sparkler trying to amp things up with some clingy dresses and sexy heels. I had a sudden, vivid image of Ethan's face when he got his first glimpse of Cat—there was definitely blinking and staring. A slow grin seeped over my face as I imagined a repeat performance, maybe even upping the shock value just a tad. Then again, I couldn't go crazy; this was a wedding, after all.

I spent the rest of the day task-hopping between grading papers, de-cluttering the apartment, and imagining romantic pair-ups among my acquaintances. I never would have had the nerve to throw people together the way I planned to if not for the journal . . . and Gypsy Jane. But now here I was, almost giddy with excitement. The journal was obviously magic—there was no other way to explain words disappearing, pages reappearing, or advice mysteriously arriving as needed—and I had wondered, more than once, whether it had somehow bewitched me. Whatever that meant.

I was overwhelmed to have fallen into an opportunity to pair up with the phenomenal Jane Austen, particularly in this quirky, puzzling, romantic way. It was as if Jane had rolled up—to the Austin Trailer Park & Eatery, no less—with a funky, gypsy vibe and settled in to tell romantic fortunes from behind a makeshift crystal ball (i.e., magical journal). I suppose that made me the medium. Who'd recently started to dress like a siren. Nowhere, but in Austin.

By the time the knock came at seven, I was totally transformed.

Ethan gave me a long look that felt like a slow perusal before saying a word, which was lucky. I was hoping his own distraction made my gauche gawping at the sight of him in charcoal gray khakis and vest a little less noticeable. His shirt was rolled up to his elbows, and he wore black Converse sneakers on his feet. I just wanted to rumple him all up. As it was, he actually looked kind of adorably sexy. . . . "Which one are you?" The question derailed a rather awkward train of thought.

I rallied. "Which one do you think I am?" I'd rifled through the dry cleaning bags and picked a simple style with Grace Kelly glamour. The dress had a fitted black bodice, dipping in front and back into matching V's, and three-quarter-length sleeves. Beneath its patent leather belt, it flared out in layers of tulle and chiffon in palest beige, edged in frilly black lace. Paired with my highest black slingbacks and a décolletage-dipping necklace, I figured I matched him sexy for sexy.

His eyes roved around again, and the backs of my ears started to burn. "Well, your mouth is putting off a Cate vibe, but that's definitely a Cat dress, so I give up."

Interesting.

"How about I go easy on you, and I'll be Cate, dressed for a date?"

The side of his mouth quirked up. "Will you be rhyming too?"

"Maybe I will, for you," I parried, grabbing the fringed shawl I'd laid on the chair by the door.

He pulled the door open and waited for me to go ahead of him, and my heart felt suddenly heavy, which was ridiculous. Ethan was a total gentleman, and somehow always managed to have a door open for me before I even realized there was one to be opened. But wearing The Dress, and The Hose, and The Heels, it felt different. Nervy. Almost like a first date.

As I passed him, he murmured, "Is that how you dress for all your dates?"

I shot him a sideways glance, my lips quirking up on the same side, and didn't answer. It was obvious we both felt a little awkward. We just needed to get back into our nerd zone and we'd find our footing.

"So," I started, settling into the leather bucket seat of his car, "what'd you do today?"

"Nothing much. Some computer stuff." He glanced over at me and quickly away again.

"What sort of computer stuff?" I'd long wondered over the mysteries inherent in the words "computer stuff."

"Just general maintenance, upgrades, that sort of thing."

I sensed an attempt at a brush-off was being made, and I braced myself against it, fully determined to dig in and ferret out the bits he wasn't telling me.

"What'd you upgrade?" I made it sound so casual, like I had a clue what I was talking about. I could have tacked on a "dude" at the end and nodded like a bobbleheaded gamer, but the reality was he could have said anything, and I wouldn't have known the difference.

As he slid to a stop at Riverside Drive, Ethan turned again to look at me, probably to gauge the seriousness of my question. Little did he know, I fully intended to go terrier on him. The brush-off was not going to save him this time.

"Why do you want to know?" He seemed genuinely confused.

"Why don't you want to tell me?" I countered.

I could see the confusion warring with exasperation on his darkened profile. "How about we start over, and you be Cat for the evening?" He glanced over at me with a single eyebrow raised, clearly pleased with his subtle poke.

"All right," I agreed, letting the words roll off my tongue in a slow, throaty drawl. I pitched my voice lower, wispier. "You can *show* me. I'd love to see your new and improved . . . *computer*."

I could sense him stiffen in the seat beside me. But, give the man credit, he rallied quickly.

"After the reception? It'll be pretty late." His tone was all business.

"Oh, I'm sure I'll be wired." I tamped down on the fit of giggles I could feel bubbling to the surface and said suggestively, "And what better way to talk upgrades."

After two solid beats of silence in which Ethan's grip on the steering wheel tightened considerably, Ethan cried uncle. "I changed my mind. I'm not ready for Cat. I'd rather take my chances with Cate."

I grinned in the darkness. "How about we both come over?"

I thought I heard a muttered curse word as he shook his head and stared momentarily out the driver's side window. "Why? Why do you want to come over tonight?"

"We could talk about the journal. . . ."

"Have you gotten another little pearl of advice?"

"No, but I did some reading up, and I'm even more convinced that the journal once belonged to Jane Austen."

Ethan shot me a quick glance. "Meaning what?"

"Meaning that every owner pours out her love troubles, and matchmaker extraordinaire Jane Austen finds a way of getting her a happily-ever-after."

"That's it?"

"What do you mean, 'that's it?' That's awesome."

"So what advice do you think she's giving you?"

I blinked. Initially I'd been under the impression that I was being briefed for some sort of spy work . . . and after that I'd just assumed the advice was urging me to make a few love connections between friends. Ethan's question had me stymied. How could I be making such sweeping statements without even considering my own situation?

"Have you been pouring your heart out?" Ethan prompted.

"What?! No!" I snapped, still stuck on the first question. And I wouldn't be prepared to answer *it* until I'd answered it sufficiently for myself.

I couldn't think—couldn't remember. I needed to see all the little snippets side by side to figure this out. What was Gypsy Jane's MO? Could she be matchmaking me? With Jake, or . . . ? I let my gaze stealthily slide over to look at the man sitting in the dark right beside me. Ethan??

"Oh crap."

Judging by the swift turn of Ethan's head, there'd been no volume control on my savvy assessment of the situation. "What?" he asked.

"Nothing," I fibbed, plucking casually at the folds of my skirt. A minute ago, I'd been willing to use the journal as a springboard straight into Ethan's house, but the bounce had gone completely out of that idea under the weight of one little question. Which meant I needed to backpedal quickly and find another way in.

I honestly had no idea what I might find at Ethan's apartment that would commence the demystification, but the very fact that I'd never been there seemed sufficiently telling—and suspicious. Enough so to push my luck.

"We could watch an old movie—a black-and-white one . . . with dames and dramatic pauses."

"What are you hiding?"

"What am *I* hiding?? Dude, you've seen me without makeup, and on occasion, without a bra. You get the lowdown on every guy I date and on every parent who inspires voodoo thoughts. What do I seriously know about you? You could be anyone—alien, witness protection enrollee, the teacher version of *Dexter*. . . ."

He froze, just for a moment, and I could feel his defenses going up, and then he cut his eyes around at me. "Alien? Clearly I need to set the record straight." His voice was friendly but tight.

"Agreed. And while you're at it, you could stand to host a play-date or two."

I'd been thinking Scrabble when the words popped into my head, but as they popped out of my mouth, the board game had been replaced by other, considerably more nefarious, activities. Activities that had no business lodging themselves in my brain while I was on a favor date with Ethan. I bit my lip, thankful for the darkness and the distraction of navigating through downtown. Maybe Ethan wouldn't notice.

Judging by the little half smile that now played around his lips, he noticed. And was even now trying to craft his response to my perfect setup. I closed my eyes, slumped ever so slightly in defeat, and waited. It wasn't long in coming.

"You're right. It's definitely time to even the score. It's unlikely I'll be up for Scrabble tonight, but I suppose I could take a stab at convincing you I'm not a serial killer." He turned to look at me, and the reflected twinkle in his eye from a passing streetlight was eerie. I felt vaguely as if I'd lost control of the conversation.

"Fine. Good," I said with a conviction I was no longer feeling.

"Where is this wedding anyway?" I asked, needing to make a clean breast of things.

"Whole Foods."

I stared at him in disbelief. "In a grocery store?"

"On the roof, actually."

"Who's marrying them, the produce manager?"

"Actually it's the DJ, who earned his officiant credentials on-line. Rob and Jules thought the whole thing would be 'humorously ironic.'" Judging by the look on his face, Ethan thought they were a couple of kooks. "Their perspective on the wedding itself is 'git 'er done and git to partyin'.'"

"O-kaay. Is it BYOB, spirits conveniently available for purchase one floor down, right along with the beef jerky and barbecue? Remind me again how you know Rob."

"I've known him for a long time—we used to work together."

"Doing what?"

A pause. "Disposable jobs right out of college."

"Like delivering strip-o-grams, that sort of thing?"

"Similar, but with fewer singles and more dignity."

"Gotcha," I said, nodding. One more question artfully dodged. I narrowed my eyes with determination. One day soon, I was going to blow this thing wide open. Maybe even tonight. Wouldn't that be humorously ironic.

I could suddenly feel the beat of my heart as if, in the soundtrack of my life, there'd been a transition to adventure music. I glanced down at myself and felt, suddenly and paradoxically, both underdressed and overdressed. I couldn't help but wonder if superheroes ever felt like that.

As I skimmed my toes—the heels had been slipped off long ago—through the seeded grass growing on the downtown rooftop of Whole Foods and slowly sipped a mango margarita, I had to admit that this was a lovely spot for a wedding reception. Crisp white linens, fairy lights, dainty pots of pansies, rosemary topiaries decorated with white pom-pom garlands, and tall outdoor heaters positioned as sentries, guarding against the early November chill. And above us, the glow of the city, reflected back against shimmery, opalescent clouds, the pinpricks of starlight shining like rhinestones in a violet sky.

A few couples were dancing, trying to keep up with the bride and groom, but I'd yet to be asked. Ethan was taking his best man job very seriously: mingling, taking care of things, being the responsible one. I couldn't help but think he needed an alter ego of his own. I'd give him five more minutes, and then I'd sidle up to him, lay my hand on his arm, and lean in to whisper in his ear. It would totally freak him out, which would be just as satisfying as the dancing, if not better.

"That's a plotting smile, I can tell. I wonder if I should be worried?"

I swiveled my head around in true distracted fashion and found myself staring up into the twinkling eyes of Jake Tielman, the sparkle of the Milky Way spread out above him.

I popped to my feet in surprise before it occurred to me that I needed to stay in character. I might have been waffling between Cate and Cat in one great big tease with Ethan, but right now, I needed to be Cat Kennedy, Woman of Mystery. I slipped slowly back into my heels and took my time in answering.

"I wouldn't if I were you. You've only just appeared. Give a girl some time." I fought to hang on to the reins of my smile to keep it from going all delighted teeth and gums. Jake appeared unconcerned and flashed me a doozy.

"So what do you think—coincidence or fate? There must be some explanation for both of us showing up here on this particular Saturday night."

A little tickle at the edge of my mind murmured, *"Or magic . . ."* Shooting Gypsy Jane a subliminal *thank you*, I smiled.

"Too soon to tell," I murmured, turning to retrieve my drink from the table to sip delicately.

Another grin. "I lost track of Grace, but you knew that." He tipped his head down with an endearing touch of bashfulness. "I chased another classy blonde, but couldn't get her to agree to be my date." He took a sip of his own drink, which looked like it could be straight Scotch.

I peered up at him over the lip of my glass and tried to pin him down. It was clear that he didn't take himself too seriously, so I decided to follow his lead.

"Was she scared of birds . . . or heights?" I quizzed, wondering if he'd catch my Hitchcock references. "Because either could have been a problem up here."

He got it, judging by the way he tucked his lower lip under his teeth and gazed off over the rooftop before answering. "Honestly? I don't think she's afraid of anything." He lifted his glass in a private little toast.

I'd take that compliment! Evidently I had at least one man fooled. Meanwhile, Ethan was listing in and out, not entirely sure how to pin me down, and I was enjoying the hell out of it.

"Bride or groom?" I quizzed, wondering at the degrees of separation that had pulled me into his orbit tonight.

"Step-cousin of the bride," he admitted. "It was a courtesy invite. But I wanted to see the city from up here. I tried to get a date, but luck didn't smile on me," he said pointedly.

"That's too bad," I agreed. "But *I* will." And I did. It was showy—with teeth—and a little bit out of character for Cat, but I let it slide.

"Any chance we're kissin' cousins?"

The blush rose up my neck and flushed my cheeks with heat.

"Only if being a friend of a friend makes you a cousin." I smiled apologetically.

He leaned into me, and I held very still. But it was a false alarm. He set his empty glass on the table behind me, and his hand grazed my bare arm under the fringe of my wrap. A trail of goose bumps cropped up in its wake, and I shivered. A good shiver.

"I'm guessing that means you're not here alone. Will your plus-one mind if I convince you to dance with me?"

I didn't even bother glancing around. At the moment I had no thoughts to spare for Ethan.

"I don't plan on asking him. That is, if you can convince *me*."

His grin was quick and cocky, and I braced myself for his attempt.

"You know I'm not above playing to your sympathies," he said. "Cut a guy a break?" He opened his arms in a gesture of encouragement. "I'd consider it a kick-ass consolation prize."

I stalled a moment and pretended to be considering before I set my own drink down and said saucily, "I suppose I could use a break from masterminding," and then let him lead me to the dance floor.

As I slid into his arms, he murmured, "This way I can keep an eye on you. And the advantages of that, Ms. Kendall, are innumerable."

A warm, melty feeling spread out over my body, and I relaxed into his hold, enjoying, for once, the feeling of having a little confidence in my own sex appeal. Sadly, it shot off almost instantaneously, like escaped air from a balloon, complete with mocking raspberry. And my heart screeched to a halt before double-timing it back to normal.

He'd just called me Ms. Kendall . . . not Ms. Kennedy, which was how, I was quite certain, I had introduced myself on Halloween. Had I somehow given away my true identity?? *Shit.* That had, very specifically, *not* been a part of the plan.

I let my gaze shift slightly to look into Jake's face, to see if he had any clue what sort of havoc he was wreaking on my "sexy time." His smile was warm . . . tempting, and I knew if I kept ogling it, I'd end up kissing him, real names or not. And I'd end up regretting it. I was, after all, here with Ethan—fake date or not—and it seemed a little tarty to kiss another guy. I was just going to have to make damn sure I got another chance.

At the precise moment I realized that Jake was referring to my make-believe stint as Hitchcock's Eve Kendall and not my—coincidentally matching—real name, I was subjected to another heart-stopping jolt.

Ethan suddenly loomed large right beside us. A minute ago he'd been MIA, and now, suddenly, the moment I'd started flirting with another man, he was Mr. Attentive, with a rather forbidding-looking jawline. Ethan spoke first, edging out all pleasantries with his brusque manner.

"May I?" His tone implied it wasn't a question, more a dismissal. His whole demeanor was very Darcy-esque—the arrogant, insufferable side of the character—and I wasn't at all impressed. Jake graciously gave way, and I offered him an apologetic smile.

"How do you know Jake Tielman?" Ethan asked, moving us determinedly across the dance floor.

"How do *you* know Jake Tielman?" I demanded. "And who cuts in?" I wondered in confusion. "My dance card has been empty all night, Chavez. Where have you been?"

"Let's just say I know him by reputation. And I'd prefer his name didn't come up over Sunday Scrabble."

"So we'll pick a new topic," I snapped. "Maybe we'll talk about *your* romantic conquests for once."

"I'm serious, Cate."

"Spell it out, Chavez. Are you forbidding me from dancing with him? Seeing him? Sleeping with him? *What?*" My jawline had tightened up nicely—now we were a matching set, with both our eyes flashing fire.

Ethan stared down at me, obviously debating whether to back off, and as I watched, the heat in his eyes was gradually banked. "I'm not forbidding you to do anything, Cate. I'm just suggesting—as a friend—" His hand tightened fractionally around my waist. "That he's a career charmer—all style, no substance." And then he couldn't help himself. "Out of curiosity, did he get to meet Cate or Cat?"

I couldn't help myself either. "He was getting *re*-acquainted with Cat when you cut in." I smiled, and it felt justifiably brittle, and then I looked away from him and gave myself permission to smolder a little with outraged anger. At times I'd wondered why Ethan and I had never made the leap from good friends to friends with benefits and beyond. Why we had never connected romantically. Thinking about it always felt strangely bittersweet, although honestly, I couldn't pinpoint why.

He wasn't exactly my dream guy. As a girl who'd grown up watching old movies, I was sort of partial to the charmers, to the men who understood that while life was serious, they didn't need to take themselves too seriously. Ethan was always serious, at least as far as I was concerned. He acted more like a big brother than a potential lover. Which was good. Every time I started looking curiously—even longingly—at Ethan's flexing biceps or really excellent ass, he put the kibosh on by launching into a discussion of income tax or hybrid cars. Which was a relief. I didn't want things between us feeling even vaguely incestuous. Which brought us back to Jake.

While Jake seemed to thrill in the mystery, Ethan went all Sherlock Holmes on me. And it was a real mood killer.

I tilted my head slightly to peek at Ethan from the corner of my eye. We'd be friends forever, I was absolutely certain, but it was obvious things would never go beyond that.

If I was here by myself, I might still be dancing with Jake. Or we might have decided to flirt over another drink. As risqué as it seemed, I might have even let him seduce me. . . .

As the song slid to a close, I was jolted back into the awareness that I was here with Ethan tonight, not Jake. And as agreed, I'd be going home with Ethan too. Which meant something entirely different than going home with Jake. Ethan dropped his arms and checked his watch, a very expensive-looking number that somehow seemed incongruous against Ethan's sensible, frugal persona.

"Give me fifteen minutes, and we'll go. Unless you want to wait to see if you can catch the bouquet," he teased, smiling in that boyish way he had that always had me forgiving him much too quickly. I set my mouth in a tight line and tried for unforgiving. Never one to give up, Ethan leaned in, his lips just skimming my ear and his breath hot on my neck. A spike of electricity shot up my spine with enough juice to shake my lips loose and offer up a breathy sigh.

"Go find Mr. Tielman and treat him to fifteen minutes with Cate Kendall. See if he can keep up." And then he walked away from me.

It took me five full minutes to recover from those ten seconds, and by then Jake Tielman was nowhere to be found. Coincidence or fate . . . it could have been either. But my money was on magic.

Chapter 10

Ethan's house was one of those sleek new "green" houses—the sort made from reclaimed materials with a teensy carbon footprint. (Me? I was still living in Mom's chunky footprint.) It was all straight lines and right angles, and only five minutes from Mom's. Curious that I never knew that. And even more curious that this house seemed way out of a teacher's pay grade. Even a teacher as multilingual and multifaceted as Ethan. This was rapidly turning into quite the little mystery.

Knowing I wouldn't get any clues out of Ethan, I kept my comments confined to the sort offered up by the casual visitor. (It should be noted that I no longer considered myself anything of the sort.) I insisted on the deluxe tour—and even had a couple of minutes to myself when Ethan changed out of his best-man garb—but the only thing that popped out at me was Ethan's collection of vintage globes and maps—his entire home office was papered in them. Interesting.

Clearly I was going to have to come up with some sort of strategy to discover precisely what Ethan was hiding. And I was going to have to go about it with a certain amount of flair.

What I needed was a distraction. . . .

"So . . . ? Does it live up to all the hype?" Ethan asked, striding back into the room in a T-shirt and pajama pants.

"If the hype you're referring to is me insisting I get to come over, then yeah," I told him, nodding, "it does."

"Okay, well then good. And I assume you didn't see any evidence that I've been killing people in my spare time? No grudge-bearing bulletin boards, surgical tools, random tarps . . ."

"That's true. Although all that computer equipment in your home office could probably contact your home planet . . . *if* you were an alien," I countered.

"Would you like to see if you can pull off my human head to find the reptile alien beast beneath?"

"Maybe later."

"So what's it gonna take, Cate?" he asked, seemingly resigned as he headed to the kitchen. I followed, glancing around me, full of curiosity. I wanted to skim my fingers over the volumes in his bookshelves, get the story on the trio of miniature elephants that traipsed across his mantel, and get culinary with his countertop herb garden. I wanted to know the him I was missing. But short of asking questions and watching him artfully dodge them, I hadn't a clue how to proceed.

I wondered, fleetingly, if I could get him to let me crash on his couch, giving me an after-hours, unsupervised window of opportunity. But I had serious doubts as to Ethan's agreeableness to the idea. *Think, Cate!*

He set a glass of orange juice on the counter for me, and I climbed onto the closest bar stool to pick his brain, even though my own felt like an old sweater, recently de-pilled. I gulped down half of the juice, hoping the vitamin C would give me a little problem-solving boost.

I laid my hands flat on the counter and tapped out a quick little beat. "So." I looked up at Ethan—sipping his own juice, barefoot in his eco-modern kitchen, a dark shadow of stubble shifting on his jaw—and had to regroup with another fortifying sip of juice.

"I would actually like to take a look at that journal again. Full-sized."

"I think it'd be good for you. It's mostly about girls outsmarting boys."

Ethan smirked, likely at all those poor, delusional girls, me included. "And which boy are you outsmarting?"

I ignored that question. I didn't have an answer for either of us. "You'll have to tolerate quite a lot of romance," I warned, glancing up at him. I didn't predict such a casual statement might be awkward, but it was, and I looked away first to stare into my quickly dwindling OJ. "That's Gypsy Jane's specialty."

"Gypsy Jane?"

"The last entry I read today likened the journal's omniscient and prophetic advice to the fortunes told by traveling gypsies. When I remembered how we found the book smack in the middle of the Trailer Park, I considered it a fitting nickname for the reincarnation of Ms. Austen here in Austin." I smiled, raising my eyebrows in challenge.

Time for a little change of subject. I decided to let Cat do the honors.

"Now, how about I slip into something more comfortable," I purred.

Turns out it felt as awkward as hell, sitting in the cozy glow of Ethan's spotless kitchen and facing his intent stare. So I shifted gears. "Seriously, Chavez. Cut a girl a break. Do you have a pair of sweats, or maybe some satin pajamas I could borrow? I'm wearing vanilla body lotion, so I guarantee they'll smell yummy when I give them back to you." I took another quick shot of OJ, tamping down on the urge to giggle. I'd been weirdly flirtatious all evening, pushing the limits of his comfort zone, but now the teasing felt almost beyond my control.

Ethan put his juice down on the counter. "Just how long did you plan on staying?" he inquired with a sardonic lift of his brows.

It was obvious I was on his last nerve, but having finally stepped into the man's secret lair, I planned to hunker down for a little stay—who knew when I'd be invited back.

"Just long enough for me to pick your brain a little."

"Uh-huh." He seemed skeptical. "Let me see what I can find. It won't be satin pajamas," he warned.

The second he was out of sight, I did a little victory dance, but I was back under control, finishing up my juice, when he returned with a pair of plaid pajama pants and a sweatshirt with "Virginia" emblazoned across the chest.

"What happened in Virginia?" I asked.

"Plenty," he said wryly.

"Why do you have a Virginia sweatshirt?" I clarified flatly, wondering if the man could answer a single question without suspicion or misdirection. It felt like I was forever firing missiles and he was forever launching countermeasures.

"I lived there for a little while after college," he said.

This was news to me. "Were you teaching?"

"No." No doubt in reaction to my steely-eyed stare, he clarified, ever so slightly. "I worked as a translator."

"Really?!" Here was an interesting little tidbit. "What language?"

"Several."

"Look at you, Chavez! You just got interesting. A translator for whom?"

"Lots of companies need translators for their overseas operations."

"Uh-huh. And who needed you?"

"Evidently you did," he said, gesturing to the sweatshirt in my hands. "You going to change into that?"

I leveled him with a determined stare. *I'm going to break you, Chavez, just wait.*

"Fine," I said, swiveling on my bar stool. He was throwing me scraps, and we both knew it, but I'd take them. And bide my time.

I slid the clothes off the counter with an irritated swipe and strolled down the hall to the guest bathroom. It took me all of ten seconds to slip out of my frothy dress and into the warm comfort of Ethan's clothes. The sweatshirt smelled like him, spice and soap, and I breathed deep before padding back down the hall, dropping onto the sofa, and curling my feet up underneath me. I pulled a pillow onto my lap and waited for Ethan to mosey in from the kitchen.

"I bet we could use your expertise as a linguistics major and recently discovered translator in deconstructing the journal."

"That expertise hasn't been particularly useful in helping me deconstruct this conversation," he pointed out wryly. Leaning toward me from his seat on a leather club chair, planting his forearms on his thighs, Ethan pitched his voice low, to a shiver-inducing pitch. "You're bullshitting, Cate. You don't want to talk about the journal. You know that, and I know that." His eyebrow rose ever so slightly, and I gritted my teeth. "The truth is, you're here hoping to ferret out a couple of irrelevant little details about my life because you're on some Girl Friday kick. Admit it."

I tipped my head slightly, keeping my eyes on him, and finally decided to come clean.

"Fine. You've outwitted me, Chavez. Happy?" I sighed deeply. "How about you cut me a break and throw me an irrelevant little detail?"

Ethan held my gaze, his eyes unblinking behind his lenses for an uncomfortably intense moment, before leaning back in his chair and indulging himself in a good, long eye roll. He was clearly exasperated, but he wasn't asking me to leave, so I decided to press my luck even further. I'd exasperated him plenty of times before, often with good results.

"Twenty questions." I probably didn't have a shot in hell at getting him to agree to that, but it had worked pretty well with Jake, even though we hadn't gotten around to all twenty. "Yes-or-no only," I offered. "But you've only got one pass."

"Isn't that what we've been doing for the last five minutes?"

"Similar, but without the evasion tactics."

"Fine," he finally agreed. "But you only have two minutes."

"Done," I said, willing myself not to get overly excited. Otherwise the adrenaline was going to trip me up.

"Okay. Starting now?" My hands were fluttery.

Ethan glanced down at his expensive watch, pushed a couple of little buttons, and said, "Go." And oh, he looked smug.

"Did your teacher's salary pay for that watch?" I asked, winging one eyebrow up.

If he was surprised by the question, he didn't show it. He was enviably calm. "No."

"Are you a trust-fund baby?"

"No."

"Did your last job set you up for life?" I remembered the conversation I'd had with my class suggesting I could be a millionaire, teaching for the fun of it. It was going to be ironic as hell if that description fit Ethan.

"No."

"Did you steal that watch?"

"No."

"Get it as a gift?"

"No."

"Is it *MIB* issue . . . or the like?"

"Or the like?? Seriously? Is your question, did the watch come from some sort of interplanetary protection force?"

I nodded and tapped the spot on my wrist where my expensive watch should be.

He pursed his lips, completely baffled, irritated, and exasperated. If I learned nothing at all from this inquisition, I'd always have this moment.

"No."

"Did you buy it?" Just to confirm.

"Yes."

"So you have another job, besides teaching and IT work at the school?"

I almost didn't catch it, but he blinked an extra time before answering.

"Yes."

Now we were getting somewhere. I sat up straighter, pushing the pillow away from me.

"Is it computer related?"

"Yes." Now I heard a slight edge in his voice.

"Are you a translator?"

"Yes."

"Do you work during the week?"

He waited a beat before answering.

"Yes."

"On weekends?"

"Yes."

"Is that where you were this week—at this other job?"

"Yes."

I was on fire! Now if I could just pin down who he was working for. . . .

And then I had an epiphany.

"Other than your desire to cultivate an air of mystery, are you keeping this job secret for a reason?"

I didn't actually see any beads on Ethan's brow, but I had a feeling I was making him sweat, and that felt *awesome*.

"Yes."

"Will you get in trouble if I pin you down in this game of twenty questions?"

He briefly considered his answer. "No." He checked his watch, and I swooped in for the kill.

"Do you work for the government?" My head was suddenly swimming with thoughts of *Burn Notice*.

"Yes."

My heart rate, which had been steadily increasing right along with the titillation involved in juicy secrets finally revealed, was beating out a rapid, encouraging tattoo.

"FBI?"

"No." This was literally gritted out. I was closing in, and I knew it. And so did he.

"CIA?"

After our impromptu rapid-fire Q&A, the next few seconds felt like they played out in slow motion. Ethan's cell phone buzzed from the kitchen counter, and we simultaneously looked over at it. Then, with a quick, unreadable glance at me, he was up out of his chair to retrieve it.

"Answer the question," I called after him.

With a glance at the caller ID, he checked his watch and announced, "Time's up. And I've gotta take this. Give me five minutes."

Before the ringing stopped, he was down the hall, closing the door to his office with a quiet tap. And I was all alone on the couch, staring after him, wondering if I'd just imagined that whole back-and-forth.

Shit.

I'd rocked that round of twenty questions, but rather than pump my fist in the air, I shifted so that my head was propped against the side of the couch. Was it possible he was playing me? Concocting a story that cast him in the role of a sexy, mysterious computer geek? Well, it had worked like gangbusters. I'd assumed the shivery thrill I'd felt as the questions started to roll fast and furious were caused by the excitement of the moment, but now I knew the truth. I was a little turned on.

Then again, it was possible I was going into shock. The way this evening had been going, it could be either. I'd gotten all dressed up for a wedding, danced under the stars; I'd sipped champagne and slipped into something very comfortable. . . . And then one of my best friends had confided that he was living a whole secret, *sexy* life separate from the one I knew about.

First of all, *what the hell?* I'd known the man for two years, during which he'd been in the loop on virtually every aspect of my life while I had been shut out of everything but school and Scrabble. Had he been intentionally keeping secrets from me, or had I simply been too self-involved to pay attention? The significance of this suddenly hit me full force: *Ethan has an alter ego.* Admittedly it was as a computer geek, but still. It made me wonder if he only wore his glasses to teach, stripping them off for top secret . . . translations . . . or upgrades . . . I shut my eyes in exasperation. I still had no freakin' idea what the man did. I just knew he did it for the government. And that my head was starting to hurt.

Ethan was going to be back in probably three minutes, and I was going to have to sit here and look at him, and finish out the twenty questions, and hide the fact that in my head, I was wondering if computer geeks who worked for the government in real life were as buff as they were in the movies.

I let my mind float. Away from the surreal quality of the entire evening and onto a little mini-vacation. I checked into the Hotel San José, a cool oasis nestled at the heart of South Congress. I'd never actually stayed there, but it had been the site of many little escapes, with its boxwood-trimmed bungalows, crisp, cool sheets, and calm . . .

Next thing I knew, I smelled coffee, and pearly light was waiting just beyond my eyelids to be let in. I had a crick in my neck, and my bra was MIA. And as curious as that was, it paled in comparison to the reality that I'd spent the night at Ethan's, and the slightly fuzzy memory that I'd uncovered some rather juicy little secrets.

When I finally staggered bleary-eyed into the kitchen, after a quick search-and-rescue mission involving my bra, I was charmed to see that Ethan had set a mug out for me. Realization came swiftly: He'd no doubt hoped to curtail any potential snooping. Smirking ever so slightly, I filled the hefty navy blue mug halfway up with coffee and then scrounged through the refrigerator looking for something to use as creamer. Skim milk was the closest thing I found, and that was disappointing. Next I rifled through various cupboards and every shelf in the pantry (so much for not snooping) looking for sugar and ended up utterly exasperated. I was well aware that Ethan drank his coffee black, and it was now obvious that he wasn't prepared for guests. At least those who took the liberty of inviting themselves.

I took my first warming sip and felt my tongue try to reject it—this brew had run roughshod over the pale, thin dollop of skim I'd added. I looked down at the mug of coffee, giving my mouth a chance to acclimate, seriously thinking about checking the freezer for some vanilla ice cream, and that's when I noticed.

In bright white relief against that handsome navy blue background, a seal stood out on the mug. A shield, topped with the profile of an eagle's head, was encircled with the words "Central

Intelligence Agency, United States of America." I stared as my synapses slowly snapped to attention, pondering the possibilities. I took another sip of coffee and nearly gagged. Slipping onto the nearest bar stool, I set the coffee down, pushing it slightly away to save me from myself.

When Ethan had found me asleep on his couch last night after he'd finished his phone call, had he decided to steal the thunder of Question #18 by leaving this mug for me to find? Or had Ethan found this at a souvenir shop and been amused by the implications? Impossible to tell. I'd just pretend I hadn't seen it and pick up where we'd left off as soon as Ethan found his way out of bed. Until then, I had every intention of making myself a coffee milkshake.

My hand was literally on the freezer door when Ethan appeared, wearing the same pajama bottoms, now paired with a CIA T-shirt. As I stood staring, sizing him up, my eyes jerking from his face to his chest, Ethan propped a shoulder against the wall and crossed his arms over his chest, scrunching up the "C" and "A," while the "I" stared back at me.

"Morning," he said, looking me over.

I ignored my rumpled state and answered in kind. "Good morning. I couldn't find any sugar or creamer, so I was checking for some vanilla ice cream. Do I have a prayer?" Refusing to wait for an answer, I whipped open the freezer door and tipped my head forward, letting the frigid air cool my face and the search give me a moment to regroup.

By the time I resurfaced, without ice cream, Ethan had set a tiny little canister of sugar out on the counter.

"Where'd you find this?" I demanded.

"In its normal spot," he said calmly. "Ready to talk, or are we pretending last night never happened?"

This sounded so off in my head that I was distracted all over again, imagining—for one harmless moment—that we'd spent the evening on other, more hands-on means of discovery. I imagined that would have made this conversation considerably more awkward, so it was lucky the option had never presented itself. I stared again at his chest and then pulled my gaze farther up to his expectant smile.

"Oh, it happened," I assured him. "What's with the props?" I said, gesturing between the incriminating mug and T-shirt.

"Thought I'd save you a question."

"How thoughtful," I said. "If only I could trust T-shirts to give me the whole story." I paused for effect and was surprised to find myself suddenly caught up in a wave of shyness. "So, you really work for the CIA?"

"Yes."

"For as long as I've known you?"

"Yes." His voice was soft but level. And suddenly I wasn't over-awed with him any more—I was irritated. And hurt.

"*What the hell?* Were you *ever* planning on telling me? And don't you dare tell me I'm over my limit of questions."

Now Ethan looked slightly uncomfortable, which was just fine with me.

When he didn't immediately answer, I snapped, "Yes or no."

"Yes." That one little word felt like it had been wrenched out of him. I felt pretty wrenched myself. But I rallied.

"Okay!" I said, turning and tipping my coffee out into the sink. "Pretty painless, huh? I am going to change back into my own clothes and then jog home for a real cup of coffee. Because I really need my coffee." I plastered on a bracing smile and dodged past Ethan on my way out of the kitchen.

Seconds later, I was back, looking considerably rougher than Grace Kelly at her absolute worst. Turns out I could slip into the dress as easily as I could slip out. Good to know. I came out babbling, not really wanting Ethan to get a word in, because right now, I wasn't ready for anything he had to say. I ended on, "Not sure about Scrabble tonight—call first!" And then I was hoofing it up and down the hills of Travis Heights, all dolled up, walking home in the sharp glare of a Sunday morning.

Chapter 11

I couldn't decide if I wanted to think about it or if I wanted to avoid thinking about it. I'd stormed up the steps, a woman on a mission, and beelined for the kitchen. Brewing myself a cup of hazelnut coffee and dousing it with crème brûlée creamer, I'd traded the dress for a sweatshirt and pj's of my own and dropped down onto the couch to take the first steadying sip.

Better. I breathed deep and let it out slowly, trying to relax.

Now came the dirty work. I was essentially going to have to go through a post-date analysis, and Ethan wasn't going to be able to help me with this one.

Rather inexplicably, I'd had a change of heart. Last night I'd been psyched, thrilled to have finally cracked the mystery of Ethan Chavez wide open, and this morning, not so much. Maybe I'd been floating on the bubbles from the champagne, maybe I'd been distracted by the chance to flirt with Jake again, or maybe I'd simply been thrown for a loop when I'd entered Ethan's secret lair. I didn't have a clue.

All I knew was that I now felt unbearably awkward. Ethan and I had been friends for two years—*good*, close friends. Before this morning, I would have said best friends without the slightest hesitation, but now I couldn't. How could I? Friends don't keep gargantuan secrets from each other. Yes, I had toyed with the idea of keeping my sexy new alter ego a secret, but that had lasted less than a week, and for all I knew, Cat Kennedy might not last out the month. Ethan's situation was soooo different from mine, notably because mine was more or less make-believe, and his was seriously real.

Never would I have imagined Ethan as a Darcy, but I did at that moment as I self-righteously slurped down my latte. The Pre-Smackdown Darcy, before he gets a taste of the force of nature that is Elizabeth Bennet, when he's unfeelingly dismissive, intolerably arrogant, and oblivious to everything that matters. I took another, steadying sip of coffee. How could he possibly imagine I'd be cool with being made to look like a complete idiot?

He probably figured I was used to it, but dammit, it was different when I did it to myself.

This was exactly the sort of thing that could ruin me for Mr. Darcy. There was an element of Frank Churchill in this too, I remembered, *Emma*, as it was, being fresh in my memory. Frank had been keeping secrets too, playing fast and loose with Highbury's good opinion of him. Knightley had never been fooled. Knightley, the constant, steady influence, the confidant, the sexy neighbor who was never more than a brisk walk away. *Where the hell is my Mr. Knightley!?*

I recognized that I was being a trifle two-faced, seeing as my epic search for Mr. Darcy had just fizzled two seconds ago.

My thoughts touched briefly on Ethan and ruthlessly skittered away again. Knightley would never keep such a secret; he had too much respect for Emma. Which was rather depressing when you considered my current predicament.

Perhaps Jake was Mr. Knightley material. . . . And if not, I might just be willing to forgive and forget if it turned out he was a Darcy. I lifted my latte for an imaginary toast and decided it was time to have a little chat with Gypsy Jane.

Reaching under the couch, I set aside my near-empty coffee cup and pulled forth the dust bunny–encrusted volume. I wasn't in the mood this morning to pore over anyone else's happily-ever-after, so the key, which I'd been keeping inside the front cover flap, stayed put.

I skimmed back over the first few pages of the journal, now sporting only a spotty collection of words imbued with some sort of hidden meaning.

> *at times the answer is hidden in plain sight*
> *an unexpected development can change everything*
> *a perfect match demands an open mind*
> *absence may In fact produce a very desirable effect*
> *puzzle it out between you*

Reading them all together, it seemed possible that they could be referring to my friendship with Ethan and the secret he'd been keeping from me and—*I assumed*—everyone else. As clues went they were pretty nebulous, and a couple of them didn't even really fit in that context. Ethan and I were far from perfectly matched. As best friends . . . or *not.* And there was nothing romantic going on between us. At all. Perhaps it was all part of the puzzle. This whole thing was going to be a sore subject for a little while, and ambiguous or not, I needed a little advice.

When Courtney insisted that we all needed secrets, I heartily agreed. After all, I had a juicy, exciting one of my own—which I've since shared with both of my best friends.

I lifted my pen and stared down at those last two words. Best friends. *Were* we still best friends? Could things go back to the way they were? If not, I was going to be spending a lot of time with Courtney and her ghosts . . . or Mom and Mr. Carr . . . and potentially the Geek Freak if my laptop went wonky on me. Oh crap. I let my head fall back in self-pity before righting myself, determined to get on with it. Things were just going to have to go back to normal—I had too much invested in Ethan to quit him now. But I could punish him a little. . . .

But now, I think I'm ready to change my vote. There is something so distancing about a secret. It immediately calls trust into question, and that automatically puts both sides on the defensive, inspires grudges, and causes all sorts of little problems. I'm currently stalled out at this stage and associate it with the bitter taste of unsweetened, blackish coffee. Blech. Incidentally . . . I could have used a little heads-up. If I'm interpreting things correctly, you knew about Ethan's secret. All I needed were three little letters, Gypsy Jane. Three little letters. There are a lot of ways I could play this with Ethan, but I think I'm just going to assume his "secret life" won't keep him from Sunday-night Scrabble, a stint as an expert journal witness, or an occasional barbecue. And I suppose I do still have a couple of secrets left up my sleeve. Ethan doesn't have a clue that I've taken up matchmaking, and he doesn't know about Mom and Mr. Carr yet either. Fun times ahead!

After last night, Jake Tielman is no longer a secret . . . now evidently he's *forbidden*. By the man with the secrets, aka P.S. (that's Pre-Smackdown) Darcy. Nice. Well, I want to see him again, despite what Ethan has to say. Despite the possibility that he's probably a Darcy too, and I've switched to Team Knightley. I may be ready to say good-bye to the brooding, tortured hero, but I could stand to see a few more intense, lust-filled stares. . . . Just a couple more, then I can make a clean break.

A new e-mail pinged its way into my in-box, and needing just a moment's distance from this topic, I grabbed my phone to check it.

Crisp, bright days, rich autumn color, and stacks of flapjacks . . .
Sleep late, lounge for a while, read the paper, and then . . .
Join us for a casually stylish brunch
at a private Austin residence on the cliffs of Lady Bird Lake.
Pancake Bar
celebrating autumn spice and winter fruit . . .
Applewood Bacon
celebrating bacon . . .
French-roast coffee and fresh-squeezed grapefruit mimosas.

Sunday, November 14, 2010
11:00 A.M.–1:00 P.M.
Reserve your spot with $20 by Thursday, November 11, 2010

My smile bloomed as I read the details and imagined the plea-
sure of showing up with Jake after we'd slept late and "lounged"
for a while. I envisioned the novelty of Sunday plans that didn't involve Scrabble. But I quickly tamped down on the possibilities,
forcing myself to deal with my current reality instead. I'd give myself a few days to think about it, weigh the pros and cons, then I'd
decide. Spirits slightly buoyed, I turned back to the journal.

There's an e-mail from Pop-up Culture in my in-box. I simply need to
RSVP, and Cat can suit up again. Ethan is not in any position to say a
word. Besides, if I refrain from mentioning Jake at Scrabble, our little ro-
mance will be my little secret. Ethan will never know. Clueless . . . weren't
we all.

I tipped the journal closed, feeling very mysterious—roguish,
but ladylike. I'd whiled the morning away on good coffee and bad,
exposed secrets and covert decisions, and now I really needed to
get a few things done. But I couldn't resist a little peek at someone
else's happily-ever-after.

Retrieving the key from the inside cover, I slid it, ever so slowly,
into the keyhole and silently watched the magic happen. I watched
a different kind of secret come alive and felt thrilled to be a part of
it. I flipped past Miss Piano, ready to move on to someone new,
and when I found her, I settled in to read.

If she had scoured all of England, the wilds of Scotland, and beyond,
Letty could not possibly have produced a more insufferably arrogant din-
ner companion. If he did not happen to be her brother-in-law I'd want to
steep her tea with something that would send her into a fit of the hiccups.
But he warrants something stronger. A swollen tongue would be fitting in-
deed. . . .

I should probably leave that bit out of my diary, but then I've little experience when it comes to diaries, and I'm not about to scratch it out now.

To think I'd confided in him my aspiration to one day be elected to the Royal Society! The nerve of the man to tell me I'd be better served in less lofty pursuits! To insist that my penchant for botany and chemistry should be "usefully directed" towards timely discoveries in medicine instead of some "elusive research" was dismissive and short-sighted. The pity his limp had inspired in me was promptly squelched by his snide commentary and asperity of manner. He didn't want sympathy, that much was clear, but whether he'll admit it or not, the Great War had made its impression. His eyes, when they weren't snapping in irritation, were sad and lost in memories.

Enough! I will not make excuses for him . . . no matter how much my heart stuttered when I caught a glimpse of those same eyes crinkling with amusement as he held his newborn niece. I'm traveling to London to begin work at King's College in less than a fortnight. I haven't any time to be mooning over a pompous jackanapes, no matter that he is devilishly attractive.

I pulled back, intrigued. This one sounded feisty. I was poised to flip the page and read on, the day's to-do list be damned, when the phone rang. It was Dad. I balked and considered sending him to voice mail but, on the last ring, decided to pick up.

"Hey, Dad," I said, patently chipper. I unfolded my legs from under me and examined my toenails, promptly deciding I could use a pedicure. "How are you?"

"Hey, Sprinkles." The nickname, barreling down the phone lines, made me smile and ache just a little. But I knew what was coming and braced myself for the eye roll. "Better than I deserve." Dad was obsessed with Dave Ramsey, and no amount of nagging had convinced him to relinquish his favorite, irritatingly overused quote. "And you?"

"Great," I assured him. "School's the same, but good. Mom's"— I briefly debated how to phrase this—"dating, but I'm not. Ethan is good, and Austin is weirder than ever." It was pretty much the same spiel I gave him every time he called. Well, minus Mom dating.

"Who's your mom dating?" he asked. He sounded genuinely curious and not the slightest bit jealous. I supposed that train had left the station for parts unknown a long time ago, but I couldn't seem to squelch the wishful thinking.

"A teacher from school. History. You'd like him." And he would.

"Well, if he's smart, he'll hang on to your mom, and I'll get to meet him before too long."

"Yeah. Maybe," I allowed, wishing he'd been smart enough to hang on to Mom himself. "You dating someone better than you deserve?"

When he answered, I could hear the smile in his voice. "No, not dating. But I do go country and western dancing with Chris's mom most Saturday nights." Chris was his assistant manager and most experienced zip-line guide.

"How come you and Mom never went dancing?" If Dad thought it was a weird question, he didn't say. Mom and Dad had been friends for years before they'd gotten married, and they seemed to have everything in common . . . until, suddenly, inexplicably, they didn't.

I couldn't help but wonder nervously if that was what was happening to Ethan and me. Minus the part about being together . . . married.

"We were busy doing other things, I suppose. We were always happy, Cate. I hope you know that."

"I do," I assured him. And I did. I just wish they could have been happier together for a while longer.

"So when are you coming up here, Sprinkles? It's beautiful with the leaves changing. You could bring Ethan . . . stay the weekend," he suggested.

"I thought I'd wait and come up with Gemma the week of Thanksgiving. No school."

"That'd be fine, but nothin' says you can't come twice. It's only about an hour's drive up here, you know."

"I know." I also knew I should make a better effort. "Let me look at my calendar. Definite maybe, how's that?"

"I'll take it!" he said. "Maybe your mother wants to come, with her history professor," he offered.

"I'll see," I promised. "Have a great day, Dad!"

"See you, Sprinkles."

I clicked off and sat staring into the middle distance, thinking about happily-ever-afters and the alternative, until the morning's coffee took effect and I had to pee.

And then I slipped back into the journal for just one more passage. . . .

I confess I'm no longer certain that this diary was the well-intentioned gift I'd imagined. I'd wondered at Olivine's insistence that I refrain from pursuing any scientific journaling in this little book, but rather save it for my own personal thoughts and opinions. She knew I wasn't the type to indulge myself in a running commentary on daily life, but then quite suddenly, I was. I certainly don't claim to understand what has happened to my first, vaguely incriminating, diary entry, nor can I explain the odd nature in which a few words remain, and rather coincidentally (when read in order all at once) form a strange bit of advice. Advice, it just so happens, I've taken, without intending.

We came upon each other unexpectedly in the rose garden. The rain had been pummeling down for what seemed like days on end, so when the sun fleetingly made an appearance, I slipped out to enjoy it. It seems he had the same idea. And seeing as neither of us cared to relinquish the opportunity for a sliver of sunlight and a walk in the dewy air, we resolved politely to endure each other's company.

Turns out he is surprisingly sufferable after all. We very deliberately didn't discuss the war or my studies, keeping our conversation confined to common interests, of which, funnily enough, there are many. We both adore horses and love to ride, so it wasn't long before we agreed to abandon the garden in favor of the stables. We were late in to dinner, brushing the hay from our bums, having spent the entire afternoon having a cozy little chat. It was quite embarrassing to be teased over doing something else entirely. I felt the flush warm my whole body.

His eyes are a murky, almost turbulent green, as if they're changing color before your eyes . . . and perhaps they are. And his passionate nature, when not set up in opposition against me, was rather arresting, appealing even. I confess, I almost wish my visit was to be longer than originally intended. I simply need to get refocused. The country air is making me feel giddy and utterly irresponsible.

I would have loved to have pushed on and discovered what Gypsy Jane had in store for these two, but enough was enough! Between the fascinating real stories and the fortune-teller-style advice, this journal had the potential to become a *tremendous* time suck. Which reminded me, I was currently in limbo. . . .

I carefully closed the journal and twisted out the key, riveted by the shrinkage. And then, just as carefully, I paged forward until I came to the latest word from Gypsy Jane.

There are secrets, and then There's Clueless

I sat for a moment and considered, trying to hit on an interpretation that wasn't a jab at my prowess at sleuthing or awareness . . . or *something*. It was a little ironic, or perhaps apropos, that I'd used the term "clueless." Here I was, embroiled in a matchmaking scheme, falling for the wrong men, i.e., the Darcys of the world, finagling my mother's love life—not to mention teaching *Emma* to my seniors—hell, I *was Clueless*. I hadn't realized how very much my life was beginning to mirror the novel . . . or the Hollywood adaptation.

I smirked at the thought of Paul Rudd playing Ethan, but quickly sobered. Ethan was not my Mr. Knightley. I closed the book, full up on Jane for the moment, and decided to go out. I needed groceries unless I wanted to spend the week eating bagels and hummus, and I wanted to pick up a couple of things before the evening's Scrabble match, assuming there would still be one. I could make dinner, but that might be awkward, while a pizza delivery was likely to snap things back to normal in a hurry. I'd just check in with Ethan.

I wasn't ready to talk, even over the phone yet, so I texted him:

Still on for tonight?

His reply, when it came back, was as casual as mine:

Yep.

I bit my lip, relieved. Now I had about seven hours to dispense with any hurt feelings, grudges, awkwardness, and all-around clue-lessness. I slipped on jeans and a sweater and my favorite scarf and stepped out the door into the crisp autumn sunshine, feeling suddenly giddy and irresponsible.

When Ethan walked around the corner and onto the patio, I was ready for him. I had the Scrabble board all laid out, a couple of microbrews on ice, and Groucho Marx glasses, complete with plastic nose, perched on my face.

Ethan broke into a grin, just as I'd hoped, and immediately plunked down a peace offering of his own: the CIA mug from this morning filled with autumn-toned ranuncula. My heart tripped on an excess of sentimentality, and I was glad for the disguise to hide that fleeting moment of awkwardness.

"We good?" I asked, sliding his pair of glasses over to him. "For undercover work," I clarified.

"We're good," he said, ignoring the glasses and eyeing the beer. "Anything else you want to know?"

"Uh-uh. At least not right now. Or is there a narrow window of opportunity, and if I don't take it now I have to forfeit my chance forever?"

"Why don't you wait," he suggested calmly, selecting a single tile from the Scrabble bag.

I did the same, and when we flashed each other our tiles, his

"A" was a winner, so he started. Almost immediately he'd lined his tiles up down the middle, spelling "HYBRID" for thirty-eight points.

As I stared with a mixture of awe and irritation, he popped the top on his beer, selected six replacement tiles, and settled back in his chair with a self-satisfied smirk playing on his lips.

I felt a compulsion to knock him off balance a little. "So, are you officially considered a spy?"

His eyes met mine, each behind our respective glasses, his real, mine pretend, and the smirk broadened into a smile. "Couldn't help yourself, could you?"

"How hush-hush does it really have to be? Because you're hiding your light under a basket, my friend. Girls would eat that up." I took a sip of wine, played "YODEL," and raised an eyebrow, poised to deliver the punch line. "Especially if you have the body of an agent."

"Is that right?" he said, leaning forward in his chair, settling his arms on the table. "Well, you're the only girl who knows, and you've seen about as much of my body as anyone recently." And then he lowered his voice and I felt goose bumps running rampant. "Planning to jump me?"

I was going to have to keep these damn glasses on all night the way things were going, and the way my lips were twitching from the itchy little mustache, I couldn't possibly be taken seriously. Then again, maybe I could play that to my advantage.

"Do I need clearance first?" I said, twitching on purpose to fight the bubble of laughter that threatened.

"You checked out," he said, focusing on his tiles.

I immediately abandoned the teasing flirtation. "You had me checked out??" On the one hand, I felt I should be outraged, or at the very least offended, but on the other hand, I had to admit, I was a little thrilled.

"No."

"Oh." My shoulders slumped. I told myself it was in relief, but I think it was more likely disappointment.

"I checked you out myself," he confirmed. "I am officially a 'spy,' and can do my own dirty work."

I opened my mouth to bluster out a protest at the same moment he laid down his tiles, using my "L" to spell "LEVERING" on a double-word space, using all his letters and earning himself a fifty-point bonus, effectively stealing my thunder. Closing my mouth, I gazed calmly at him. It was unlikely I was going to come back from this. He knew it, and I knew it.

"Are you impressed yet?" he asked.

I blinked at him. If he wasn't my best friend, I'd be flirting up a storm right now. What can I say? Words impress me, "spy" having particular impact. But this was Ethan . . . goofball, computer geek, Mr. Secrets Ethan. I glanced over at him from beneath my two caterpillar eyebrows and imagined sitting on his lap, pulling off his glasses, running my fingers along the edge of his jaw, leaning in . . .

My hand jerked suddenly and sent my tiles tumbling off the table and onto the patio stones. Thrilled to have a momentary escape, I ducked my head and tried to pull it together as I gathered the little vowels and consonants.

But when Ethan's head suddenly dipped down to my level, I started again, rapping my head on the iron table and shooing all thoughts of Ethan from my head. Except perhaps the blameful ones.

"Shit! Oof." Gritting my teeth against the pain, I snatched up the remaining tiles, went topside, and violently repositioned my tiles, spontaneously deciding to play "VAIN" off his "V."

Cradling my head and gulping down wine in a determined effort to dull my senses, I silently added a string of curses to the first.

This was all his fault. Friendly competition was one thing, but it was hardly fair play given that he'd had formal government training (it didn't matter that I had no idea in what exactly), and I was just a civilian. It occurred to me that my crack on the head might have knocked something loose. Something kind of critical.

I let my eyelids shutter closed—just for one peaceful moment. When I opened them again, Ethan was watching me, and I was ready to change the subject.

"How about I order the pizza, and you play both our hands?" I suggested.

"Why don't we just put the game away and do something else?"

All the conflicting thoughts I'd been having about Ethan, prompted by the recent Knightley daydreams and the spy guesswork, were starting to wreak havoc on my palling around with him. I was reading innuendo into everything, imagining the two of us in compromising positions, and tripping over myself in every situation. It had to stop. And I knew the perfect way to stop it.

"You up for a little experiment?"

His eyebrows shifted slightly, but otherwise he didn't visibly react. "Possibly. I'm going to need a little more information."

I glanced toward the house to make sure my mother was busily occupied and then settled my gaze on Ethan.

"Okay, here's the deal. Things are a little garbled right now, between the journal and . . . you . . . and even me," I admitted, thinking of Cat. "And I admit, the journal has inspired me to do a little matchmaking among friends. . . ."

Ethan's posture relaxed and he looked away, clearly amused.

"Seriously? You're trying to set people up?"

I couldn't decide if the stress had been on the "you're" in that sentence and whether I should be offended, but Ethan didn't give me time to figure it out.

"The experiment isn't about you trying to set me up, is it?" he demanded.

"No!" I assured him, rather huffily. "Not exactly. And give me a little credit. I may be an amateur, but I'm consulting with a professional." I squared my shoulders and straightened the Scrabble tiles on the board. "I'm getting backup advice from—" I paused. "Gypsy Jane" didn't sound particularly reputable. "Jane Austen."

"What?!" Ethan exploded before quickly reining himself in. He settled back in his chair and crossed his arms over his chest, waiting, no doubt valiantly fighting a giant eye roll from overtaking him.

"It's already working," I assured him, a little smugly. "Mom had a date last week while you were out of town." I tipped my head saucily.

"With whom?"

"Mr. Carr," I said, daring him to find fault with the situation.

"From school?" He seemed baffled.

"Yep. They hit it off marvelously. In fact, you can see for yourself on Wednesday. He's coming over for a barbecue dinner . . . and maybe a little *Burn Notice*."

That last bit threw him a little, but he shook it off.

"I think maybe I will," he said, looking a little smug himself. Then again, Ethan often looked a little smug, and not always for good reason. I decided to ignore it.

"Anyone else?" he asked. Drawled is probably more accurate.

"I'm working on it," I said cryptically, not really wanting to share the rest just yet. "But the matchmaking is only part of the madcap muddle. Then there's the whole 'secret spy' situation with you," I said, using air quotes while lowering my voice and glancing around nervously.

The corners of Ethan's mouth lifted in amusement.

"What about it?"

"Let's just say it's adding to the confusion."

"The confusion over what?" He seemed genuinely interested.

"You and me." Now I was avoiding his gaze, which I knew was leveled in my direction and as sharp as a laser.

"What about us?" he asked quietly.

My heart was beating quickly now, and I wanted to just blurt it out, but at the same time I wanted to sound casual and confident.

"About the potential for more between us than just . . . Scrabble."

I fiddled with the tiles in front of me, switching, rearranging.

Now his voice was low and tight, and I wondered how mine sounded.

"More, as in . . . ?"

And then I couldn't take it anymore—I just wanted to know. Businesslike and matter-of-fact, I scraped my chair back, stood up, and leaned into Ethan, pausing once, just barely touching, before laying my lips determinedly on his.

I hardly had a moment to gauge the situation before Ethan's competitive spirit fired to life, and he had reached over, hooked his finger in the belt loop of my jeans, and tugged me toward him.

My mouth opened in a gasp of surprise, and that was all it took for my little experiment to become a full-fledged project.

And then we were egging each other on, pushing each other's buttons, looking for a reaction, craving attention.

My lips rasped over his jaw and down his neck. His hands skimmed softly over my waist and then shifted down to settle firmly, possessively on my hip. I was done imagining—I was literally ready to tear his clothes off.

With considerable effort, I pulled myself away.

"Come upstairs," I murmured, feeling flushed and light and happy.

He stood, laced his fingers with mine, and tugged, leaving the Scrabble determinedly behind.

With each stair, my pulse beat out its encouragement, and by the time we reached the door and slipped inside, it was all I could hear. Until Ethan spoke.

"There's no going back after this."

"No," I agreed. "But you said it yourself: We could be friends with benefits."

"Hell yeah, we could," he said, grinning.

"And we should probably find out . . . just see . . . whether there's anything there . . ."

I fully recognized how ridiculous this sounded, coming only moments after our spontaneous interlude on my mom's back porch, given the fireworks we'd started, but as justifications went, I thought it worked.

Ethan evidently agreed, seeing as we launched at each other at precisely the same moment. He had me backed up against the wall beside the door, clinging to him like a monkey, hoping his touch would quell the fluttery little shivers coursing over my body.

I slid off his glasses, feeling very Lois Lane, and then tugged up his shirt, pressing my (slightly chilly) hands against the planes of his stomach. He winced, which made things down there feel even sexier and had me biting my lip in hot anticipation.

He was busy himself, unbuttoning the cardigan sweater I'd thrown on to go out this morning and unhooking my jeans, but now he paused, stripping off his shirt and looking me over.

"I pegged you for lacy underwear," he said.

I glanced down at myself, blushing.

"If I'd known the day was going to go like this, you can bet it would have been." As it was, I was standing in front of him in white cotton, feeling slightly less sexy.

"Then I'm glad you didn't know, because I like this," he said.

He was charming me, slowly and deliberately, and like it or not, it had me wondering how many other women he'd looked at in just this way.

And then I looked at him—I mean really looked at him. The man could have been Mr. November in a fireman's calendar! For all I knew, he was, although probably not in a fireman's calendar . . . maybe in a spy geek calendar. *How could I possibly have missed this?* It didn't matter, because I didn't intend to miss a thing right now.

Before we could attack each other again near the doorway, I pulled him along into my tiny bedroom, pushed him backward on the bed, and climbed up to straddle him.

He reached his hands around to cup my ass, and I leaned over him, propping myself up by my elbows.

"Ve haf vays of making you talk," I teased.

"I bet you do," he agreed. "But I have a question of my own."

"Ask away."

"How spontaneous was this?"

"Oh, very," I assured him. "My intention for the evening was to make up, and maybe engage in a little merciless teasing."

"Has this ever crossed your mind before?"

I sat up straighter and looked him shyly in the eye. "Maybe a couple of times—in a vague, nebulous, it'll-never-happen kind of way. What about you? Did I just totally blow your mind?" I grinned.

"Not as much as I expect you're going to," he admitted, "but you definitely took me off guard. You want secrets? I've been imagining this for a while now."

"Since when?"

"Since the first time I saw you smile—a real, can't-hold-back smile."

"You're kidding!" I said, pushing myself up.

"I'm not," he said, matter-of-factly, bumping out my elbows with his and reaching his hands up to cup my face and bring it down to his. "I hope you're worth the wait," he said, all dimples. And then he flipped over on top of me and all thoughts of teasing fled.

Chapter 12

We were lying splayed out on my bed, playing footsie, when someone knocked. Someone being my mother.

"Cate? What happened out here? It looks like you two just lost interest in the middle of the game."

I sat up guiltily, glancing over at Ethan, who was smiling at me, one arm folded behind his head.

I felt suddenly, flamingly self-conscious and yanked the sheet over myself, daring not even to look at Ethan's naked body in my bed.

"We got hungry," I called. Ethan squeezed my hand, and the shivery chills were back again. "Ethan went to get a pizza."

This got a reaction out of him. I shrugged and made wild eyes at him.

"Why didn't you just order one?"

"Home Slice doesn't deliver, and we needed a little space," I said, racking up the little white lies as Ethan shifted his bare leg to press up against mine. "We had a little tiff," I added, hoping this would explain the condition of the table.

"So are you licking your wounds in there?" she pressed.

I closed my eyes, not wishing to see the amusement that was certain to be written plainly on Ethan's face.

"Something like that. I'll be down in a few minutes to clean things up," I promised. "It's a little chilly, so I'll come in when I'm done and we can wait for Ethan inside," I added, hoping to give Ethan a clean getaway.

"Maybe you should bring the pizza back up here and spend the time making up," she suggested softly, as if talking to herself, but loud enough to make sure I heard. Thankfully, the next sounds I heard were her footsteps on the stairs.

I shut my eyes and bit back a smile, before turning to look down at Ethan. "So I guess you heard all that."

"Most of it. And I vote with your mom—let's bring the pizza up here. Hell, let's get a pizza delivered—I don't need the time to lick my wounds." He tugged me back down on top of him and cupped my hip through the now-tangled sheets. "So what do you think?"

I stared down at him, baffled. "Are you looking for a critique?"

"Not exactly," he said. "I'm more interested in your feeling on doing this again."

"Right now?" Damn if the man *wasn't* a superhero!

"I'd prefer it if you'd give me a few more minutes," he said wryly. "Let me rephrase. How do you feel about keeping the 'benefits' option open?"

"Good," I told him, considering. "Very good."

"I'd kind of hoped you were going to need a little more convincing," he said. Judging by his expression, he wasn't referring to a well-constructed argument.

"Why don't we just call it catching up?" I suggested and fell into him all over again.

We decided the story would be that Ethan came back with the pizza and we ate it alone in my apartment. In reality we ate squeeze cheese on Ritz crackers, red grapes, and Nilla Wafers with milk, sort of a postcoital picnic. And afterwards we lingered at the door, knowing that things would be different once it was opened.

"So . . . can I tweet this?" he asked with a face that couldn't hold a serious expression.

"Only if I can tweet your alter ego, Double-oh Chavez."

"Secrets all around, then, huh?"

"Secret handshake? Pinky swear?"

"I trust you," he said, running a finger down my cheek, sending a shiver up my spine. I offered up a wobbly smile. "See you at school, Cate."

I watched him walking down my stairs, his dark hair silvering in the moonlight, and thought of Cary Grant . . . and Hitchcock's *North by Northwest*. Ethan was sliding almost effortlessly into every conceivable, dreamy role my imagination had conjured over the past couple of weeks: superhero, government spy, Cary Grant charmer—even, it seemed, Mr. Knightley.

I watched him sliding through the shadows until he disappeared from view, and then I shut the door, the weekend now officially at an end. Tomorrow I would return to normalcy.

But what was normal, anyway? Not much since Cat had sidled into my life, followed closely by Gypsy Jane and Agent Chavez. My head suddenly hurt, and I moved to the couch, planning to throw over the journal tonight in favor of a little mindless television.

The second I dropped, my phone rang from the bedroom, so I pulled myself up again to catch it before it went to voice mail.

"Hey, Court, how was your weekend?" I asked, staring at my much-rumpled bed with its froth of white sheets.

"Lovely," she said. "Sexy too."

"Are we still talking about your weekend?" I asked dubiously, suddenly aware that those adjectives could rather adequately describe my own weekend.

"We are," she said mysteriously.

"What a coincidence," I countered, equally mysterious, "mine too." I dropped down onto the bed, considering how much to reveal.

"Want to come down here tomorrow after work, and we can trade stories?"

"Accepting your invitation doesn't in any way compel me to participate in any ghost-hunting activities, does it?"

"No. But I may make you tag along. Goggles are optional."

"Maybe you could just hit the highlights right now," I suggested, hoping I could make my decision based on the preview.

Courtney waited a beat before answering, no doubt wondering if this would play to her advantage.

"Okay. Remember the guy from the elevator? The not-so-amateur ghost hunter?"

"Yeah," I said warily.

"We went out last night, and afterwards he let me play with his equipment."

"What?!" I blurted. I came up off the bed with a guilty start and stood waiting, desperate to hear the rest.

"His ghost-hunting equipment, Cate."

I honestly couldn't say if this was an improvement over my original assumption, but it was clear I was going to need to suit up again (the goggles were a must for preserving a modicum of dignity) to get the full story.

"See you tomorrow around six-ish," I said, not yet ready to share my own equipment story.

When I hung up I opened today's e-mail from Pop-up Culture and skimmed over it again. I had no idea how Syd and Company had pulled this off, but it was the opportunity of a lifetime, and I didn't plan to miss it. Each time I'd canoed on Lady Bird Lake, I'd gazed longingly up at those houses, imagining the views of the Austin skyline to the east and the winding path of the lake to the west as it flowed down from the Hill Country.

I hit Reply and quickly typed in my info, my finger hovering over the box to specify "number attending."

I sank back down on the bed, Ethan back in my thoughts. If things were normal, I'd RSVP for the two of us and check with him later. But things weren't normal—we might as well have been in the Twilight Zone for all I could grasp what was going on. Besides, if Ethan and I had merely upgraded to friends with benefits, then that meant that we were just casual, and that I could attend this dreamy weekend brunch with bona fide single status.

But it would be loads better if I could turn "single" into "couple." It couldn't hurt to give Mr. Tielman a call. . . . could it?

There'd been no mention of love, romance, or exclusivity; it had been like make-up sex, no strings attached.

Before I let myself consider that analogy too carefully, I slid out of bed, darted into the living room, and rummaged through a disarray of lollipop sticks and their crinkly-wrapped heads to find my secret phone. Before I could second-guess my strategy, I dialed his number, retrieved from voice mail, and readied my voice.

"Hello, Jake, this is Cat Kennedy. I had a little idea of how we could wrap up our twenty questions without interruption. . . ." I felt a twinge of guilt, thinking of Ethan. "I've just RSVP'd to the Pop-up Culture brunch this Sunday. If you'll be there, come find me." I waited a beat, and then decided to leave it at that.

I smiled giddily to myself as I dropped the phone back amid the candy, stirring the mix until its trim black case slipped out of sight.

I told myself I could ignore even the smallest twinge of guilt. I was unarguably unattached. Ethan and I were undisclosed and uncommitted, and the fact that I'd promised to drag Dmitri along with me to meet Syd was barely relevant. He was an operator, not likely to hang around with me when there were "pretty people" and Austin Movers and Shakers in the crowd. So I was good.

I settled back on my bed and picked up my real phone, now officially committed. I typed "2" in the RSVP box, entered my credit card number, and hit Send. It was done; I was going; and I had no reason to feel guilty. Ethan would understand, and Jake didn't need to know the backstory.

I quickly texted Dmitri the details of our brunch date, suggesting we might want to ride separately, just in case. I thought it best to keep my options open.

Slipping under the covers, I curled in on myself and tried to imagine how this evening fit in with the sudden whirlwind of crazy in my life.

There are secrets, and then There's Clueless

Was it possible that Gypsy Jane was familiar with Alicia Silverstone's portrayal of Emma and had been trying to hint around the fact that I might want to give Ethan a second look? Well, subliminally, it had worked like gangbusters.

But as much as our little experiment had brought the wow factor, bubbling over like a homemade volcano, it hadn't exactly left me with the feeling that the landscape of our friendship was irrevocably changed. While it might be true that we couldn't go back, going forward into unknown territory wasn't necessarily a foregone conclusion. It might be that fate had dealt the two of us a really good friendship . . . with the occasional bout of requited lust.

Maybe we'd just hover comfortably right where we were.

Or maybe this evening's little trial run would blow up in our faces, burning the both of us beyond recognition. . . .

Promising myself I'd dial down the drama, I groaned dramatically and buried my face in my pillow. And I tried not to think about any of it.

Luckily I woke on my own, because setting an alarm clock had been the absolute least of my concerns. I hadn't gotten around to removing my makeup either, but I thought the raccoon eyes paired nicely with my tangled wreath of hair. Groaning again, this time for entirely different reasons, I staggered into the shower and mentally prepped myself for the day ahead. Or attempted to. By the time I stepped out of the shower, I still wasn't entirely clear on my strategy. I think I'd decided to keep Mom in the dark, keep Ethan at arm's length, and keep Courtney from playing with any foreign equipment.

I waffled over jotting a little note to Gypsy Jane and finally gave in despite the certainty that it would mean lounge coffee instead of a vanilla latte. It had to be done. My entries of late had been entirely self-focused, and Gypsy Jane had consequently homed in on my own little romantic situation. If I was going to keep up with a little matchmaking on the side, I needed to get her back on track. I needed an alternative for Sportcoat.

Clearly I have some things to work out with Ethan and, if I'm lucky, maybe Jake too, but I could use a little insight into luring Courtney away

*from her latest crush-of-the-moment. A shared fascination with ghost hunt-
ing is not the solid foundation of a long-lasting relationship. Okay, I take
that back . . . maybe it is online. Let me clarify: I'm talking about a romantic, in-person relationship. Courtney needs a sweet, serious, stable guy
to walk into her life right now. And I would be thrilled to facilitate that.
So if you have any hints, tips, or suggestions, work your magic, and I'll try
to figure them out.*

Satisfied, I smiled down at the journal, tipped it shut, and
tucked it into my carryall along with another ninja-style ensemble
for tonight. I'd check for any new advice on my off period.

For a Monday, the day was particularly surreal. As I was pulling
the door to my classroom closed on the first bell of the day, Ethan
shoved a foot in the door, handed me my favored coffee drink, and
let a silent message flash in his eyes. But it remained indecipher-
able. After that I saw Ethan in the hall, in the lunch line, even in
the lounge, and other than the secrets banked in Ethan's dark
eyes, we behaved like perfectly normal, respectable high school
teachers. But when the final bell rang, we turned, like werewolves
at a full moon.

Suddenly we were horny and irresponsible.

An after-school visit to the computer lab to ask about my slug-
gish Internet connection turned into a fumbling free-for-all in the
shadows. We kept it PG-13, but just barely. Afterwards, Ethan
boosted my connection speed and we parted ways. It couldn't
have been more casual. And yet, by the time I reached my classroom, I was definitely feeling it: some sort of delayed reaction to
my bout of risky business with Ethan. I dropped shakily into my
desk chair and dragged the journal out of my bag, just now remembering it. I needed to focus on something other than Ethan
and certain recent developments. . . . Gypsy Jane clearly did not
have my back.

Ethan is sweet, serious, stable. work your magic

Unavoidably my thoughts fluttered back over the past twenty-four hours with Ethan as I bolted for the vending machine and an Orange Crush. It was difficult to know for sure, seeing as the other messages from Jane had been directed to me, but I assumed, given my request, that this one was meant for Courtney, with me facilitating.

Courtney and Ethan. I had suggested it myself a week ago when she was looking for a tagalong companion to her Roaring Twenties event, but this was bigger than that. And things were a little different now. A week ago Ethan had just been a cool but geeky guy who rocked in the friend department. Now he was bona fide boyfriend material. And he was sleeping with me. Scratch that—we'd had sex once (well, twice) and pawed each other in the computer lab. He was not my boyfriend, which is not to say he wouldn't be perfect as someone else's.

As the orange soda fizzed loudly in its bottle, I made the mature decision: I'd step back and away and let Ethan and Courtney decide if they could be more than friends with really good benefits.

I washed down the lump in my throat with a swallow of Crush and then glanced at my Jane Austen action figure, standing primly beside my pencil cup. Craving a little harmless violence, I aimed her leg for a sharp kick and watched my now-empty soda bottle sail into the trash can. Short of pulling it back out of the trash and repeating the little fit of pique, there was little left to do but go and see a girl about a ghost.

I transformed from school teacher to ninja in Courtney's office, and decided to introduce Ethan into the conversation as a counterpoint to Sportcoat, aka the Ghost-hunting Guru.

"Cate, he really is adorable. We talked for hours that night in the Driskill Café, and he's been back twice since to give me some pointers. We even spent fifteen minutes closeted together in the elevator, trying to get a reading on P. J. Lawless," she told me importantly.

"And did you?" I asked, wondering if the Guru extraction would be more difficult than I'd assumed.

"Um. Not exactly," she admitted, clearly flustered. She'd

shrugged off a royal blue jacket in favor of the pseudo-ninja garb underneath, and the pale contrast of her skin against the black set off the sudden rosy blush on her cheeks.

"Wrong time again?" I asked, tongue-in-cheek.

"No. In fact, he may have been there, and we just . . . didn't see him."

"How is it possible," I said, knowing full well precisely how it was possible, "that the two of you could be in an elevator with an infamous ghost—around here anyway—and not notice him?"

"Well for one thing, Micah's equipment was going haywire," Courtney snapped, lifting Casper the Friendly Ghost Finder onto the table and turning knobs and flipping switches in a semiprofessional manner. Either she'd learned something from Sportcoat or she was faking it really well.

"And for another . . ." I prompted, rather enjoying myself, even though I was going to have to bust this up. It was one thing for Courtney to have a ridiculous hobby that she indulged in in the safety of a respectable hotel, hooking being the exception to that rule. It was another to engage in said pastime with someone who took it a little too seriously, or worse, someone who thought nothing of playing a role to take advantage of a pretty ingénue.

"Let's just say we weren't fixing the equipment, Cate," she admitted, fighting a smile.

I moved closer and dropped into the chair across from her desk, perched on the edge. "Do you really think you should get involved with a ghost hunter?"

She leveled me with a steady gaze. "You're involved with one," she said, her eyebrow lifting in challenge.

"Only as a favor," I reminded her. "And you're just messing around," I countered. *Please let that be all you're doing.*

"So's he. He's just better at it." Her mouth curved into a crescent, framed on one side by a sweet little dimple.

"So he's not a 'professional ghost hunter'?" I hoped she couldn't hear the quotes in my voice.

Her smile morphed into a disbelieving smirk. "No! He's a freelance writer, published regularly in magazines like *Wired* and *Pop-*

ular Science." Seeing my raised eyebrows—one quite possibly higher than the other, likely coming across as dubious uncertainty—she added, "I looked him up online. He has a web page, and his picture is featured with one of his articles in *Wired*." Now her eyebrow was up, and I had no choice but to lower mine in momentary defeat.

"Okay, fine," I said, starting over, splaying my hands on the smooth mahogany of her desk. "So you like him, and he's a solid possibility. I still think you should maybe see if you and Ethan could hit it off as more than friends."

I swallowed past the lump in my throat. Technically "friends with benefits" was "more than friends," and I'd say Ethan and I had knocked it out of the park. But that was irrelevant—we weren't romantically involved and didn't intend to be. He was fair game, and so was I.

Courtney's brows knit in a mixture of confusion and exasperation.

"What is the deal with Ethan?" she asked patiently. "Why the recent push to get the two of us together?"

"You're already friends, and neither of you is in a relationship. I just think there might be the potential for something more." It pained me, just a little, to admit that.

"You're better friends with him," she pointed out, now a little bit sassy. "And you're not in a relationship. I say you've got dibs. And I think Ethan would agree and thank me for saying so." She let this settle in for a minute before tacking on the death blow to my matchmaking scheme. "Besides, I think I sort of am in a relationship." She grinned and shifted her focus back to Casper.

Well, I'd tried, so the matter was settled—it didn't seem kosher somehow to broach the subject with Ethan right after we'd taken our friendship to the naked level. I started rummaging for candy corn and ignored the fact that the evening felt marginally celebratory from that point on.

I trailed Courtney for thirty minutes before it happened, my only concessions to the hunt a pair of goggles and a clipboard. I'd volunteered to jot down any findings as an alternative to using a tape recorder, but so far had nothing on the page but a selection of bird and butterfly sketches. I was leaning over the balustrade on the stairs leading up to the second level, waiting for instructions, when a man came through the doors of the Brazos entrance. Tall and broad-shouldered, he carried himself with an almost cocky attitude. He glanced up on his way to the elevators and saw me watching him. It was the man from the other day. I let my mouth curve into a casual, passing-stranger, "I feel like I should remember you, but I don't" smile, but he didn't return it. In fact, he turned sharply away, stepping into the elevator and out of sight. Weird.

I had too many things on my mind to let a cranky stranger's bad manners bother me. By the time the really weird stuff started happening, the incident was already completely forgotten.

We were in the mezzanine ladies' restroom, Courtney attempting to extract an eyelash from her right eye and me washing my hands with the fancy soaps, when it happened.

A little shimmer appeared in my peripheral vision, and I glanced up curiously, searching the gilt-framed mirror for the source. But there was nothing, so I finished washing and picked up one of the upper-crust cloth-style paper towels arranged in a neat stack on the counter. As I rubbed my hands dry, the shimmer teased my subconscious a second time. Curious, I switched my focus back to the mirror. There was still nothing reflected there, but shifting my gaze slightly, I noticed that something was in the room with us, and, skeptic or not, I couldn't ignore the evidence that it looked a *lot* like a ghost. Or at least how I thought one might possibly look.

I started, as if someone had snuck up on me, as I supposed, someone had. Or some*thing* that had once been someone. Creeepy. My heart rate, having launched into a panicked reaction, didn't bother to settle, and I stood, blinking with a vengeance, half-hoping that with just one more twitch of the eyelids, she might disappear. And half-hoping she wouldn't.

This vision, with her wide, intelligent eyes, mischievous mouth, and willowy, ladylike stature, was clearly not the ball-bouncing child of hotel legend. So who was she?

I glanced back at Courtney, who was leaning over the sink, rubbing and rinsing.

"Court," I said, keeping my eyes on our ghost and trying to take deep, calming breaths, "You're probably gonna to want to see this."

"I can't see anything right now, Cate. Between the eyelash and the mascara running into my eyes, visibility is very low right now. Not to mention the fact that I can't stop winking! Shit!"

"I think it might be a ghost," I murmured in singsong, keeping things light and friendly and backing up ever so slightly toward Courtney.

"What?! Are you serious?" She pivoted in my direction, dribbling water all over the pristine marble countertops and floor, squinting in a deranged sort of way. "Try to take a picture!" she screeched, frantically cupping her hands under the faucet and aiming palmfuls of water at her eyes, sending most of it cascading down into the V-neck of her black T-shirt. "Use your phone, and hurry! But don't spook her . . . stall for time!"

"Yes, ma'am," I said, fumbling as I pulled my phone out of my pocket. I snapped two shots with shaky hands and didn't bother checking them. In all likelihood, I'd blurred them or she had, simply by virtue of being a ghost. I spared a glance for Casper, currently sitting on the floor at the feet of our translucent mystery guest and decided it wasn't worth the trouble. Clipboards were both user-friendly and nonthreatening. Turning back to the person-shaped shimmer, I smiled winningly and started jotting notes.

Monday, November 8, 2010, 6:45 P.M.

Ladies' Mezzanine Bathroom, Driskill Hotel, Cate Kendall, ghost hunting with Courtney Reynolds. Who is currently occupied by a freakin' eyelash. Okay, what to write . . . *Visitor is female, mostly transparent, with no discernible reflection. She also appears to be hovering.*

Her dress is a pale, shimmery blue, with a short, high bodice and a floor-length skirt . . . very nineteenth century. She's wearing a pretty cap over her brown curls. She looks vaguely familiar (can't place her), and she's obviously curious, looking directly, disconcertingly at me, very possibly smirking.

With that officially recorded, I looked up, conscious that I should probably try to make contact.

"Hi, I'm Cate. Who are you?" I clenched my teeth, bracing myself for an answer.

It could have been my imagination, but it seemed like her mouth, already edged up slightly at the corners, edged up a bit more. It was tough to tell, seeing as I was also looking right *through* her, at the flowered wallpaper hanging behind her. Seems I needn't have worried. Beyond the subtle shift in her facial expression, she didn't answer. Maybe she was shy.

"Um, do you come in peace?"

With this question, I was sure of it: She definitely smiled, and it was a saucy smile. I think there might have even been a nod of agreement.

I smiled an awkward half smile, spared a quick glance for Courtney, prayed for a quick search and rescue, and then glanced down again, jotting *"Friendly"* on the clipboard. I wondered suddenly how she had died, and a shiver crept up my arms. What if it was violent—gory, even? What if she was angry . . . or crazy mad? I was now officially freaked out.

"Shit!"

That one word, emanating from the sink behind me, echoing my sentiments exactly, worked like two paddles to the chest and broke me out of my funk. This wasn't exactly the House of Usher. I was in the ritzy bathroom of a historic landmark hotel in downtown Austin, with Hollywood lighting and fancy soaps . . . conducting an interview with a ghost. *Get it together, Cate. It's not like it's a vampire.*

I jotted the questions as they occurred to me, desperately hoping she wasn't toying with me, biding her time, poised to launch into a terrifying medley of ghostly behaviors.

"Is your intention to be avenged?" I asked, holding my breath. *No.*

"Remembered?" Possible shrug.

"Just put your eye under the faucet, Courtney, and blink the damn thing out!" I said in an urgent aside.

"To make an impact?" Wider smile . . . maybe a wink.

"*On whom?*" Not a yes-or-no question. "*On us?*" That seemed doubtful. *Kind of looks like she raised her eyebrows—can't be sure.* Her stance seemed to indicate that she was waiting for something . . . possibly for me to get to the good questions. Or get the hell out of the bathroom.

I was beginning to wonder if there was any point to this . . . and the irony did not escape me. A ghost had found *us* and we—well, *I*—had no clue what to do with it. Where was Sportcoat when we needed him??

I heard the water switch off, and as I glanced back at her, Courtney was pulling a paper towel off the stack and dabbing the water from her raccoon eyes. Thank God!

Tossing away the trash, she slowly inched forward to retrieve Casper and lifted the strap over her head, busily tweaking and fiddling. She gave me the universal sign for "you're on a roll—keep it up," and I almost seethed with frustration. But I dutifully turned back to my insubstantial and uncooperative new friend.

"So . . . do you hang out strictly in the ladies' room? Or do you like to spook the guys every now and then?" I didn't even bother writing that down.

There was a snicker from Courtney, but I ignored it. It wasn't like she was coming up with any material. Our ghostly visitor answered with a shy smile and averted eyes. I should have known she'd have nineteenth-century sensibilities. Then again, I wouldn't be caught dead hanging out in the men's room either.

I glanced down at the clipboard. I didn't feel like I was closing in on anything.

"I'm definitely getting some EVP," Courtney said, tossing out the acronym that had stumped her less than a week ago. "Keep talking." She was nearly squeeing with excitement.

"Right," I said, utterly exasperated. Difficult as it was to believe, the novelty of seeing an actual ghost had pretty much worn off. With the absence of any spooky—or even mischievous— behavior, this one-sided conversation could just as easily have been occurring with my own reflection. *Suck it up for Courtney's sake. If for no other reason than to give her something titillating to discuss with Sportcoat.*

Pen poised over the clipboard, I pulled out a new question.

"Is there a message you want to deliver?" Oh my God, did she just nod?! *Yes!*

I scribbled onto the clipboard.

"Can you give it to me?" Another nod. *Yes!*

My blood pounded through my veins, proof that Courtney's excitement had rubbed shamelessly off on me. But as the moments passed and nothing happened, my whole attitude slumped in exasperation. Clearly I was going to have to pry the message out of her. But how? I stared down at the clipboard, fidgety with frustration, doodling in the margins. I knew that if I had to continue this ridiculous Q&A session, I might just lose it, ghost or no ghost.

"How about a hint . . . enough to get me started?" I scribbled the words out, simultaneously sending subliminal messages, willing to try anything at this point. I figured it was worth a shot. Evidently it was the million-dollar question, because her entire demeanor changed as soon as the words were out of my mouth. She tipped her head in a Mary Poppins sort of way—a sort of polite arrogance—unlaced her fingers, and gestured for me to look again at my clipboard.

I was midway through my follow-up question before I bothered to look, but it was never added to the formal ghost-sighting minutes because I was completely derailed by the once-friendly clipboard that had gone over to the other side. One by one, starting at the most recent and moving backward toward the beginning, the words were disappearing off the page as I watched. I would have dropped the clipboard if my hands hadn't curled into white-knuckled fists.

"Court!" I yelped, looking back, holding the clipboard out in front of me like it was a dead rat.

"I'm trying to get a picture of her," she said quellingly.

"That can wait," I insisted. "Get a video of this instead."

But the words were disappearing quickly now, almost flying off the page. And Courtney wasn't particularly keen on giving up her photo op, so by the time she'd switched to video mode and had her camera positioned over the clipboard, it was too late. The words were gone, only a handful left to grace the page, fodder for an utterly stagnant video, highlighting a scattered cookie-less fortune.

He is your K . . . Is it enough?

Chapter 13

"What the freakin' hell?"

That was Courtney. Unlike me, she wasn't yet used to words disappearing willy-nilly—she didn't know about the journal or Gypsy Jane. Me, I had a good hunch on the identity of the ghost two sinks down. The ghost of Jane Austen was here—in Austin, Texas—barely three feet from me, and I hadn't recognized her! Although in my defense, circumstances were slightly extenuating. Journal or no, she was probably the last person I would have expected to arrange visitation in a hotel bathroom, and yet it was unquestionably her. And I suspected I could read between the lines of this latest supernatural message.

Jane Austen is matchmaking me!

Evidently I'd made some poor assumptions, jumped to all the wrong conclusions, and failed to register that she was bent on setting me up with my Sunday Scrabble partner! A shocking, almost out-of-body revelation had me wondering, *Was it* her *idea that I hook up with Ethan?* Had those little fortunes brainwashed me into an ill-conceived romance? I'd admittedly been the one to suggest we try out the benefits, but the idea had seemed to come out of *nowhere*. Did her talents extend beyond the written page? Because word games I could deal with—mind games were going to be problematic.

I tipped my head back up, away from the latest snippet of advice, to see if I could wring even the tiniest bit of explanation out of her: Why Ethan? Why Austin? And why the silent treatment? To say nothing of, what's next? I was all over the map, but after the last couple of weeks, could she really blame me for having a surfeit of questions? Either way, she clearly wasn't in the mood to answer them; her little "smirk and shimmer" was gone as quickly as it had appeared. The pop-in was over.

Over a huge plate of nachos ordered off the room service menu, I filled Courtney in on the Gypsy Jane situation. Well, some parts. I was keeping Ethan's involvement out of it—for now. I was having a hard enough time dealing with the reality that Jane Austen herself, or more specifically, her ghost, had likened Ethan to the adorably dependable Mr. Knightley. Did that also imply that I was the Emma of the scenario? Because Emma wasn't my favorite of the Austen heroines—she was pushy and overconfident and utterly misguided. My thoughts whizzed about, skimming over the last couple of weeks as I attempted to keep up my end of the conversation.

"That night at the Trailer Park . . . you, me, and Ethan?" Courtney quizzed, wanting all the details. "You found a magical journal, enchanted by the *ghost* of *Jane Austen?* That tells fortunes and makes words disappear? All after I left?"

I nodded, confirming every bit of it with my lips pressed snugly together. The reality spoke for itself, and explanations were both disappointingly absent and superfluous.

"*Why the hell didn't you say anything?!* You let me drag you around the hotel, the two of us hunting ghosts like a couple of goobers, when you had one at your damn beck and call??" Her voice had risen to a shrieky pitch and then fallen off again, hurt and betrayed.

I sat up straighter in my chair, eager to defend myself, figuring now wasn't the time to press her on the goober thing. "Okay, first of all, I didn't know what I had for days. And I'm too embarrassed to even admit the ideas that flitted in and out of my brain in an attempt to explain the crazy behavior of that journal."

"And second?" Her face had softened slightly, and in answer, the tightness in my chest had relaxed just a bit.

"If we hadn't gone hunting, we never would have run across Sport—er, Micah." I smiled big to cover my bobble. "Or his equipment," I added, with a wink.

"And possibly not even Jane herself," Courtney finished, crunching into a chip heavy with cheese and black olives.

"Very true," I agreed. My eyes met hers, and together both pairs rounded like saucers. "That was beyond, beyond," I said, having no coherent words for what we'd just experienced.

"Damn eyelash," Courtney groused. "Damn camera. Damn slow reflexes. We essentially got nothing." She bit her lip, holding back a chuckle that if released would, no doubt, be at my expense. "Except the transcript of your exclusive, hard-hitting interview: 'Do you come in peace?'" The chuckle could no longer be held back and actually took the rowdy form of a guffaw.

We smiled at each other, truce called, and spent a quiet moment, each lost in our own thoughts.

"So do you have any idea what today's fortune meant? Who's 'K,' and who's 'he'? Is it Ethan?" she asked, clearly giddy with I-told-you-so potential.

"No idea," I lied, punctuating with a shrug and feeling only vaguely guilty. What was one more little white lie, after all? I wasn't even 100 percent certain that Courtney had read—or even watched—*Emma* (although she'd definitely seen *Clueless*), so confiding in her could well be pointless. I needed to work this out on my own.

"You don't have it with you, do you? The journal?" Her eyes lit up with vicarious possibilities, and sparkled and fizzed like fireworks when I drew the unassuming book out of my bag. I ate quietly amid the rasp of pages, the gasps of disbelief, and the oohs of junior high–style teasing. When she was all caught up (I hadn't mentioned that there was a key), she slapped the book closed, leaving her finger to mark the place, and leveled me with a steely-eyed stare.

"No idea? Seriously? You're either clueless or lying." She tipped the book back open to the saved page and read, *Ethan is sweet, serious, stable. Work your magic.* Then she tipped her head to the side and said, "You idiot—'he' is obviously Ethan."

"Really? So who is 'K'?" I countered, truly hoping that reference had stumped her.

She pursed her lips, thinking hard. "K, K, K . . ." She looked at me with a triumphant light in her eye. "Could it be a character in one of her novels?"

I shrugged, striving to look clueless. "Could be."

"Let's look it up!" And suddenly she was pushing away from the ignorant bliss of our nacho huddle to the business end of her computer. Her fingers hovered over the keyboard, and within two seconds, I'd caved under the weight of my guilty conscience.

"K is for Knightley!" I blurted, wondering if I'd have any secrets left by the time we parted ways. Clearly Ethan never should have confided in me—I could not be trusted.

"Uh-huh." She smirked, simultaneously searching her memory and gloating. "Knightley's the hero of *Emma*, isn't he? The best friend—the trustworthy neighbor—the sexy secret crush. Sounds about right." She reached for her travel mug. I wondered if she'd be able to stop grinning long enough to prevent water from dribbling out around her teeth. Then again, our bathroom fun had left her prepped and ready for a wet T-shirt contest, so it probably wasn't of particular concern.

She rallied quickly, as I'd imagined she would, no longer so inclined to be indulgent.

"Hold up! Less than an hour ago, you were trying to hook me up with Ethan. What the hell, Cate?"

I sighed. I'd known we'd eventually come back to this and was now feeling slightly crappy that I was telling lies of omission and disappointed that I couldn't dish on my secret life with Ethan.

"I thought the All-Powerful Jane was matching the two of you, so I was . . . facilitating." I smiled ruefully. "Now, I'm just in shock."

"Oh, we are so gonna make this happen, chickie. This has been a *long* time in coming. Now, you can go one of two ways with this, but both rely on the element of surprise and some serious flirting."

I'm sure I looked skeptical, feeling, as I was, that my life was already full to overflowing with the "the element of surprise."

"Option one: Bake him a plate of irresistibly fudgy brownies, because brownies are known to attract quality men. It's a fact."

She pressed onward, ignoring my eyebrows, which were turned down in disbelief.

"Are we talking special-ingredient brownies?" I asked coyly.

"No, just normal brownies."

"Has this method been recently tested on Micah?"

She blushed and fiddled with the nachos, trying to even out the toppings among the remaining chips.

"With great success," she said definitively, marginally distracted by her own thoughts.

"What's option two?" I pressed. I needed to wrap this up and get myself out of there. Parent Night was tomorrow, and I didn't want to be dragging by the time six-thirty rolled around.

"Option two is to offer up a little sexy surprise. And I'd say you've already got a jump on that one. Just send in Cat Kennedy," she suggested, a single eyebrow raised. "Let her do your dirty work."

I fought hard to keep my face impassive and my secrets well hidden. I tried pensive, dubious, and even shocked, feeling that none of them was a sufficient camouflage to cover my guilty-awkward feelings. And ironically, I think the indecisiveness was my undoing.

Courtney's gaze sharpened within seconds. If this had been a duel, she'd have had the tip of her rapier at my throat, insisting on the full disclosure that honor between friends demanded.

I shifted uncomfortably and distractedly reached for an olive.

"You've already *done* the dirty, haven't you? You are just full of naughty little secrets tonight, aren't you?"

I didn't answer. I couldn't. I hadn't a clue what to say to her. *It would have worked if you'd have given it a chance. . . . You and Ethan as the adorable couple, and me playing the mistress. . . .* I was really hoping I could blame that little lapse in judgment on Jane Austen, but I wasn't even sure she condoned "benefits." Difficult as it was to admit it, this might have been all me.

Courtney sat back in her chair, not judgmental, not angry, more . . . concerned.

"You need to figure a few things out, Cate. I think you're a little in love with Ethan—which doesn't surprise me at all, by the way—and you're afraid to take that next step. Maybe you never planned on ending up with Mr. Knightley, but that doesn't make it the wrong choice. I bet you can't even give me one definitive reason why he wouldn't be perfect for you."

I stared into her eyes, secrets fairly swirling in the air around us. I couldn't answer her—couldn't confide that the biggest reason was classified—a secret that, until two days ago, I hadn't known myself, and even now I wasn't sure what to do with.

"His feelings on brownies are unconfirmed," I finally answered.

"First things first, then," she said, managing a look of bossy compassion. "Full disclosure: *How was it with Mr. Chavez?*" She grinned at me.

"If Chavez is Clark Kent, then I found his phone booth, figuratively speaking." I giggled, wishing I dared to order a glass of wine and while away a couple of hours with a little buzz and a lot of girl talk.

"I could see that," Courtney said, nodding, her eyes nearly crossed in an effort to picture that. I snapped my fingers in front of her face in an attempt to derail the wanderings of her imagination and stood up, suddenly exhausted.

"I better escape while I can before word gets around that I'm interviewing ghosts, asking the hard-hitting questions. Right now I don't want to think about anything more confrontational than a bubble bath and a hot cup of tea."

I'd slung my bag over my shoulder and had my hand on the door when I turned to look back at Courtney.

"Court, are you good to keep all this between us—well, at least the bits about Jane Austen and Ethan? The sighting is fair game, as long as you keep it anonymous. I don't know exactly what I'm dealing with here, but I'd prefer to work things out without the whole world looking over my shoulder, if you know what I mean." I rolled my eyes. "Imagine all the amateur ghost hunters who would crawl out of the woodwork in response to a little leaked interview with you know who." With the CIA crawling out right behind them over an entirely different interview. But then Courtney didn't know about that. . . .

"Take your time. Just out of curiosity, is he in possession of a good fortune?" she teased.

She'd be surprised.

Tuesday I spent the hours between the last bell and the start of Parent Night in my classroom, grading papers and jotting down little notes on each student, making sure to have something positive to relay in addition to the struggles and expectations.

At six o'clock, an e-mail pinged its way into my in-box with a subject line I couldn't resist: "The Lost Work of Jane Austen." It was from Ethan.

It was a stop-motion video, starring my very own Jane Austen action figure (the hem of her white dress was stained pale orange as a result of an accidental spill), and the grin that broke over my face at the idea of this never faltered for the entire minute and a half of Austen antics.

He'd paired her with a G.I. Joe action figure, and together they conspired to send coded messages for secret missions while saving the world from bad romance. It was hilarious. But at the end, I could feel the prick of tears and a lonely lump of uncertainty in my chest. Ethan really was my K—nobody got me like he did; nobody could save me from myself like he could. But I couldn't afford to be as flippant as Gypsy Jane because it was impossible to know if that would be enough.

Somewhere along the way, it seemed that my search for the perfect guy had been hijacked. And not just by Ethan over Sunday-night Scrabble—by me. I'd seen too many people grow apart, reinvent themselves, get bored, and change their minds, and it was spooking me. As a result, I wore my insecurities on my sleeve, second-guessing every romantic prospect. Very recently that had come to include Ethan. I wanted forever, with a guarantee, and I was determined not to settle for less. So what did that mean for Ethan and me? I didn't even know what was going on with his life right now, let alone his past, so how could I predict how it all might change in the future?

Closing the e-mail, careful not to cry, I blinked away potential spillage, pushed back from my desk, and went to get a bottle of tea from the vending machine, figuring it was more respectable than my regular Orange Crush. I should at least try to give the illusion that I was a grown-up.

I left Jane to fend for herself, resting a proprietary hand on a bruised green apple, and she was still there thirty minutes later when parents started arriving.

Mostly the evening went as expected. I gave the same unre-hearsed mini-presentation six times and introduced myself to a hundred or so parents who came out to see just what it was we were teaching their precious babies. Things got interesting during my fourth-period class meet-and-greet. I'd just finished speaking to Raj's father about his son's sudden fascination with the Bolly-wood versions of Jane Austen's novels when Piper approached with her parents in tow. As she was introducing them, I felt a little click of recognition. I'd seen her father before—recently. It wasn't five seconds before I realized where: stepping into the Driskill as I'd been rushing out, in a hurry to distance myself from the ghost-hunting geeks . . . and Jake. And then again, slipping into an ele-vator as I'd watched from the mezzanine stairs. I smiled, on the verge of making the connection, when I noticed that the woman standing beside Piper, with matching green eyes and wide smile, was not the woman in the clingy coral number he'd been ushering possessively into the hotel. Mental math done, I fought to keep my expression from betraying any suspicion that I'd caught Piper's dad cheating.

There could be other explanations. I couldn't think what they might be, but that didn't eliminate the possibility that they existed. . . .

I swallowed, blinked, and lifted my chin, conscious of all of it. *Keep calm and carry on.* Piper's dad seemed awfully conscious of it too, but I powered through, chatting away with Piper and Mom, all while Dad eyed me suspiciously, as if expecting I might rat him out at any moment. It was painful. And as they moved away, I realized how very tense I'd been with the uncomfortable effort to ignore a stranger's secret. I smiled and imagined the adult beverage I'd be enjoying in less than an hour.

During the fifteen-minute rotation scheduled for my off period, I started packing my things to enable a quick getaway at the end of the night. I had my head tipped down behind my desk when I heard my classroom door click shut. I glanced up, relatively certain it was Ethan, and was rather shocked to discover that it was Piper's dad, back again. My heart fluttered nervously as I imagined an awkward confrontation, and I took a swig of tea, hoping to look relaxed. I almost choked on it.

"Hi!" I started, hoping my smile looked winning and unthreatening. Wishing his did too. "Back again?" Well played, Cate. Golden.

He didn't respond until he had his hands planted on my desk and he'd leaned his stocky, football player's body in to speak in a lowered voice.

"Why don't we skip the bullshit?" he demanded. I felt, suddenly, as if I were in the crosshairs, caught in an appalling attack of bad manners. "I'd have sworn it didn't register, but obviously it did. Your poker face sucks."

Then came the second click. Both our heads swiveled around to see who it could be. This time, it was Ethan. And the way he looked now, I had no trouble imagining him in the role of a secret agent.

He walked forward casually, but I could tell he was wound tight.

"I can't argue with the statement—just how it was made,"

Ethan said calmly. "And I can tell you that it's unlikely—if not downright ridiculous—that Ms. Kendall has not been truthful with you."

"Who the hell are you?" Piper's dad demanded, pushing himself up off the desk.

"Mr. Chavez, foreign language teacher. And you are?"

"Talking to Ms. Kendall alone." My name might as well have been a slur. "If you don't mind."

"But I do," Ethan said, coming close and then leaning back against the whiteboard running along the side of the classroom, crossing his ankles, seemingly completely relaxed. That made one of us. My heart was tripping along at a frantic pace, and my lungs had switched off a couple seconds ago.

Señor Bad Manners was silent for a moment, and then all bluster. "Okay." He glanced back at me. "Fine with me. You're both in it, then. I am a deputy superintendent of this school district, and the two of you can consider yourselves under investigation. You want to get into my private affairs—I'll get into yours!" He jabbed his finger, first at Ethan, then at me. I snapped back as if struck; Ethan didn't even flinch. "Get your skeletons ready for their close-ups. And enjoy your jobs while you have them."

He said all this in a hard voice, with a maniacal glint in his eye, and I could only stare in shock as he swept past Ethan and out the door, leaving it to bang on the wall in his wake.

"*Shit!*" I heard Ethan bite off the curse before looking at me and demanding, "What the *hell* was that?"

"A whole lot of crazy," I said, half-distracted in wondering if I actually had any skeletons worth digging up. Other than Gypsy Jane—and she wasn't exactly buried.

"Seriously, Cate, what did that guy want?" Now it was Ethan who was leaning over my desk, and the recent confrontation was edged out of my mind by a little impromptu fantasy. I blinked at him and looked away, focusing in on the carryall that still sat, half-filled, on my lap.

I shook my head in disbelief. "It was nothing. He knows I saw him go into the Driskill last week with a woman who is not his wife." I shrugged and rolled my eyes. "So he's a pig. I don't care—other than as it affects Piper, who happens to be in my fourth-period class," I clarified.

"Well, obviously *he* cares."

"So he's a prick. I still don't care. As pathetic as it may be, I don't have any secrets. He can damn well bring it on!"

Ethan stared hard at me, and the silence between us was like a roar.

"Wha—?" I started, shaking my head in confusion. And then I got it and slumped back, a little deflated, in my chair. Ethan did have secrets. Big ones.

I opened my mouth, unsure what might come out of it, but was saved the trouble of any response at all. The door was suddenly pushed open and voices swept in from the hall—free period of Parent Night was over. Ethan pushed himself off my desk, and with his mouth in a thin, angry line, dodged incoming parents to make his escape. I stared after him, overwhelmed with a feeling of stunned shock.

What just happened here? The entire five-minute episode had been utterly surreal. Was I truly facing investigation? Could my job honestly be in jeopardy? Could Ethan's? All because I'd been a pushover for Courtney and refused to be one for Ethan. I never would have recognized Bad Manners if it hadn't been for the ghost hunting, and if I hadn't pushed for answers . . . and benefits, Ethan might not have been so quick to come to my defense. Although, knowing Ethan, he still would have. Was this my fault? I preferred to believe it was the fault of Piper's overly ballsy father, but Ethan did seem a little ticked with me.

Maybe if I put my head down on my desk and whimpered pathetically, all of these students and their parents would want to disappear. . . . Crap. That was no good. It would probably be played to my disadvantage in the investigation: "Ms. Kendall shirked her obligations to parents during Parent Night." So I would smile and silently curse Bad Manners with all the dirty words in my repertoire, and then I'd go find Ethan and assess the damage. Maybe set things straight.

Or maybe not. Thirty minutes later, I'd fulfilled my responsibilities and gone in search of Ethan, but he wasn't in his classroom, the IT room, or even the computer lab. I texted him, got no response, and finally checked the parking lot for his sensible hybrid vehicle. Upon ascertaining that it was missing, I decided he'd gone off grid. No way was I going to chase him back to his house. It was possible he'd gone to check in on his other life. I would not be interfering.

I would go home and see what Gypsy Jane had to say about all this. Maybe I could convince her to make a little ghostly appearance in honor of Bad Manners, perhaps during a crucial moment of one his Driskill visits with the hussy . . . scare the crap out of him. Probably not the way she had imagined putting her talents and ghostly existence to work, but judging from her novels, she was quite a fan of the comeuppance. I wouldn't rule it out.

If she did put in another appearance, I hoped I'd handle it better this time.

Chapter 14

How on earth could a little against-my-will ghost hunting have taken such a wrong turn? I'd take last night's freak-out or even this afternoon's weepy confusion over this. I mean, what can I even do with this, besides stay on my best behavior and try to be there for Ethan? Or maybe it's better that I keep my distance, hope Ethan will drop off the radar and leave me to deal with this little bout of adulterous stupidity. To be the surprise superhero.

I let my hand go limp and tipped my head back against the couch cushions, utterly spent. I barely even wanted to think it for fear of jinxing myself, but honestly? I kinda wanted a little break from all the secrets. I clearly wasn't cut out to be a secret agent, and I seriously doubted my capacity to handle a "beyond benefits" relationship with one.

And maybe, in this particular instance, the job of the superhero is to create a diversion. At a pancake brunch, far away from Ethan.

I felt the familiar churnings of guilt that seemed to glom onto every aspect of my relationship with Ethan, but I plowed on. I hadn't even heard back from Jake, so there was no guarantee I'd even be engaging in any guilt-worthy behavior.

While it's true that Ethan and I dove headfirst into the "benefits" with our eyes wide open, keeping my little crush on Jake a secret is—perhaps—a little deceitful. I know how Ethan feels about Jake, and whether I agree with him or not, I should respect him enough to tell him. There probably shouldn't be any more partaking of the benefits either—at least until I can figure a few things out (and Ethan can deal with whatever a spy like him might deal with).

I tried to resist my gaze straying through my bedroom door and my thoughts straying two nights back, but it was impossible. My willpower is woefully nonexistent when it comes to sexy men, particularly geeky, sexy men . . . with glasses . . . and irresistible flashes of charm. . . .

I forced myself to stare hard at an electrical socket to get back on track. And realized that I'd never confronted Gypsy Jane about her Monday-night haunting. No time like the present . . .

Change of subject. What's the story on the ladies' bathroom at the Driskill? Honestly, that could have gone sooo much better. For one thing, you could have identified yourself from the get-go. Maybe I should have recognized you, but when it was clear I didn't, why didn't you just speak up? Questions could have been answered, plans made . . . just keep it in mind for your next visit.

Um . . . will there be a next visit? If so, I'd appreciate a little warning. Unless you're up for a more ghoulish haunting and want to teach a certain cheating someone a scary little lesson. . . . Let me know, and I'll hook you up.

I smiled ruefully to myself and tossed the pen onto the table, sparing a longing glance for the Dum-Dum bowl and its still-buried burner phone. Feeling like I should occasionally get something out of that bowl, I pulled out a cherry cola lollipop, unwrapped it, and popped it in my mouth. I was too wound up to try to sleep yet, and the absolute last thing I wanted to do was grade papers, so I unearthed the key to the journal and turned until I found where I'd left off.

It would almost seem as if pixies are at work, both in this journal and in this particular corner of England. The barest mention of prolonging my visit and a rather unexpected romantic crush, and here I am, fallen victim to both. Gifted with sunlight for the second day in a row, I fully intended to indulge myself in a ride about the glistening countryside. After all, it wouldn't be long before I was off to London . . . or so I imagined. I hoped I might find a riding companion—one in particular—hanging about the stables, but had no such luck, and so set off on my own.

I enjoyed a perfectly lovely ride until a motorcar blasted its horn from the nearby roadside, causing my up-to-now gentle-spirited horse to go positively berserk. I was unavoidably thrown and, I suppose, rather lucky to get away with merely a broken ankle. Luckier still that a certain someone had shared my desire for a ride and happened to come upon me, helplessly engaged in prying off my boot, like a conquering hero. Despite my protestations (and the silent ones of his leg), he managed, with some difficulty, to get me up onto his horse and then mount up behind me, but manage he did, and the ride home across the parkland was pleasantly awkward.

The doctor has visited, and I am instructed to stay off the ankle for at least a fortnight, and therefore obliged to postpone my trip to London. My knight in shining armor has since plied me with books and puzzles . . . and even a heady bouquet of roses from the garden. I fear the pixies have bewitched me. Either that, or the strange magic of this journal, whose workings I have yet to grasp fully, is responsible for my grand infatuation. I am not complaining. Not one bit.

While my eyelids fought to the bitter end, I eventually had to concede defeat and save all subsequent entries for another day. I'd pulled out the key, shrunk the journal, and was sliding it, out of habit, under the couch when it occurred to me that perhaps I'd had a little visitor while I'd been otherwise occupied.

Flipping to the relevant page, it was clear that I had. All she'd left me with was *it's the little surprise s that tell the story*

I could only assume that the "s" hanging by itself was meant to be attached to the "surprise." Evidently, I hadn't been as accommodating as a certain someone would have liked. Beyond that conclusion, this latest snippet had me stumped. It could be sheer exhaustion that was boggling me, and with luck I'd figure it out in the morning, but it was far more likely that I wouldn't, seeing as Gypsy Jane had made a habit of stumping me on a regular basis. Things might just have to play out on their own.

Wednesday went relatively well, considering Tuesday. I dressed normally (if possibly a bit more conservatively), acted normally (minus the Orange Crush), and tried hard to exude normalcy and respectability, despite having been recently threatened with joblessness and gifted with some nebulous life advice from an author the world considered dearly departed, but who was, in some ways, alive and kicking.

I didn't particularly care for surprises, unless they involved gifts . . . or cake. The discovery of a journal channeling the spirit of Jane Austen had been an exception, but I'd been reconsidering my position for days. Cake never gave me any trouble. Gypsy Jane, however, liked dishing it out on a regular basis.

What was the purpose of getting a little prophetic advice if it merely hinted at surprises? Unless you were Alice Cullen, life was full of surprises—that wasn't exactly a news flash. And it didn't help me with Ethan, Jake, *or* Bad Manners, whose nickname I was seriously considering switching to Big Shit.

When my free period rolled around and I still hadn't heard from Ethan, I went looking and found him holed up behind a posse of computer screens in the IT room. Judging by the intense look on his face, he wasn't doing a kitty puzzle.

"Hey," I said, my voice sounding shy and uncertain.

"Hi," he said patiently, his face shuttered, his hands still on the keyboard in front of him.

"Everything okay? Want a Coke . . . or an Orange Crush?" I was kidding, but it wasn't obvious that he noticed.

"I'm drinking water." It figured. Not fortified water, or flavored water, just water-water. Probably straight from the drinking fountains.

"Okay, so . . . I just wanted to remind you of tonight's little barbecue get-together at my mom's house. You still up for it?"

His gaze shifted away from me to the computer screen and as I watched, his eyes tracked back and forth across the screen. Three seconds passed. Eight. He didn't make eye contact again for thirteen seconds.

"What time?" he asked, clearly making an effort to be polite.

"Six-thirty," I said shortly. Then added, "Just bring your charming self," before stalking off.

I felt a little petty after that. He definitely had more at stake than I did. I assumed. What did I know about the lives of CIA agents? Only what I'd learned from the USA Network. As a peace offering, I dedicated my afternoon to making a chocolate layer cake with buttercream icing, Ethan's favorite. I also switched out of my lacy underwear into a pale blue cotton set. In the interest of comfort . . . and on the off chance there might be benefits. Naughty benefits.

I was, in fact, regretting that moment of weakness when Ethan stepped through the back door. Mr. Carr hadn't shown up yet, and Mom had just stepped onto the patio to fire up the grill, so for the moment, it was just me and him. And a truckload of awkward. Funny that a brush-off should be more potently awkward than sitting astride your best friend in white cotton underwear.

He'd brought a bottle of wine and proffered that first, perhaps as a peace offering of his own.

"You okay?" he asked.

"Yeah," I said, turning to set the bottle on the counter. "Is the wine a substitute for your charming self?" I teased.

When I turned he was behind me. In fact, his body had me trapped against the counter. I'd just heard a truck door slam, so there was a good chance Rodney had shown up. I crossed my fingers that they'd be flirting and chatting at grillside for a few moments, but I'd definitely need to disentangle myself soon. I'd promised myself I'd resist Ethan, no matter what, but I hadn't counted on him being *pressed up against me.* That wasn't playing fair, so as far as I was concerned, all bets were off.

I looked up at him as he lifted his hand to cup the back of my neck. He gave me two long seconds to refuse. I didn't.

I was tentative first, feeling my way. Nobody had reviewed the code of conduct with me for situations like this. On the one hand I felt like I should balk at this offer after Ethan's standoffish behavior recently, and on the other, I had no self-control whatsoever. I'm pretty sure Ethan wasn't keeping score, so it was an easy decision.

Two more seconds and I was up on the counter with him between my legs, and we were kissing like he was freshly back from a tour in the Middle East. I couldn't stop my fingers in their urgent quest to be everywhere at once, and I could feel my lips chapping against the stubble already shadowing Ethan's face, but I couldn't resist him. My mind was lost to everything but him.

It was actually the oven timer going off right beside us that had us springing apart, and me off the counter, my legs nearly buckling under me. Ethan caught my elbow until it was clear I'd rallied.

I'd been feeling particularly flushed and had attributed it to my reaction to Ethan, but evidently part of it could be blamed on a four-hundred-degree oven. But with nothing in the oven, we were left to assume that Mom had set herself a preheating timer . . . and she would shortly be in the kitchen.

Much as I felt like I should be looking anywhere but at Ethan, I ignored my own instincts and stared up at him, wanting to assess the impact of our impromptu make-up session. He didn't look flustered the way I felt flustered, but he definitely looked affected. It occurred to me that I could ask him what he thought about the journal's supposition that he was my Knightley. I suspected it would be rather fascinating to watch his expression when faced with that news. But I decided to go for show over tell—if nothing else, it was a way to get him upstairs.

"You want to come upstairs after dinner? I want to show you something. In the journal." My thoughts were already tripping me up.

Ethan stared down at me with a twinkle in his eye that I read as optimism that he was "getting some." I didn't disabuse him of the notion; I merely wondered if I had a matching twinkle.

"Can you pour me a glass of wine while I see if I can figure out what goes into the oven?" I asked, moving toward the refrigerator. I found some sort of Saran-wrapped casserole but, given that it wasn't readily identifiable, I wasn't enthusiastic about sliding it into a hot oven. "You want a beer?" I asked, holding a bottle in Ethan's direction.

"Okay, I'm stumped," I said, trading the beer for my glass of wine. "It looks like we're going to have to break up Mom and Rodney's romantic little tête-à-tête beside the propane tank if we're ever gonna move dinner along."

He moved with me to the door and stepped out right behind me to witness something so utterly bizarre that I simply stood gawping.

Mom was lying across the patio table with apparent disregard for the effort I'd gone to in setting the table, not to mention hygiene. Silverware was askew, napkins had flown off the table and were now caught in the shrubbery, and as I watched, two plates slid off the table to crash and scatter on the pavers below. And that wasn't even the unbelievable part!

Rodney was on top of Mom. Okay, he was bent over Mom, kissing her passionately—and somewhat obliviously given that he hadn't let up since we'd walked onto the scene. And even worse, his right hand was gripping Mom's left ass! Left *side* of her ass. Whoa! By the looks of things, Mom had gotten used to the idea of being set up, and sex was definitely not off the table. I'd bask in the rosy, contented glow of a match well made, but it was seriously all I could do not to drop my wineglass and consign its pieces to the fray. I tore my gaze from the sight that was now officially burned into my retinas and turned to Ethan, both shocked that he should be seeing this and relieved that he should be seeing this with me.

His eyes wide behind his glasses and a quirked smile playing about his mouth, he tipped his head slightly in the direction of the house. Excellent plan. We'd go in, pretend we hadn't been traumatized by the sight of two active seniors going at it on the patio table, and come out again a bit later . . . or not. At this point I was happy to leave them to it and just go for pizza.

We'd just pulled open the back door when I heard shifting behind me, then a creak, and then laughter, slow chuckles at first, that quickly turned into hysterical, gasping-for-breath giggles and guffaws as Ethan and I turned back to stare at them as they helped each other up off the table.

I eyed them both dubiously, silently wondering if they were both on some sort of sexual stimulation medication with a side effect of uncontrollable laughter. "You know, Ethan and I can go get pizza," I offered. "You can have the place to yourselves."

"Evidently we were too convincing," Rodney said, a huge grin splayed over his face.

"Well played," Mom said formally, offering him her hand.

"What are you two talking about?" I asked, wanting to be let in on the joke.

"This was just our way of telling you that we're not looking to be set up," Mom told me quietly.

"Well, you might try another strategy," I suggested, "because I'm not convinced." I glanced at Ethan, who looked to be biting the side of his mouth to hold back a smile.

"Why don't you get the chicken from the fridge, Rodney, and I'll break it to her gently," she said, winking at him. I frowned as she turned back to me. Judging by the way she took my arm and turned us toward the table, I could tell she was going to suggest we sit down, but I preferred to keep my distance from the patio table for the time being. Ethan drifted off into the shrubbery, ostensibly engaged in some activity with his phone. I wasn't fooled, but I was jealous. I'd like to vanish into the shrubbery myself.

"Break what to me gently, Mom?" I started, tipping my head to the side in irritated confusion. "I was here last week, Mom—you and Rodney hit it off great. So, why are you faking a passionate embrace—on the freakin' patio table?" It wasn't clear to me exactly what I was angry about, but I was definitely angry.

"It was just a joke, Cate."

"His hand was on your ass, Mom!" I nearly shrieked.

My mom forcibly squelched the humor on her face and switched to defensive posture. "So what if it was? If I gave the go-ahead, what do you care?"

I closed my eyes and shook my head, willing the two of us to reach common ground.

"Okay, so let me see if I can break this down. You're trying to tell me you don't want me to play matchmaker in general, and specifically not with Rodney, but I shouldn't freak out if I come across the two of you going at it on the patio table. That about it?"

"More or less, the point being that you won't be coming across me and Rodney doing it again." My relief was palpable. "But that doesn't rule out anyone else." Mom had switched to cagey, and I countered with suspicion.

"What are you not saying, Mom?" I had a sudden vision of a living room in utter disarray and a chocolate cake destroyed. "Are you seeing someone?" I quizzed, my voice raised in accusation.

Mom's chin jutted forward. "I am, yes."

"Who?" I demanded.

"Brady," she admitted with a soft smile.

"Brady? Is that someone from the garden club?"

"You met him, Cate. He's my Geek Freak," she said simply.

I couldn't have been more shocked. If I was any judge, Brady was a good five years younger than me. That meant my mom could be his mother. It also meant my mom was a cougar. Oh my God! I actually fell into a chair at the table and then looked over at the jumbled cutlery and wrinkled napkins and bolted right back up again. If her little grope with Rodney had been just for laughs, things with Brady could have gotten way more serious on this table. Naked serious. I shivered.

"What could you possibly have in common with him?" I asked.

"We both really like sex," Mom deadpanned before smiling mischievously. "I like going to Zumba, and he likes the results. He bought me a black lace thong, Cate!" That last part was confided in sotto voce as Mom leaned in companionably.

"Oh, dear Lord!" It was all I could manage. Until I thought, "What are you going to do when Gemma shows up?" and actually said it aloud.

"Introduce her," she said with a shrug. I'd had all I could take. I was taking my chocolate cake and going upstairs.

"Okay. Okay, Mom. This needs to sink in a little, I think. And seeing as you and Rodney don't need a chaperone, I'm just going to skip dinner and head upstairs. Ethan can decide for himself, but there is no way I am eating a meal on that table tonight. I'll scrounge for something."

I was certain Ethan had heard that—had heard all of it—so I slipped back inside, grabbed Ethan's bottle of wine, and found him in the shadows.

"If you want to have dinner with Mrs. Robinson, just come up after you're through. I've got the wine," I said, holding it up for display.

"I'll follow you," Ethan said, pocketing his phone.

"That was positively diabolical!" I was setting glasses on the coffee table, and Ethan was letting me rant. "And I am never going to get that image out of my head—not to mention the ones I'm imagining now that I know about the Geek Freak. What's the visual version of '*lalalalalalala*'?"

It suddenly occurred to me that I'd left the cake. I was just going to have to suck it up and go get it. And hope everyone was fully dressed and keeping their hands to themselves.

"Believe it or not, I have to go back down there. I'm not giving up my chocolate cake—*your* chocolate cake, seeing as I baked it for you. If I'm not back in five minutes, come looking."

"Would you rather I go?" he asked, the veritable picture of chivalry.

"No, I'll go. She's my mother," I said, sounding, I'm sure, very much put upon.

I left him smiling on the couch.

Nothing was the same when I returned, barely two minutes later.

As I breezed in the door, feeling light and happy for the first time in almost twenty-four hours, he was standing near the door, waiting. Wordlessly he held something out to me, and I glanced at it before refocusing on him, wondering at the total transformation. That he was angry was obvious, but I thought I detected a little hurt too, maybe even exasperation. WTH?

"I took a call for you while you were retrieving your cake," he told me, his voice cold, his eyebrow hiked up in a full-on confrontational manner.

I'm sure I looked confused, but then I glanced again at the object in his hand and recognized it for what it was—my burner phone. The one I'd hidden in the bowl of Dum-Dums sitting smack in the middle of my coffee table. The one whose number was a secret from all but one person, rather coincidentally the person Ethan had warned me away from on the day before he'd slept with me himself. I couldn't see this conversation ending well.

"How come you answered the phone?" I asked quietly, rewriting the last few moments in my mind, desperately wishing he'd just let it go to voice mail.

"Honestly? I thought it was you playing a practical joke. A burner phone in a bowl of lollipops—who the hell wouldn't answer that?"

"Who-oo was it?" I asked, my voice catching a little on the shameless misdirection. There was only one person it could be, barring a wrong number, and something told me Ethan hadn't gotten worked up by a drunk guy only able to muster a slurred "Duuude."

Ethan's lips curved up into a slightly scary smile. "It was Jake Tielman. But I suspect you already know that. He's returning your call. Wanted to let you know that he'll be at the brunch on Sunday. He hopes the two of you have a better chance to chat this time around."

I gripped the cake plate with both hands, frantically trying to hit on some way to fix this, to remind him that when we'd agreed to benefits, there were never any promises or any guarantees. But judging by the look on his face, there was nothing I could say that would make a difference right now. I needed to let him go.

When I didn't answer, he leaned around me and set the phone down on the little table beside the door. My eyes tracked his movements, and the smell of buttercream made me nauseous. Finally he spoke. "You could have warned me you planned to cast me as Rodney in the reprise. Gotta love a surprise ending," he said with a brittle half smile. "Thanks for the bit part." And then he turned and quietly stepped into the dark.

That was how Wednesday ended, and it pretty much set the tone for the rest of the week. About the only good thing that could be said about it was that Courtney and her ghost-hunting beau managed to score a forty-five-minute exploratory session in room 525. Apparently, they'd only managed to detect a vague supernatural presence before succumbing to the irresistible romantic allure of the double suicides rumored to have taken place in that room, not to mention the other freaky, unexplained phenomena. That was true love.

Clearly my matchmaking was going disappointingly awry. However . . . I suspected my mom had put the moves on Brady before Rodney was in the picture, and Courtney had obviously been keeping her hands off Ethan in some sort of misguided notion that I was in love with him myself. It was time to start fresh, with virgin territory. Dmitri was first on my list, and Gemma was right behind him. I hadn't settled on a potential match for her yet, but I still had a bit of time to figure something out. I chatted with her Thursday afternoon and hung up with renewed determination.

"Hey, Gemma," I'd started. "Is this a good time?"

"Anytime is good when it's you calling," she assured me in a slinky voice.

"Quit it, Gem. You know that creeps me out."

"Whatever you want," she gushed, and I could picture her licking her lips.

"Tell me you haven't been completely corrupted and that you

know how to turn it off," I begged. The last thing I needed was to introduce her to someone and have her huskily encourage him to talk dirty to her.

"Of course I can turn it off," she protested. "But I can also turn it on," she added suggestively.

I refused to respond to that, and the line went silent until she quipped, "I'm done, okay? I'm *done*. How are *you*, Miss Priss?"

"Just checking in, hoping to hear your plans for Thanksgiving."

I heard her murmur something on her end and prayed she wasn't multitasking with a customer on another phone.

"It's a quick visit this time—I'm a little behind in my research. My flight gets in on Tuesday afternoon, and then I'm leaving on Friday morning."

"Were you planning to drive up and see Dad?"

"I'll probably go up straight from the airport and then drive back to Austin on Thanksgiving morning. Anything I should know before I get there?"

I considered the question and decided to keep my answer simple. Maybe I'd catch her up over some s'mores. "Judging by our last phone chat, Dad's pretty much the same—I haven't been up there in a little while. Thought I might go up when you do. Mom is officially a cougar and is dating an undergrad computer geek named Brady."

"Go, Mom!" Gemma said laughing. "Tell Mom to invite him for Thanksgiving dinner. And Ethan too." There was another beat of silence as I tried to pin down her MO. She spoke before I did, changing the subject and making me wonder if I was being overly suspicious. "How do you feel about picking me up from the airport? I didn't want to inconvenience anyone, since I'd planned on driving up to Dad's, but if you're going anyway . . ."

"You have to promise *not* to talk dirty to me."

"What about flirty?" she countered.

"Not interested," I said, standing firm.

"Fine. But there are things you could learn from me. . . ."

"I know how to find you if I'm in pinch," I said drolly.

"Ooh! Sorry, but I gotta take this, Cate. Booty *calls!*" As ridiculous as it was, Gemma's naughty play on the overused "duty calls" never failed to lure a smile out of me.

"Bye," I said to dead air.

She needed a strong personality, quirky would be best. Someone not easily offended. No one of my acquaintance came immediately to mind. I'd have to give it some serious thought. Not to worry, I had time . . . and no one to spend it with.

I'd had an awkward chat with the school principal, wherein I'd tried to talk my way around the situation with the school board, without revealing that I'd seen Bad Manners skulking through a downtown hotel with a woman of questionable morals. I would have preferred not to give away the reason for my own evening visit to the Driskill, but decided it best to come clean and so launched into a babbling summary of my ghost-hunting activities. It was impossible to tell whether I'd gained an ally or ensured that Principal Ruffio would be keeping a close eye on me in the future himself.

Ethan stayed away, and I decided, for the time being at least, to respect his space and privacy. It was unfortunate (and damn awkward) that things had played out the way they had, but I couldn't help but think that maybe it was easier this way, and less awkward in the long run. I'd been second-guessing the "benefits" all along, and now I was even wondering if I'd made a slight error in judgment by throwing Mr. Darcy over so quickly in favor of Mr. Knightley.

I didn't bother writing in the journal—I was confident I could predict Gypsy Jane's response. She'd somehow finagle my next entry into a suggestion to apologize to Ethan (likely suggesting I grovel if need be), and get him back. I wasn't in the mood.

Friday night and Saturday I held a Jane Austen film festival all alone in my apartment. My intentions were threefold: I watched the Gwyneth Paltrow version of *Emma* to pin down the most direct way of separating the men in my senior British Lit class from the boys. The men were classified as anyone choosing the novel over a movie adaptation, and as a group were, rather ironically, dominated by the fairer sex. I watched the Keira Knightley version of *Pride and Prejudice* as a counterpoint, and found myself comparing Darcy and Knightley frame by frame. And finally, I watched *Clueless*, pondering Jane Austen's influence on modern culture, wondering whether I should reconsider my quick dismissal of her rather highhanded approach to journalistic integrity.

I'd give it some thought. But first I was giving it one more shot with Mr. Jake Tielman. In truth I was attempting to muster up the courage to kiss him. For real this time. I knew how Ethan's kisses made me feel—even the *anticipation* of one made me feel fidgety, achy, and on the verge of something wonderful. And while kisses weren't enough just on their own (and neither were *really* amazing benefits), they were a deal breaker. If Jake's kisses didn't inspire the same feeling of exuberant possibility, then I was cheating myself.

So that was my plan. Dress like a knockout and act like a siren. And remember this was a Sunday brunch. Should be interesting . . .

It took me a little while to work up the courage to abandon the security of my car and walk around the side of the house, through the garden gate, and out onto the wide expanse of tiered decking. The views took my breath away (well, the little I had available given my intentions), and I stood rooted to one spot gazing east toward the city skyline and then northwest along the river snaking its way into Texas Hill Country under a wide-open November sky. I wished, a little bit, that I was only here for the pancakes and the views. But I wasn't, and I needed to get on with it. The coffee was calling to me, and Dmitri was nowhere in sight.

There was a cold snap in the air today, and I'd been worried about chilly November breezes blowing over the cliff tops, so I'd tried to balance warmth with va-va-voom. I was wearing a curvehugging hunter green sweater dress, cinched at the waist with a cream and coral scarf, paired with dark tights and heeled loafers. I'd clipped my hair back in defense against the wind and wore little makeup besides deep red lipstick. I felt particularly autumnal.

There was a good-sized group already congregating around the mimosas, and I slipped in among them, looking for a familiar face.

I accepted a cup of coffee from Willow, who told me with an overly bubbly smile that Syd had just stepped into the kitchen. And there was Olivia, manning an impressive makeshift griddle on the home's outdoor barbecue grill. The smell of bacon was beginning to distract me.

I wondered if it would be good strategy to eat first and seduce on a full stomach. Then again, bacon breath might be a turn-off. I stared down into my coffee cup. Not to mention coffee breath. I rolled my eyes in utter exasperation. Not only did I not have a mint—I hadn't remembered my lipstick either. I couldn't help it; I wasn't used to getting my vixen on at eleven in the morning.

I turned to the buffet table, looking longingly as my stomach rumbled its opinion. On the end was a chalkboard menu, listing all the options, pancakes, and toppings. There were stacks of white plates just waiting to be plied with pancakes and bacon, bowls of fresh fruit garnished with mint, and a mind-boggling array of homemade syrups and compotes. I decided to risk it. I'd seen enough romantic comedies to know that guys actually preferred girls who liked food. Heck, I loved food—maybe a pile of pancakes smothered in blueberry syrup would play to my advantage. Afterwards I'd force myself to chew on a mint leaf and then scrupulously check my teeth before I put my plan into action.

In a quirk of perfect timing, I'd just finished discreetly swishing some ice water through my teeth when I turned to see Jake slip through the garden gate looking adorably cozy in a deep red sweater and butterscotch tan corduroys. I decided to waylay him before he had a chance at the coffee—for what I had planned, I needed him all to myself.

I'm proud to say I sashayed right up to him. My hair caught on a ruffly breeze, along with a handful of red and gold leaves from a towering pear tree, and for just a moment, I felt that the morning couldn't be more perfect. I couldn't have been more wrong.

"Good morning. Remember me?" I said, holding my hands behind my back in full-on flirt mode.

"The secret agent looking for Cary Grant? You are impossible to forget," he informed me, his eyes scanning the deck and the yard beyond. It didn't register that he might be looking for someone other than me.

"I'd hoped to have you to myself for a few minutes," I confided, my pulse suddenly riotous with nervous energy. "Before you go pancake-crazy."

This brought his gaze quickly back to me. We shared a secret smile. "I'm yours," he said, dipping his hands comfortably into his pockets.

"Excellent. I had a little experiment in mind." Feeling distractedly déjà vu, I remembered Ethan . . . and the kiss . . . and cursed myself for an utter lack of creativity.

"What sort of experiment?" Jake asked, his eyebrow adorably quirked with curiosity.

I stepped forward—one step. I was simultaneously working up my courage and playing the tease. "I'd like the answer to something I've been wondering about ever since you rolled up in your pajamas," I admitted slyly. I looked up at him from under my lashes.

"And what might that be?" Jake's smile hitched up at the corner.

I took another step, moving determinedly into his personal space.

"I'd like to know," I leaned slowly, inexorably forward, "what sort of k—"

"Jake!"

The familiar voice, coming unexpectedly from behind me, nearly tipped me off balance, but the awkwardness of getting caught in a compromising position at a pancake breakfast rallied me. I stepped back and swung around in one motion, feeling like I'd been spun out in a clumsy dance move. Only to see Syd approaching in black utility boots, with a belted wool skirt and vintage red ruffled blouse, her miniature sleeping dragon tattoo just peeking out from beneath the right cuff.

"Hey, Cate," she said, linking her arm with mine. "I've been stuck in the kitchen, dealing with a dishwasher disaster." She bumped her hip against mine. "You're a regular Pop-up Girl now, huh?" She turned to Jake and grinned, her face glowing with happiness. I glanced up to find him grinning back at her. I felt my lips curving into a grin just so I wouldn't feel left out.

"We can let her in on the secret, right?" Syd asked him.

"Why not," he agreed, expansively.

And suddenly I wondered if this had all been a setup. Jake had said he was a Pop-up regular . . . maybe Syd had told him about me, and I'd sauntered into that Hitchcock party all dolled up and raring to flirt and played right into his hands. Figuratively. I hadn't quite made it, literally speaking. . . .

Syd spun to face me and smiled with her lips while leaving her teeth locked tight together in a zany sort of grin. "It's gonna blow your freakin' mind," she assured me, probably mistaking the rigid set of my jaw for curious uncertainty.

"Blow away," I told her, conscious of the double entendre.

Her left arm shot out and hung there between us, her hand flexed and fidgety. I glanced at it and slowly registered the ring on her third finger—an artsy ring with a lovely, faceted ruby set in warm gold. It wasn't a typical engagement ring, but I knew instinctively that that was precisely what it was.

I looked up at Syd's shining, fresh-scrubbed face and smiled against the hurt. I held her chilly hand and examined the ring, not really seeing it, and then engulfed her in a fiercely protective hug. "My mind is freakin'." I admitted. "And blown."

By the time I stepped back, Dmitri had walked up behind me in navy jeans, a layered ensemble of T-shirts and sweaters, and Converse sneakers. He was also sporting a brand-new shock of neon orange hair gelled up in casual fashion. The man's timing was impeccable.

Once the introductions were made, it took him all of two seconds to size up the situation. Two seconds to realize that the pair of us had reached our lowest common denominator—as of right now, we were both here for the pancakes. And I'd already eaten.

We left the happy couple to dispense its news to other unsuspecting friends and even strangers, and Dmitri pulled me away to gossip over grapefruit mimosas. We stood on the farthest, chilliest corner of the deck, and I told him everything—refusing to leave even Ethan out of the confession. I was chilly and wishing I'd skipped the dress, glamorous as it was, in favor of pants and a sweater. And I discovered the hard way that Dmitri didn't dish "poor babys".

"So, you got your feelings hurt. Well, I'd say Ethan's got you beat. And that Jake dude was never going to be your 'one true love.' Because he's a Willoughby and you're an Elizabeth."

I turned away from the view and looked at him, intently curious. And more than a little shocked.

"You can stop your second tier wondering as to whether I'm gay. I went to college; I took British lit." His friendly bluster suddenly turned into a vaguely disconcerted defense. "Okay, I was curious about the world's fascination with Colin Firth. And I knew that if I could work even the smallest Jane Austen reference into casual conversation, you'd be impressed. And confused. And you'd won-der . . ." He dimpled at me, slung his arm around my shoulders, and turned us back in the direction of the food.

"Okay, now that I've played the part of your gay friend for the morning, I think I should be rewarded. I want pancakes. Stacks of pancakes. And bacon. And coffee. You might as well have another plate yourself. You're gonna need your energy if you want to se-duce Ethan a second time," he said with a wink. Luckily, any blush that comment might have elicited was simply swept up into the pink already staining my cheeks on this chilly morning that had gone completely and utterly awry.

Chapter 15

I didn't speak to Jake Tielman again. He simply disappeared. But after I'd hugged Dmitri good-bye, thanking him for his tough love and promising to be on the lookout for someone more suited than Syd to his unique personality (I'd told him that part too), I snuck into the kitchen and volunteered my services as a dishwasher. And that's how I got the whole story.

Syd had met Jake at the launch party for Pop-up Culture and been utterly swept off her feet. They'd spent a wild weekend at the Hotel San José (I did not need to hear that) and she thought that was that. But then he showed up at the next event, and the next, each time pretending they were strangers, flirting heavily, seducing her, and then disappearing. Until the next time. I didn't bother to ask whether Halloween had been an exception—I simply didn't want to know.

After a month or so of this, Syd looked him up (just as I had), pinned him down, and they'd talked. For lack of a better term, he was a trust-fund grown-up, hoping to springboard off his family connections and bank account to make a name for himself. But he was still, somewhat, in his mother's pocket, and Syd wasn't the sort of daughter-in-law she'd let quietly slide by without objection. So Jake was keeping Syd secret and finding other girls to attend high-profile or family events with him (which was why he'd invited me to his cousin's wedding).

Syd did what any self-respecting girl would do. She invited Mum to tea and sorted the whole thing out. Turns out Jake's mom *did* approve of Syd, thought she'd be a wonderful influence on her son, "despite the tattoos and occasional, indiscriminate use of the f-bomb," but encouraged Syd to keep that confidence between the two of them.

Jake had proposed the night before, apparently secure enough in his manhood to take on a firecracker like Syd, not to mention his mother. Syd was over the moon, while keeping two feet on the ground and both eyes open. She knew his faults—both the ones she'd discovered for herself and the ones his mother had thought prudent to mention—and thought it might be her job to fix him.

This confession sent a jolt right through me. He *was* a Willoughby, and everybody had seen it but me. How could I be an Elizabeth, worthy of a Mr. Darcy, if I couldn't even identify a Willoughby? Although, come to think of it, Lizzie had been bamboozled too, at least at the beginning. As wishy-washy as it sounded, I was beginning to think I really was an Emma . . . in love with a Knightley.

I didn't bother admitting to Syd that I'd almost kissed her recently landed fiancé. In all likelihood, she would have taken it in stride. But *I* wanted to forget. I'd made way too many mistakes lately, and I was facing a long lonely evening, with no Scrabble *or* benefits. Things were bad enough just as they were.

After that my schedule opened up again. I'd had a whirlwind couple of weeks, but now it was over, and I was floundering. Ethan had turned into the equivalent of a high school crush. I wanted him from afar, but didn't act on it, unsure of how he'd react. Courtney was busy ghost hunting with an *experienced* amateur who offered side benefits I couldn't, and Mom was instructing Brady on the care and feeding of cougars. And I was taking a break from Pop-up Culture for a while—Cat Kennedy was officially on hiatus.

I'd decided that my stint as a superhero slash sexy spy slash matchmaking siren had run its course. I'd even steam-cleaned all the glamorous vintage couture I'd had on indefinite loan from the shop and returned it—including the midnight blue dress that had started it all. I knew now that it wasn't critical to the happily-ever-after I wanted. The burner phone was unceremoniously tossed in a Dumpster.

The highlight, by far, of the week before Thanksgiving break was a Thursday/Friday screening—complete with teacher commentary—of the Gwyneth Paltrow adaptation of *Emma*. When gossip started swirling on screen about Jane Fairfax and Frank Churchill, I paused the movie for a little discussion.

"A piano is a pretty significant gift," I began offhandedly, strolling back toward Alex's desk with my arms crossed and the remote cradled on top. "Why do you think Frank Churchill sent one to Jane Fairfax, particularly when he barely knew her? Alex?"

I could feel a classroom full of gazes switching back and forth between me and Alex, and I waited, confidently curious.

Alex smiled at me. "But he did know her. He'd met her months ago at Weymouth and they'd gotten secretly engaged. He sent her the gift because he couldn't express his feelings in person. Same with Knightley hanging around Hartford all the time. Sort of like the way Mr. Chavez brings you coffee in the mornings."

Suddenly panicky, I swiveled my gaze around the room to gauge the class's reaction to this latest "connection." Quite a few weren't paying attention to my little sideline chat with Alex, but rather waiting to get on with the movie, but several students were nodding, ostensibly in full agreement with Alex's assessment of my relationship with Ethan.

I schooled my reaction, despite the *WTH?* flashing through my brain and the nervous, edgy feeling any mention of Ethan conjured. "Mr. Chavez *occasionally* brings me coffee, because we're friends. I do the same for him . . . *occasionally*," I told them, hoping that quelled any further commentary on a secret love life playing out between Ethan and me. *These kids are too damn perceptive.*

"And after Emma learned the truth of all this," I continued

briskly, "she felt guilty in gossiping about Jane Fairfax. What specifically had she and Frank Churchill speculated on, with regard to Jane Fairfax?" I stared down at Alex from my high-heeled perch, the classroom dark and silent, the movie on hold.

"What? Me again?"

"Why not? You're doing great," I encouraged, really hoping I could catch him with this one, shoot him the teacher glare, and get on with the movie.

He shrugged and answered. "She felt guilty hinting around that Jane Fairfax had fallen in love with her friend's husband." There were a couple of outbursts from the guys—a sort of audible shakedown—but I narrowed my gaze on Alex.

"You read the book, didn't you?" I accused him in a quiet murmur.

Alex feigned surprise and mild offense. "Of course I read the book!"

I leaned down, bracing my arms on his desk, and muttered, "There was no archery in the novel, Alex."

"I wondered if you'd pick up on that," the little smart-ass replied. Evidently, no one in my life was as they seemed. And secrets weren't necessarily secret.

I pushed myself off his desk, conscious of a new, grudging respect for him and the conflicted feeling of being outed in my "bonus feature" relationship with Ethan. Part of me wished I could still pretend it was our little secret, and the other part thrilled in the knowledge that these kids could see in Ethan the beginnings of a little crush. I just hoped it hadn't been trampled by everything that had happened. If I could just talk to him—explain about Jake, and what a fool I'd made of myself—maybe we could try again.

Feeling very wistful, I pressed Play and let myself imagine—in the dark—the sexy dependability of my own Mr. Knightley.

That bittersweet bubble burst when the bell rang, hurtling us all unceremoniously back to the twenty-first century. I slung my arm over Piper's shoulders as she moved slowly toward the door.

"Everything okay?" I asked.

"Not great," she confirmed, looking up at me. "My parents are acting kind of weird."

My heart took up an erratic beat, as naturally I was wondering if it had anything to do with my awkward confrontation with her father. Was a posse of investigators using her house as a headquarters to plan and execute my downfall? Or had her mother figured out that her father was a cheating bastard with delusions of grandeur? I kept my voice steady. "Maybe things will get back to normal during the holiday," I suggested randomly.

I gave her shoulder a commiserative squeeze, bestowed a heartfelt "poor baby" smile and an offer to talk if ever she needed it, hoping her situation wouldn't escalate and require a parent/teacher conference. In true head-in-sand fashion, I'd been tiptoeing around, trying not to call attention to myself, imagining that if I didn't catch anyone investigating me, then maybe no one was. Maybe it had all been a lot of bluster. I was also counting on the impending holiday season to work in my favor. Things would get dropped and forgotten, and I was hoping to be one of them.

Except where Ethan was concerned.

I had a sudden, urgent need to see him. He might not be ready to talk to me yet, and honestly, I wasn't decided on the best way to approach him, but right now there was a big awkward void overshadowing every day. In one way or another, he'd managed to insinuate himself into almost every little part of my life, and now all the bits were broken and I was having trouble putting them all back together again. Particularly as he was still the missing piece. . . .

I strode down the hall, cautiously optimistic, wondering if I could lead with the "secret love" bomb Alex had just dropped during last period. We could shake our heads in disbelief over the relationship savvy of kids today, and then, just maybe, concede that perhaps we shouldn't be so surprised that people could see the connection between us.

This little soda fountain fantasy fizzed off like a shaken up bottle of Orange Crush when I came around the corner and heard Ethan on the phone.

"Are you flirting with me?" A pause and then a warm, deep laugh. "You know that could get us both in trouble, right?"

I instinctively flattened myself against the wall outside the IT room, and then I bolted, running down the hall in heels, my A-line skirt shifting and sliding and my French-striped boatneck coming quickly untucked. Back in my classroom, I collapsed onto my chair and dropped my head in my hands.

Either Ethan had already moved on or else I'd never had him to begin with. Clearly my seniors had a bit more to learn about romance, because they were way off with us. With a tightness in my chest that I wondered if I could technically claim as a heavy heart, I packed my carryall for the long Thanksgiving break. I was powering down my computer when my phone chimed with a text from Gemma.

Did you invite everyone for Thanksgiving dinner? Dad's a no, but what about Ethan? And what about Brady?

I stared down at my phone, now feeling baffled *and* sad. Since when did Gemma care about holiday dinners with specific guests? We were lucky if she was around for the whole thing. I texted quickly back.

Not sure about Ethan. He might be busy. I'm sure Mom's asked Brady unless she's moved on to younger, meatier prey.

I was unlocking my car when I got her unexpected reply. There hadn't really been anything more to say.

Why not ask Ethan . . . he'll tell you if he's busy.

I rolled my eyes, not sure what her angle was, and glanced back at the school. I could go ask him. . . . No. I couldn't. I couldn't go back in there and invite him to a family dinner after I'd just eavesdropped on him talking to—*flirting with*—some other chick. I glanced down at my phone again and then threw it in my bag and got in the car, planning on drowning my sorrows in a basket of chips and queso at Torchy's.

A text came in as I was driving, and I nearly clipped an aggressive cyclist in my scramble to get to the phone, my desperation to hear from Ethan having ratcheted up considerably in the last few hours. But it was only another one from Gemma.

Bring your yoga clothes . . . downward dog forty feet in the air!

That was apparently what I had to look forward to over Thanksgiving break.

I was under the trees, braving the cold snap of a late-November breeze, staring down at the dregs in my bowl of cheese dip when I finally gave in and texted him. Giving in took all of two seconds; texting him took considerably longer. Whereas two weeks ago I would have tossed off a misspelled or autocorrected message and remained blissfully unconcerned, today I agonized over every character. Even punctuation was important. Not that it wasn't always important—as an English teacher I knew that better than most people—but it wasn't necessarily critical in a casual text between friends.

But I wasn't even sure we had that anymore. I hadn't spoken to him since the burner phone debacle. I finally decided on simple and straightforward, familiar but not forced.

You're invited for Thanksgiving dinner. And Scrabble afterward. C

I sat shivering all alone, grading papers at a picnic table in the shade until the sky dimmed to twilight purple, the fairy lights blinked on, and the dinner crowd started to arrive. I'd chosen to sit at the same table I'd shared with Ethan and Courtney almost a month ago . . . before Cat Kennedy . . . before Jake Tielman . . . before ghost hunting and Gypsy Jane. Before I'd made a colossal idiot of myself. I tipped my head to peek up underneath and check the table supports, just on the off chance that something else had been left to be found. A love potion or a magical scarf . . .

There was nothing. But if there had been, I so would have used it. I was that desperate.

I was packing up to go when his text came in:

Thanks, I'll let you know.

My shoulders slumped in defeat. Nothing. I got nothing from that. I couldn't tell if it conveyed distraction, uncertainty, anger, or a simple noncommittal maybe. Exhausted, I trudged back to my car and drove home and let one day blur into the next.

After a good amount of nudging from my mom, I called Courtney and invited her and Micah to Thanksgiving dinner. After she gabbled on a few minutes about Micah and ghosts, she asked how things were going with Ethan.

I cringed, but came clean. "He kinda found out about Jake. And then there was the cheating bastard from the Driskill. . . ." Naturally that prompted a whole new line of questioning, and a bit of nuancing to keep Ethan's secret life out of it.

"Aw, sweetie! If this were a noir film and you were still a femme fatale, you'd be ready to bitch-slap someone and make off with the cash."

"That does sound good," I admitted. "But I don't think that'll get Ethan to talk to me, particularly if he's the one to get the slap."

"Good point. What can I do? Want me to go back to the bathroom with Micah, see if Lady Jane reappears? Quiz her a little?"

"I appreciate the offer, Court, but you and Micah should probably stay out of the ladies' bathroom. Besides, I sort of have a feeling that she's connected to the journal and that she wouldn't make an appearance without it being somewhere in the vicinity."

"Gotcha. Hang in there, Cate. Knightley is a sure thing."

The sentiment was comforting. Trouble was, I wasn't convinced it was accurate.

I spent a good amount of time wearing sweats and my reading

glasses, poring over the entries in the journal. Not surprisingly, Gypsy Jane had been right all along, but I didn't need "I told you so"s. I needed practical, step-by-step instructions that I could meticulously follow in a effort to at least get Ethan talking to me again, beyond the prickly "Your e-mail is back online" I'd gotten via voice mail the Thursday before the weeklong Thanksgiving holiday.

Clearly that wasn't her style. So I let myself enjoy the romantic successes of others, feeling terribly martyred as I lay on the couch and dined on Chinese takeout.

It was miserable having to say au revoir to England, but in being so miserable I inspired Henrietta to loan me the use of her journal. This journal. I have heard about it—little snippets, odds, and ends—how it "solves problems" and "tells fortunes." I am anxious to try it out here in India, where I'm kept like a hothouse flower, away from any "damaging influences." Damn it, I <u>want</u> to be damaged . . . I do. Perhaps not in the manner Father is most concerned about, but in other ways no less diverting. I want to see a Bengal tiger and an Indian princess. I want to meet a concubine and pepper her with questions. I want to make a secret friend of the boy who brings me afternoon tea and lounge on silk pillows in men's trousers. But I need to know how to begin. A girl's imagination is only as enlightened as her experience will allow. Father says that's as it should be and an excellent reason indeed to lock me up. It's difficult to believe he doesn't realize that such a statement must be interpreted as a challenge. Which I've accepted, with your willing help, Dear Journal. Let us conspire. . . .

I read that last bit while biting into an egg roll and felt simultaneously pitiful and intrigued. I'd had a chance to conspire with someone, and I'd let it slip away. And now I was alone, vicariously conspiring, a century and a half after the fact. I flipped the page, being careful of greasy fingers.

Excellent suggestion! The perfect way to proceed. Henrietta is as absolute treasure to offer you up on loan, Dear Journal, and I wrote out an effusive letter of thanks just this morning, seconds after checking for your reply. After which I pestered Father for a visit to the market, insisting I needed a new parasol and some lighter fabric if I was expected to survive in this heat. He tried to suggest I let the house man go, but eventually I convinced him that I could not be satisfied without going myself. I'm to be escorted tomorrow. With that taken care of, I very casually foraged about the house, searching for a few items I consider necessary for the implementation of our plan. Now it is time for tea, and I have a few little thoughts of my own on how to draw out the tall, lean boy with the quick, mischievous smile. I will let you know how I get on, and otherwise behave as much as possible like a hothouse flower to divert suspicion.

Hmm. I had my suspicions as to how this would play out.

I had managed, quite elegantly, I believed, to attach myself to a hunting group that was venturing off into the jungle on the hunt for a troublesome tiger, but I didn't count on Father's deplorable lack of trust. Now I see that you tried to warn me. . . . I just wasn't clever enough to decipher the message. It seems I was spared "considerable danger and discomfort" by one of Father's junior officers, who'd been instructed to keep an eye on me . . .

That was all I could take. I didn't want to read about this particular adventure seeker and her Gypsy Jane Success Story. I could already predict the outcome: Irritation with this interfering junior officer soon gave way to an easy flirtation, and before long the pair had fallen hopelessly in love and ridden off into the sunset on the Orient Express. Not. In. The. Mood.

I also wasn't in the mood to pour my heart out only to have my words taken out of context and crafted into a little snatch of life wisdom that was completely irrelevant to my current, rather precarious situation. The truth was, I was itching for a confrontation. I'd tried calling Ethan on his cell, and when he didn't answer, I'd biked over to his house . . . but he didn't answer there either. Probably on secret assignment. Perhaps taking care of our Bad Manners problem with a little *Burn Notice*–style vigilante justice. I biked home feeling thwarted and more determined than ever to get into it with someone.

And that is how I ended up in the mezzanine ladies' bathroom at the Driskill Hotel on a Saturday afternoon. Holed up in the handicapped stall, carefully poised on a Texas Longhorn stadium seat that was teetering on the closed lid of the toilet. (I was prepared, if necessary, to vacate my impromptu headquarters, should the need arise.) I'd packed my clipboard, a bottle of Orange Crush, a bag of Chex Mix, and my clothbound Coralie Bickford-Smith copy of *Emma*. And, of course, the journal. I hadn't told Courtney I was here, nor that I was holding an amateurish sort of séance. Anyone who ventured into the bathroom would only think they were catching one side of a phone conversation. Admittedly a particularly odd one.

"I think you made the connection before I did, but now I've realized it: My life has turned into a parody of *Emma*. Every instinct I had about matchmaking was wrong, including the ones I reserved for myself. Jake was the rake in my tale of romantic woe, my Frank Churchill." I paused to take a sip of soda and lick the salt from my fingers, silently berating myself yet again for not having seen that. "And Ethan was my Knightley. *Is* my Knightley," I corrected. I was going to cling to that until all hope was lost. Gemma could just keep her hot little hands off.

"So what I really need from you," I continued, "is a little gypsy magic. I need a second chance. In other words, I need some more 'surprises' to finish out the story so I can earn my happily-ever-after. So . . . if you want to come chat, I'm here. Waiting. Hanging out in a bathroom stall." I paused in my little speech to see if anything would happen. Nothing did. I glanced around, wondering if the ghost of Jane Austen had higher standards than a little chat around a toilet. It was probably best if I just checked the rest of the bathroom.

I stood up, clutching my clipboard and ballpoint pen, and took a deep breath, feeling all jittery at the prospect of another ghostly visitation. I left the stadium seat in position and my day bag slumped in the corner and slowly opened the stall door. When I saw her shimmery nineteenth-century self perched primly on the bathroom counter beside the fancy soaps, the triumph of success was promptly edged out by "crazed celebrity fan" nerves and excitement. I was tempted to flick the lock on the bathroom's outer door to ensure that I had Miss Jane all to myself for a few critical minutes, but I couldn't bring myself to do it. If someone chose this moment to breeze in and freshen their makeup, well, she'd just have to deal.

I took a moment to bask in the unbelievability of the entire situation. I had summoned the ghost of Jane Austen. All by myself. While sitting on the toilet! That last bit would likely not make it into the retelling. Should I decide to tell anyone . . . Who was I kidding? Courtney was a must-tell, and Ethan . . . Well, if things ever got back to normal with him, I was going to use this little doozy to whip up on his logical ass! I'd never even gotten the chance to tell him about the first sighting, what with Bad Manners and the burner phone.

Suddenly my smile faltered and I was hesitant. If there'd been a secret mission associated with my turn at the Jane journal, it had been to hook Ethan and reel him in. But I'd failed. Judging from past experience with her close-lipped self, I probably shouldn't expect any poor babys. A glance at her face confirmed my suspicions. Her knowing smile and single lifted eyebrow were clearly willing me to get on with things.

I straightened my shoulders and hitched my clipboard into position. I figured if I wanted any response at all I'd need to get my words down on paper, but it seemed overly weird to chat up a ghost without a peep from either of us, and I didn't see her making any concessions, so I talked us through it too.

I'm all for skipping the small talk, particularly given that your lips are sealed and your poker face is utterly undecipherable. Presumably you have somewhere to be, and yet here you are, summoned by a chick who's been waffling between Darcy and Knightley and has misread virtually every clue you've left for me to follow.

My pen was flying over the page, scrawling out the bleak reality of my situation as my eyes blurred with prickly tears.

The last bit of advice I found in the journal was essentially that surprises make the story. I disagree. Not always. Occasionally a story plays out exactly as expected and still manages to get the job done, even wowing you in the process.

My voice had risen in urgency and was now echoing loudly through the bathroom, but I couldn't rein myself in.

Once Darcy thwarts that jackass Wickham (or at least does his damnedest in trying), I think every romantic soul in the world knows that Elizabeth will forgive him and that they'll end up together at Pemberley in a gorgeous happily-ever-after. See? No surprises there and still a swoon-worthy love story, even two hundred years later. You rock, by the way.

Come to think of it . . . I suppose Wickham counts as the surprise. . . .

Well, in my opinion, my own story has already had more than its share of surprises, and yet, it's missing the most important element. I don't have my happily-ever-after! So . . . I'm hoping that we can come to some sort of arrangement, whereby you offer up some additional, remedial advice, and I'll be extra careful to follow it. Basically I'd like to rewrite my ending.

I glanced up at this point, slightly chagrined that I was asking Jane freakin' Austen to tweak a few things. In any other situation I would readily concede her indisputable qualifications to call the shots, but not this one. Gypsy Jane could help me or not, but one way or another, I was getting my Mr. Knightley. I firmed up my smile and straightened my shoulders, hoping I was projecting confidence and determination.

My shimmery companion tipped her head to the side and glanced up to the ceiling, biting her lip. I couldn't tell if she was planning her escape or brainstorming possible alternate endings. I decided to keep jotting and hope for the best.

I haven't made any specific plans myself yet—so I'm wide open. Clean slate. Anything goes. My "secret life" might have fizzled, but I see no reason why there shouldn't be a little excitement, a little spark, a little sexy seduction. . . .

I was getting off task and so reined myself in with effort.

But as tempting as that sounds, it won't be enough. I need to prove to Ethan—and myself—that I can handle his secret life and not feel like an outsider. That I won't let my little insecurities and Austen hero crushes affect our relationship. That I love the man he is and don't want to change him.

I lifted my pen off the page and stood staring at the words I'd just written. The same words I'd just spoken aloud into the mostly empty room. Eyes wide in surprise, I let them dart around like pinballs, trying to take it in. I loved him. Somehow, amid the teasing, and the subtle flirting, and the long talks . . . and the *benefits*, I'd fallen in love with Ethan. And now he was MIA and I had no idea if he felt the same.

I let my eyes swing around to gaze in bemusement at Gypsy Jane and found her beaming at me with a ghost of a twinkle in her eyes. As I watched, she clapped her hands happily and raised her brows in encouragement.

Whipping my gaze down to the clipboard, I watched in awed amazement, with a nervous, thudding heart, as words began to disappear from the page as if sucked into the ether, to remain a secret, shared between Jane and me. Within seconds, there were only a handful left, and my eyes glazed slightly, wanting to read them, but not. An encouraging nod from my co-conspirator gave me the boost I needed.

Occasionally a man thwarts even the most careful plans. why not let him.

What the hell? That's it?? My eyes swung back up to confront my ghostly matchmaker, but she stayed only long enough to flash me a wink, and then she was gone, fading into nothing, shirking all responsibility. Shit! So her advice was to give up? What a cop-out—forget that! I was just going to have to come up with a plan on my own.

Assuming, of course, I could find Ethan and get him to agree to talk to me. Or even just let me do the talking. Maybe if I pulled out the l-word he'd pay attention. Perhaps not as close attention as he might pay to another l-word admission, but I'd take what I could get. He had yet to get back to me with an answer for Thanksgiving, but one way or another, I was going to pin the man down.

I stalked back into the stall and packed up my stadium seat and carryall, cramming the clipboard in next to the journal, spearing them both with a withering look. I was muttering angrily to myself when I carefully maneuvered out of the bathroom with all my paraphernalia and nearly collided with two blond beauty-pageant types with Texas-sized hairdos and tipsy laughs. I offered a blithe smile, said, "Watch out for ghosts in there," and hurried off, just slightly smug in the knowledge that I'd given them a little pee-your-pants excitement.

Chapter 16

I still hadn't come up with a definitive plan by the time I had to pick Gemma up at the airport on Tuesday afternoon. And from there the two of us were going straight up to Zippedy-Do-Da, my father's zip-line business in the Texas Hill Country, not planning to be back in town until early Thursday (or possibly late Wednesday). But I was confident that with a little distance and a little one-with-nature time, I would come up with something. And I had my phone. I was reachable. I might have to climb to the top of one of the canopy platforms or linger on one of the sky bridges to place a call, but I could find a signal.

Against my better judgment, and in direct opposition to the grudge I was holding, I tucked the journal into my overnight bag, just in case. I fully expected it to stay buried and forgotten, but I was kinda having an "anything goes" sort of month.

My good-byes to Mom were a little awkward for several reasons. Partly because she suspected something was up and that it had to do with Ethan, and partly because I knew the Geek Freak—*Brady*—was coming over and for all I knew the two of them were going to spend the next couple of days stark naked. My poker face was severely tested as she came to stand beside the car with a to-go bag of homemade oatmeal Raisinet cookies.

"Enjoy your road trip with your sister, and make sure your father knows he's invited for Thanksgiving," she said. "Did Ethan ever commit, one way or another? We'll have plenty of food, but it's nice to know who's expected," she added casually.

"Not yet," I said breezily, shaking my head and avoiding eye contact, easing the bag of cookies out of her hand, considering whether to stash them in the trunk instead of on the seat beside me. Where I'd be tempted to eat the whole bag while feeling sorry for myself. "I'll try to get a hold of him and let you know."

"He hasn't come for dinner in a while. Or Scrabble, for that matter." She paused. "Or if he has, you've been keeping him to yourself." The question was reaching, but I dodged it.

"I've barely seen him," I admitted, wondering if my voice sounded as watery as it felt. "He's been busy," I offered, an optimistic excuse for both of us.

"Well," I said and punctuated the single word with a deep breath let out quickly. "Enjoy your time with Brady!" An image of tossed pillows and a mauled chocolate cake flashed into my head, and I blinked and shifted, trying hard to dispel it. But as I leaned in for a good-bye hug, visions of Mom in dominatrix attire had me choking back a fit of giggles. I quickly slid into the car, but Mom held the door open.

"Two things I learned a long time ago, Cate: Don't hold a grudge longer than it takes to work your way through a pan of brownies all by yourself, and don't begrudge someone an apology if they deserve it."

"I get it, Mom. Thanks." I pulled the door quickly shut and waved as I pulled out of the driveway, already unzipping the ziplock.

It didn't take long before I blurted the embarrassment of the past weeks to an unsuspecting Gemma. I didn't mean to . . . it was mostly a defense mechanism against hearing any more fetish stories, which she was able to churn out one after the other. I very carefully kept Ethan out of it—the benefits, the secret life, the burner phone, and the flirty phone call. But otherwise, I had no more secrets.

"That sucks about Jake—he sounds like an immature prick. Trouble with the Cary Grants of the world?" She glanced at me and took a big bite of cookie. "The little shits know what they've got . . . *and* that we want it. We're powerless to resist, until we catch a flash of the man behind the charm and he's not quite the gem we imagined."

Actually this was mostly conveyed in a garbled, full-mouth mumble, but I caught the gist.

She dusted the crumbs off her fingers and resealed the bag of cookies.

"Any Cary Grants charming you over the phone?" I asked, tongue-in-cheek, but also seriously curious.

"Nah. Charm is the first thing to go when you're paying a dollar a minute for the call," she admitted, ever practical. "I'm like any retail clerk . . . taking orders and doing my best to fill them. Customer service is job one!" she said, punctuating with a jaunty fist pump and inciting a fit of giggles.

"So . . . are you seeing anyone?" I asked her as we drove past rolling fields dotted with scraggly cedars and the occasional, majestic live oak.

"Seriously? No."

"Frivolously, then?" I said, grinning.

She looked at me then, and the read I got from the quick glance I sent in her direction was that she was waffling on her answer.

"You're not going to want to hear this, but I have an arrangement with a grad student in the next lab over. Whenever time allows, and we're both hungry—or horny—we go out on a 'date,' and that tides us both over for a little while. On the rare occasion neither of us is hungry and the lab is empty, so . . ." She trailed off, and I turned to look at her, ready to comment on this.

A sexy memory of Ethan and me losing control in the computer lab quick-flashed in my brain, and I popped my mouth shut. It looked like the Kendall sisters were all about the benefits. Until they ran out.

"I'd let you set me up, but I've only got two nights at Dad's and one night at Mom's, so unless your specialty is one- and two-night stands, it's probably not a good idea."

She propped her feet on the dash, her toes sporting the chipped remains of bright green nail polish. Eye-catching, like the rest of her. She'd stepped out of the airport wearing narrow-legged khakis, zebra-stripe espadrille wedges, a pale pink, ruffly tuxedo shirt, with a dusty blue cardigan thrown over her shoulders and a necklace of chubby turquoise beads. I'd glanced down at my own denim capris and faded hoodie and grimaced. I actually *looked* like a woman scorned.

"Unless it's Ethan," she amended. "I'd be just *fine* with that. We already know each other . . . and I have my suspicions about the wild man behind that buttoned-down façade."

"Forget it," I said, a little heavy on the jealous girlfriend. "He may not even be around to fend off your advances. But you can have your way with Dmitri. He'd probably love you." I looked over at her. "With your direct—some would say slutty—approach and your worldly attitude. And with your phone sex experience, you're all set for a long-distance relationship." I chuckled to myself, and after a few seconds, Gemma finally spoke up.

"He sounds perfect!"

It was exactly the escape I needed. We stayed up late, curled up on chaises around the fire pit, and marveled at the far-flung scattering of stars in a wide-open sky. There was a brief touchy, resentful period when I felt like I was all alone in the world, abandoned by Jake, Ethan, and even literary darling Jane Austen. But that bit was short-lived. With Baileys and hot chocolate in quiet collaboration, I started warming up a little.

"I am *not* alone," I announced to Gemma, probably two hours after Dad had kissed the tops of our heads and headed in to bed. "And I'm not going to run from a fight."

"'Course not!" she agreed.

"I don't need to wait for a man to make the first move either." By now I was starting to confuse two separate problems in my mind. Bottom line, I needed to quit tiptoeing around and deal with both Ethan and Bad Manners; the order in which I accomplished those tasks was irrelevant.

"Damn straight! *You* are in charge of your own orgasm."

I squinted at Gemma, briefly considering whether that advice was useful in either case. Not likely.

"That's not what I meant," I clarified, snuffing out an impending giggle. "I meant I don't need a man to take the lead or to swoop in and save me. And frankly, I don't want to be in charge of my own orgasm—I'd rather it be outsourced."

The two of us dissolved into a fit of tipsy giggling.

"What do you need saving from . . . besides yourself?" Gemma inquired.

I looked at her, figuring I should object, but decided she was right. "A cheating bastard."

Her head swiveled in my direction. "Who cheated on you?" she demanded. "Nobody bothered to mention that little nugget!"

I felt my eyebrows dip down in exasperation. "Why would someone mention that to you? My life's not a soap opera—"

"You got that right." The comment was droll and unappreciated.

I glared in her direction. "Nobody cheated on me. I caught someone cheating and he freaked. Now he's trying to use his position on the school board to make things uncomfortable for me."

"Prick, the Second," she confirmed. "Let's deal him a crushing blow." She paused and held up her hand. "Wait. Who are you expecting to swoop in and save you? Your life's not a comic strip either—you'd be pinup curvy. Superheroes are few and far between."

"Ethan," I mumbled. "He was there for the 'outing.'"

"Ahh. Well, that's just coincidence. This is your fight. I am, however, available for consultation, and if you'd like to avail yourself of my professional expertise, I could offer you a freebie."

I sat quietly for a moment as an idea began to form in my mind.

I waffled a bit, knowing that my plan had the potential to hurt one of my students, but I convinced myself that perpetrating the deception was far worse.

Watching my face, registering the smile that signified that I was down with cold revenge, Gemma pulled out her phone with a flourish. Seconds later she pulled me to my feet as the Black Eyed Peas' "I Gotta Feeling" tumbled out of the speakers like fireworks launched into a quiet sky. We could pin down the details later. Right now we celebrated with a frenzy of arm-waving, butt-bouncing, girls'-night-out dancing, until we collapsed in awkward fashion, exhausted.

We woke up on the patio to a terrified shriek that had us bolting up off our lounge chairs, then suddenly shrinking back, lifting our arms in defense against the sunlight and eventually resuming the fetal position, certain that we'd merely heard a first-time zip-liner taking off down the wire, sailing over the trees. Anyone watching this display of ours against the panorama of scraggly oaks and spiny prickly pear likely assumed we were a couple of weirdos from Austin, practicing some sort of interpretive dance.

I'd fallen back into a groggy funk by the time the world intruded a second time. But I smelled coffee. Dad plunked down two stoneware mugs on the table between Gemma and me and shook the backs of both our chairs, making my teeth rattle.

"Did you girls sleep out here?" he said, the surprise clear in his voice.

I squinted, watching my arm snake out from under the covers to snag my coffee cup. Gemma was visible just beyond, a tousle of hair and feral raccoon eyes, watching me.

"Yes," I groaned in answer. "And my feet are like ice cubes."

"Well, it's warming up! Sun's been up for a while now," he said. I peeked up at him as he removed his hat and swept a hand through his slightly damp hair. "Some skittish ones up there today."

"We heard," Gemma said, shifting onto her back and taking a long swig of hot coffee.

"Why don't you girls stop lazin' around and get your cabooses up there? You can help me with the last few stragglers and then maybe take a ride yourselves."

Gemma groaned. "You have *got* to be kidding! Hearing one of those half-excited/half-nervous screams up close right now might be enough to have me jumping off the platform just to make it stop. There's also the possibility I might toss the screamer off. . . ."

With a headache pounding behind my eyes, I knew exactly how she felt. And shuttling through the sky on a suspension wire didn't sound doable either. I tipped my head up to smile weakly at my dad. "Maybe later? About all I can handle right now is a walk." I took a sip of coffee. "And even that's going to have to wait till I get this entire cup down."

"Well, get up, get something to eat, and come on. You got one day here, let's make it a good one!" Dad walked back inside and Gemma and I both indulged in "five more minutes," with caffeine.

Once the coffee had kicked in, things were better. The world started to feel less fuzzy and more deterministic. I breathed deep, imagined a little connection with nature, felt on top of the world. Nothing like planning a little revenge in the evening to wake up fresh. . . . Now I just needed to decide how I was going to play it with Ethan. Which reminded me, I hadn't checked my phone since before dinner last night. I had no idea if he'd called and RSVP'd.

I slid my legs over the side of the lounge chair and faced Gemma, already feeling fidgety with anticipation.

"So, you up for a walk?" I said, my legs bobbing up and down.

She peered at me out of one eye. "I can do a stroll."

"You can set the pace," I assured her. "I'm gonna get dressed— I'll meet you back here in . . . ten?"

"Fine," she agreed. Before I'd even turned away she'd flipped the blanket up over her head, evidently intent on squirreling away a few final minutes of private time. Once she was all the way under, I sprinted inside, cringing against the headache, hurtled up the stairs, and rummaged through my bag in search of the phone.

I had a single message, from Courtney, confirming her plans to be there for dinner with Micah. Nothing from Ethan. I threw the phone down in disgust, not sure who it was aimed at (the disgust), quickly changed, grabbed a hat and sunglasses, and fled.

Probably the reason I was five minutes early and she was five minutes late in meeting back up, giving me ten solid minutes to let the impotence of my situation fester. When Gemma appeared, geared up but still scoping out her surroundings like the paparazzi were after her, I plastered a smile on my face, tamped down on the coulda/shoulda/woulda train chugging out of the station in my head, and decided to enjoy this rare morning with my sister. I was fine with putting Ethan on hold—it was possible he'd already disconnected.

I shook my head, which was clearly jumbled with metaphors and crazy imagery, and took advantage of the fact that I was wearing huge, dark sunglasses. I admit, I let my eyes get hot and tingly with tears, but I refused to let even a single one fall. This was my idea of self-control.

I tried gulping in deep breaths of the cool, crisp air, drawing on the whole nature thing again, but mostly it just made me feel light-headed. Luckily, Gemma seemed distracted with her own thoughts, because I didn't particularly want to rehash it all and have it confirmed that I'd screwed things up royally. Gemma, I was sure, would get some sort of whispered lowdown from Mom during cornbread stuffing prep.

We took it easy, walking the relatively flat hiking trail around the lake. Halfway around we'd both found our stride and were pushing each other to an ever more brisk pace that, in the end, had us sprinting the last stretch, elbows out, jostling for position.

"Whew!" Gemma said, glancing around, probably hoping, as I was, that our little spectacle had gone unwitnessed. "Now I'm ready for breakfast. Or lunch. Or breakfast for lunch, yum! Let's see if Cheyenne will make waffles."

After a late lunch of pasta salad and garlic bread, with waffles promised for pre-Thanksgiving dinner, Gemma and I were sprawled on the leather sectional in the great room, flipping through Gemma's airplane reading, i.e., the impulse-buy glossy magazines she'd picked up in the airport.

"Want to ride the zip-line? Just once before it gets dark? It's kind of a tradition . . ." I reminded her.

Her face, a moment ago blissfully content, now scrunched in consideration. She glanced at her watch before posing a suggestion. "Why don't we go shower, brush our teeth, and change into our yoga duds and do a little meditation in the trees?"

I felt my eyebrows turn down in confusion.

"Why are we showering and brushing first?"

"Because you stink," she said, with a full measure of sisterly sensitivity.

"What?!"

"The sweat? The garlic? They're mixin', sweetie, and not in a good way. You'll feel better if you freshen up a little." She wrinkled her nose at me.

The possibility that I currently smelled like sweaty garlic jolted me out of complacency. I stood up, discreetly trying to smell my breath and pits on my way to the bathroom. When Gemma didn't move, I turned back. "Aren't you showering?"

"I'll be right behind you," she assured me, turning the page of *In Style* with a flick of her wrist.

"Should I meet you on One?" Technically, Portkey 1. Dad had read all the Harry Potter books and seen all the movies. After watching *Goblet of Fire* and seeing how a lone boot on a hill had transported Harry and friends to the Triwizard Tournament, Dad decided a zip-line was as close as Muggles could get to that sort of wild, free-fall mode of transportation. He refused to even acknowledge skydiving as a front-runner.

Gemma glanced up. "How about Five?"

"Is anyone staying in the cabin?"

"I do believe The Castle is to let at the moment," she returned in a stilted British accent.

The Castle was either proof that Dad was secretly a romantic at heart or that he was a keen businessman preying on the tender emotions of "those poor bastards." Built on a larger platform thirty-five feet in the air, the *cabin* was like something out of the *Swiss Family Robinson* movie. Crafted out of golden oak, the cozy little retreat boasted enough room for a queen-sized bed and a tiny sitting area. The three-sixty views were open-air, but there were gauzy white privacy curtains and a mosquito net draped over the bed, which was made up with all-white linens. Amid the rustling breezes and the sound of birdsong, it was a lovely little escape that seemed a world away—at least after the zip-liners were done for the day. Gemma and I had spent hours lounging on the down-stuffed duvet when the lofty cabin wasn't booked, each imagining a life as Roberta and debating the merits of Fritz versus Ernst.

You could only reach the cabin from Portkey 5, or a miniature bridge that led to a rustic little bathroom cottage, and in an attempt to keep The Castle experience as private as possible, we tried to avoid Portkey 5 whenever necessary. But if it was empty. . . . I was all for yoga on Five and then a zip-line ride down to the cushy comfort of the cabin.

"Five it is, then," I agreed and headed to the shower, where I let the tears finally have their way.

When I reached the top of the platform, Gemma was already there, looking suspiciously unfreshened. I narrowed my eyes at her.

"What happened to your shower?"

"I checked and I wasn't dire, so I decided to hold off till after yoga." She was fiddling with her phone, presumably cueing up some soothing music. She looked up at me. "Didn't you have any black yoga gear?"

I glanced down at myself, in purple pants and a bright, flower-patterned top. "Why? Is this throwing you off your Zen?"

"I'll keep my eyes closed."

I rolled my eyes in exasperation and laid out my yoga mat, appreciating my clean, fresh scent. Lavender mint . . . very soothing.

We took turns picking positions and specifying hold times, with

Gemma choosing the most overtly sexual of the standard poses and then adding a few of her own.

"You haven't branched out into pole-dancing, have you?" I quizzed, lying back on my shoulders with my hips up off the mat and one kinked leg in the air.

"Not yet," she said. I could hear the smile in her voice. "But I hear it's a great workout." She sat up. "Ready to take a ride?" Her eyebrows did a little Groucho Marx number.

"Sure. I'm done. My muscles feel like noodles." I reached for the harness and stepped into it, clipping it around my waist before slipping the helmet on my head. As I fastened it beneath my chin, Gemma clipped the zip-line carabiner into place at my waist. Then she turned quickly and grabbed her phone, grinning.

Seconds later, the *Mission: Impossible* theme was echoing through the trees, and Gemma was leaning in to speak to me.

"Your mission, should you choose to accept it, is to *close the deal*."

Her grin broadened and she took hold of the zip-line strap and gave it a good hard yank toward the edge of the platform.

Surprised, confused, and suddenly a little panicky, I grappled for something to hang on to. But there was nothing—even Gemma's hair was back in a ponytail I couldn't reach.

"Good luck, sweetie!" she said, right before she centered her foot on my ass and sent me flying out over a Hill Country panorama, replete with gorgeous fall color, native birds, and at the moment, a cornucopia of expletives.

The landing wasn't graceful, and that put Gemma even higher on my shit list. She was tramping on the tradition: We were supposed to sail gracefully into The Castle, like fairies, or at the very least, elegant young ladies. We were *not* supposed to catch our foot on the platform and go sprawling. Then again, we weren't supposed to be pushed either. Or squirming, *or* cursing like a sailor.

The moment I stopped I realized that *Mission: Impossible* was playing over here too. The dork. I quickly disengaged myself from the harness and removed my helmet, wanting to pummel Gemma with it. I peeked up through the canopy of leaves, toward Portkey 5, trying to get a glimpse of her, wondering if I should keep hold of the helmet in anticipation of her imminent arrival, but she'd obviously gone into hiding. Smart girl.

Now I had The Castle all to my fresh-smelling self, and I would use the opportunity to plan yet another bit of revenge. Smiling broadly with maybe a twinkle of menace in my eye, I stepped through the doorway and felt my heart stop as a thundering rush filled my ears.

Ethan was lying on the plush white down.

Fully clothed (that was the first thing I noticed!)—wearing faded jeans and a royal blue polo. He was lying in the typical hottie calendar pose, propped up on one elbow, facing the doorway. He lifted his phone, and suddenly it was quiet. Shockingly quiet. And we were alone. Glaringly alone, with only a soft, white bed between us. *Awkward.*

"Hello," I said, a world of inflection in my voice. I honestly couldn't decide how to react to this little surprise of Gemma's. I was *thrilled* to see him, but über-conscious of the fact that there were a lot of hurt feelings—on both sides—and I wasn't sure of my footing. I felt my face flush as I realized he'd seen—and heard—the unprecedented humiliation of my grand zip-lined entrance. Perfect.

"Hi." It wasn't much, but it was more than he'd said to me in nearly a week. Something loosened inside me, and I let out the breath I'd been holding. It was still a little hitched. And that's when I noticed the Scrabble board.

Lying on the bed beside him, the board already had words arranged on it with careful spacing. With each word building off another, wherever possible; it read: "I'm game, if you're game."

My gaze shifted back and forth between the board and his face. I was loath to misinterpret whatever message he was sending by showing up unannounced, conspiring with Gemma to be alone with me . . . and a bed . . . but I was also daring to be optimistic. I felt an encouraging glow of hope kindle inside me.

"What does that mean exactly?"

"It means," Ethan said, standing and walking slowly around the bed to my side, "that if you're willing to put up with my strange schedule, 'secret life,' and a nondisclosure agreement, then I'm willing to put up with your amateur sleuthing, amateur ghost hunting, and amateur matchmaking." His mouth quirked up in an amused smile, and I melted. I'd missed that smile. I fisted my hands to keep from touching him and twisted my lips in a rueful smile of my own.

"What if I go pro?"

"With what exactly?"

"Any of it." I shrugged in an "it could happen" sort of way and faced down Ethan's stare with my arms crossed over my chest.

I could hear the amusement in his voice when he answered. "You could probably win me over to your side, assuming there was no danger to your person," he admitted. "Or my reputation."

I rolled my eyes and pushed back. "Probably?"

"Very probably," he allowed, sitting on the edge of the bed.

"But there's no guarantee." Reaching his hand out, he wrapped it around my wrist and tugged gently, pulling me toward him on the bed. I resisted falling onto his lap, but just barely.

"There never is, Cate. If I'd do it for anyone, I'd do it for you. Good enough?"

I stared at his face, feeling suddenly incandescent, and grinned. "How could I ask for more than that?"

"I feel certain you'll find a way." His tone was dry and a little superior. So I pushed him back on the bed, falling over him into the pillowy down. He caught my hands and flipped me in what seemed like a well-practiced move. I was going to assume spy training and leave it at that.

The moment hung between us, our faces inches apart. We were beyond just benefits now—this was the real deal. We were going for it, the big win . . . the happy ending.

I bit my lip. "You're okay being my Mr. Knightley?"

"I've been your Mr. Knightley almost since the day we met. You were just looking for a Mr. Darcy."

"I could see that."

"*Now* you can see that." He smirked, settling a friendly kiss on my forehead.

Alone in The Castle with—I was certain—guaranteed privacy, this wasn't the time for forehead kisses. "You know, this whole thing is reminding me a *lot* of a James Bond film . . . the double cross, the riveting soundtrack, the daredevil action sequence . . ." I cocked my eyebrow up. "And now, the seduction scene."

Ethan's face broke into a giddy grin as his arms tightened around me. "Are you saying you want one of those kinky names?"

"I hate to burst your bubble, Chavez, but I'm imagining *myself* as James Bond, thus making you the Bond Girl equivalent. You just let me know if you want one of those raunchy names."

Ethan wasted no time in shutting me up, or stripping me out of my "spy duds" and finding ways to remind me that I was, in fact, the girl in this equation. But always one to have the last word, he couldn't resist uttering, "Oh, James!" as things progressed.

We spent the night in The Castle, curled up together against the chill, snacking on the provisions available courtesy of Ethan's planning instincts.

We talked through the last few weeks . . . about our impromptu slide into benefits, about Jake, Bad Manners, the CIA, and the silence. It was agreed between us that the silence couldn't happen again. If something went awry, we needed to regroup and talk it out, not simply "go dark." Ethan was being a particularly good sport over my espionage lingo, which was great, because I didn't think I'd be able to rein it in anytime soon.

He admitted that while getting that call from Jake on a burner phone buried in lollipops had irked him—"You could have told me. I can turn up the charm when I need to"—he'd really been mad at himself. I'd caught him off guard with my little Q&A and subsequent seduction. (Judging by the grin this mention brought on, I could see I'd be given full credit for this particular match.)

And then there'd been Bad Manners and his threat to investigate, "Which is nothing," Ethan assured me. "I'm taking care of it." After a quiet pause, he continued: "Honestly, I just needed to back off a little and figure a few things out. And Gemma called right in the middle of that."

That brought me up suddenly, and my hand stilled on his chest. *"Gemma* called you? Why? Was she working?" *Oh please, God, say no!*

"She may have called from work—I don't know—it didn't come up," he said, looking at me curiously. "The weird thing was she was a little flirty." He shook his head, slightly baffled. "Evidently your mom called her to discuss our 'little speed bump' and suggested she help nudge us along."

I sat up now, frustrated on two separate levels. "Why are the two of them interfering, and why the hell wouldn't they come to me?"

A slow grin settled over Ethan's face, and he tugged me back down so that I landed very cozily on his chest. "Because apparently you don't appreciate a little well-meaning help."

I rolled my eyes and tightened my jaw, silently conceding the truth of that assessment. "So Gemma called, and you answered, but you let *me* go straight to voice mail?"

"I wasn't ready to talk to you yet," he insisted, tightening his grip on my hand. "I didn't know what to say or how to say it. And I figured I was only going to get one chance to convince you to give me another shot." He reached up and tucked my hair behind my ear. "When she offered The Castle, I jumped on it. What could be more romantic than this? This is worthy of Mr. Darcy himself. Although I did consider donning a ruffly white shirt and some breeches, and walking out of the lake as you and Gemma hiked around it."

I giggled, raising an eyebrow. Clearly my insistence that Ethan watch the 1995 BBC adaptation of *Pride and Prejudice* with me had been the right decision. "Oh, really? You know you can't keep screwing me around. You're either Darcy or Knightley—you can't be both."

"Oh really?" I nearly giggled again at the pompous British accent Ethan assumed. "Why can't I be the estimable Mr. Knightley with the romantic sensibilities of Mr. Darcy? I daresay I can. That is, my dear, if that is what would make you happy."

My heart thudded heavily, and my throat was dry. As I gazed into Ethan's dark eyes, I marveled that it had taken me so very long to truly "get" him. Now that I had, though, I had no intention of letting him go. "*You* make me happy," I said honestly, and leaned down to lay my lips on his.

"What do you suppose your Gypsy Jane has to say about this latest development?" he asked huskily, skimming his index finger over my jaw.

I fought for concentration, trying to remember how I'd left it with her. Something about the man thwarting the best-laid plans. *Which is precisely how things had played out.* Not that I'd had a firm plan in mind, but I was working it, getting there. I would have. And he would have thwarted it anyway, because I hadn't been expecting him here. He was one step ahead of me, and so, it seemed, was Jane.

"I suspect she'd approve," I finally answered. The journal was tucked down into the bottom of my weekender, but we'd be having a little back-and-forth at my earliest convenience. Until then, I was on my own. Without the slightest concern for ladylike behavior.

I kissed him then with wild abandon, wanting to convey everything I felt in that one fiery kiss. As it swelled with urgency, I suddenly pulled away, caught my breath, and said, "Don't talk to Gemma on the phone."

A long time later, we'd pulled the Scrabble board out and started up a game. As usual my head was only half in the game. I fiddled with my tiles, shifting them on the rack, searching for a way to play on a triple-word score.

"What did you mean about the investigation and you taking care of it?" I said, looking up at him.

Ethan glanced up from his tiles, met my gaze and smiled. "I have a little surprise for you on Friday. You get to ride along on an off-the-books sting operation."

I raised an eyebrow in amused curiosity, but didn't say a word.

Ethan wouldn't tell before he was ready—I'd learned that the hard way—so I didn't ask. Instead, I let my imagination whirl with possible scenarios and thrilled at having Ethan firmly established in my life again.

And then I laid down my tiles to spell "DAZED" on the triple-word score, feeling that "dazzled" would have been more appropriate. Either worked. And forty-eight points was very respectable.

Chapter 17

Thanksgiving was a lovefest. Everyone but Gemma and Dmitri was coupled up, and from the looks of things, the two of them were chumming up nicely. Mom had decided to skip the turkey and cook up beer-butt chickens instead, a task she had delegated to the "boys." This basically involved them drinking beer and sitting on their butts, warming themselves near the grill while the "girls" prepped the rest of the meal in the kitchen.

"It's sort of ironic that things ended up the way they did," I said, rolling out homemade pie crust. "Okay, maybe it's not ironic. Maybe it's just weird that I envisioned a beer-butt Thanksgiving and imagined Rodney would be in charge of the bird." I glanced up at Mom from beneath my lashes, curious to gauge her reaction. "Maybe I have 'the sight,' but it's only one-eyed."

She stopped whipping her bowl of sweet potatoes, let go of the spoon, and propped her hand on her hip. "Do you know that I introduced him to my Zumba instructor, and now they're going out! I could have invited them, but I think I heard they were going to eat at IHOP today."

"No," I admitted, shaking my head in bafflement at the world in general and my mother specifically. "I didn't know that." And I wished I still didn't.

"*She's* twenty-six, so if I'm a cougar, what does that make him?"

"Young at heart?" Courtney suggested from her position at the sink, peeling potatoes. "You could use that term too."

"Oh, I like being a cougar, sweetie. It gives me a little edge." She winked at Courtney, Gemma, and me in turn. Any more winking and I'd wonder if she had a nervous tic. I held back my grin as I rolled the crust up onto the rolling pin and rolled it back off into the ruffle-edged pie plate.

"Sugar daddy?" Gemma proposed. She was supposed to be arranging a plate of crudités, but mostly she was just crunching loudly on carrot sticks. "Showboat? Casanova? Fan of flexibility?" I pinched the edges of the crust, spinning the pie plate until I'd gone around, cringing all the way.

That last one had us all laughing. Except Mom, who, troublingly enough, had a comeback for that too.

"It's funny you should say that, Gem. Because I recently quit going to Zumba—"

The three of us glanced at one another, wondering where this was going. I latched the can opener onto the can of pumpkin pie filling and twisted, waiting to hear the rest.

"—and I've been going to Pilates instead." She paused, I assume for impact. "You would not believe how tight my core is . . . and how extraordinarily flexible I've become. In just a couple of weeks. Brady is wildly impressed."

Lalalalalalalala!!

I didn't even look up. I left the can opener dangling from the can of filling and sailed around the kitchen island on my way to the door, fighting back the giggles. "I'm just going to go out and check on the beer butts." No need to specify. "Back in a few!"

As the door sailed shut behind me, I heard Mom saying, "What about the pie? The pie is what it's all about. How can any child of mine not get that?"

At that point, the hysterical giggles that were welling inside me could not be stopped. I staggered over to the group of men circling the grill who'd all gone abruptly silent. Ethan handed over his beer, and I took a long, steadying swig. Better.

"How's it going out here?"

"Fine," Ethan answered. "What's going on in there?"

"Just a little girl talk." I felt the hilarity bubbling up inside me again and took another drink of beer.

I noticed that now they all exchanged a look, probably realizing that, excepting Dmitri, they were very likely the topic of conversation. Any more time spent with Gemma, and Dmitri would be on the table too . . . so to speak. I smirked.

"I can't go back in there right now," I whispered to Ethan.

"Do you want me to go fill in for you?"

"You don't want to go in there either," I assured him.

I inhaled a deep breath of smoky November air. "Maybe I'll just take a minute to be alone. . . ." I suggested.

Ethan leaned in, turning his face away from the guys. "Is that code for something? And does it involve me?"

"It isn't and it doesn't. But if you want to start talking in code, let me know, because I'd be all over that," I told him.

The panic in his eyes assured me that we wouldn't be doing that anytime soon. I handed him back his beer and headed up to my apartment. I was finally in the mood to talk to Gypsy Jane. Settling on the sofa, in the still quiet, I waited until the giggles and the echoes of girl talk subsided.

I skimmed through the pages of the narrow little book (including the inserted sheets of notebook paper from two separate bathroom visitations), now graced solely with the advice she'd offered up in an effort to steer my path toward a happily-ever-after . . . *at times the answer is hidden in plain sight . . . an unexpected development can change everything . . . a perfect match demands an open mind . . . absence may In fact produce a very desirable effect . . . puzzle it out between you . . . There are secrets, and then There's Clueless . . . Ethan is sweet, serious, stable. work your magic . . . He is your K . . . Is it enough? . . . it's the little surprise s that tell the story . . . Occasionally a man thwarts even the most careful plans. why not let him.* She'd seen it long before I had—that Ethan was the one. She'd nudged me through my amateur investigation, hinted at his feelings for me (I suspected that's what the "Clueless" reference was all about), downplayed the burner phone in the lollipops situation (I suspected that might have been a big "little surprise"), and then encouraged me to back off so that he could take the lead on at least some part of our little dance of love. Looking back at the drama and frazzling uncertainty of the past month, I could see all the components of a quirky and elegant solution to Ethan's uncertainty and my utter obliviousness. We'd been in desperate need of an intervention.

I smiled, suddenly feeling very worldly wise, and started fresh on a new page.

Where should I even begin? Your entire association with me has involved a pattern of misguided behavior. You've witnessed every blunder and offered up consistent, useful advice throughout. I was just too blinded by my overactive imagination and a legendary love story to see it. You even mustered the fortitude, or gumption, or just plain shimmery goodness to appear precisely when I needed you. . . . (I honestly have no idea what it took for you to accomplish that, and I'm good if we keep it that way. You made Courtney's year, though—just sayin'.)

As embarrassing as it is to admit, I'm not sure if I would have reached this happy place on my own. Ethan was right there, waiting for me to notice him . . . and maybe to deserve him. I think it took a bit of a transformation, and maybe a few sticky situations, and even a supernatural event or two for me to discover what I want, and what I can do without. Things are different now: Darcy's merely a swoony fantasy. . . . Knightley's my reality. I will strive to remember that when Ethan goes dark and silent, as he is likely to do, and I'm left to ogle Colin Firth alone. (And I'd like him to remember that I'm really more a medley of Elizabeth Bennet and Emma Woodhouse than strictly one or the other.)

What I really want to say, though, is that you're amazing. Most of the world believes that yours is a legacy of six wonderful, memorable, timely novels, but the truly fortunate among us know you've written countless other happily-ever-afters. And that I happened to stumble onto the chance to be one of them is thrilling. (Or maybe it wasn't chance at all. . . .) To actually have the opportunity to "meet" you, as a benign, clever ghost with a magical touch, was <u>insane</u>. But I suppose it's time to pass this journal on to someone else. Anonymously. I'm sad to say good-bye, but it's just as *well. I think it needs to be just Ethan and me now—we need to figure stuff out for ourselves.*

But I hope this is merely au revoir. . . .

I tipped the journal closed, feeling very bittersweet. The giggles were gone. The silliness had dissipated with the feeling that I was losing a stellar sidekick. I'd have to think of a good drop spot and leave it up to Gypsy Jane to find another open-minded individual in need of a little romantic nudge. This whole thing had played out like a zany reality program: *Jane Austen's Happily Ever Afters*, and I'd played my part.

Just as others had played before me. It struck me that I'd missed a little opportunity. It hadn't even occurred to me to flip back a few pages in the full-sized journal to perform a little detective work on the person who had left the magical little book for me to find. Suddenly I was desperately curious. Extracting the key, I slipped it into the lock and waited, my breath caught, for the missing pages to slip primly back into place. Shifting the tome on my lap so that the back cover was face-up, I paged backward through my own entries until I'd reached that first world-rockin' one. My fingers quivered slightly with nerves and excitement as I turned back one more page.

Well, this is to be the end—my last entry. Despite her earlier exuberance and fangirl crush behavior, Beck decided to just "wing it" with Gabe without advice or magic or "whatever else you might be dealing"—her words. So rather than offer you up to someone else of my acquaintance, I've decided to go the message-in-a-bottle route and let you be found by some enterprising young lady (or, I suppose, gentleman . . . would that be weird?) who is looking for a Happily Ever After à la Jane Austen. I'll need to pick somewhere utterly <u>Austin</u>-tatious to facilitate the handoff of a totally <u>Austen</u>-tatious journal! I wish I could wait and watch to see who finds you, but this really needs to be a clean break with no hangers-on. I just hope whoever it is will realize the treasure they've uncovered with a little more grace than I did. . . .

Obviously the previous owner hadn't been quite as gung-ho about the disappearing words and secret messages as I had. With my dreams of femmes fatales, secret spies, and superheroes. She was probably totally sensible. I flipped back one more page and skimmed over the entry. Totally sensible. Who else mentions mutual funds in their journal? Particularly their magical journal . . .

For one split section I had visions of winning lottery tickets and my life as a day trader with a little insider information, but I quickly squelched them. That was so beneath Gypsy Jane . . . or Fairy Jane . . . or whatever her next incarnation might be. And perhaps a little illegal. I needed to be done—I had to pass the torch. Otherwise I'd obsess over the stories and the secrets forever, and convince myself that after *one more question* I'd give it all up.

I retracted the key, let myself savor the moment as the magic seeped back inside one final time on my watch, and then set the journal carefully on the coffee table. Averting my eyes, I dug around for an orange cream Dum-Dum and headed determinedly back downstairs into the fray of this year's Thanksgiving feast.

Things were precisely as I'd left them, and I slid back in without anyone missing a beat. Little did they know that I'd been chatting with a two-hundred-year-old literary legend, and that she had quite a bit of spunk left in her. Some spook too. Well, Ethan knew and Courtney knew, but neither of them knew *everything*.

I looked over at Ethan, who'd moved to the couch and was now watching the UT/Texas A&M game. I felt a little flurry of excitement spark inside me at the knowledge that this was just the beginning.

I took credit for the pie, despite having left it unfinished to escape the mother/daughter sex talk, and, topped with Cool Whip, it was my favorite part of the meal. Well, that and catching Dmitri staring fixedly at Gemma. If this had been an English country house, they would absolutely have "taken a turn" in the gardens after dinner. As it was, I think they might have groped a little in the ligustrum when no one was looking. I volunteered to wash dishes and spent the time linking each couple with a famous Austen pair. And then imagining muttonchops on all the men.

When we said good night, I made no secret of the fact that Ethan and I were going upstairs together, and we wouldn't be playing Scrabble. (It was possible we might be playing Scrabble, but that wasn't all we'd be doing, and that was kind of the point I was making.) We collapsed on the couch together, and I immediately put my feet up on his lap, remembering the night, weeks ago, that I'd been careful to stay on my side so as not to send the wrong message.

Ethan's gaze settled on the journal, sitting guilelessly on the coffee table.

"Whatever happened with the journal? Did you solve the mystery—find out how the words were disappearing?" With one hand resting on my knee, he put the other to use massaging my foot.

"No." I shook my head dismissively—somehow, it was magic, simple as that. "But that's not important. What's important— thrilling, even—is that she knew about us before *we* knew about us."

His hand stilled on my foot. I glanced at the pair and then shifted my gaze to Ethan's face. His eyebrow was raised in wry amusement.

"Jane Austen's been keeping an eye on you for two years?" he demanded, referring to the beginning of our friendship.

"It's not out of the realm of possibility," I mumbled, pulling the book off the table and gripping it with both hands. "But fine, she knew about us before *I* knew about us—happy?"

"I would have been happier if you'd been a tad more perceptive at some point in the past two years," he said seriously, starting in on the massage again.

I decided to let him have that one.

"Well, she held my hand the whole way—even when you didn't," I told him, adding a little sass. "She even showed up . . . to clarify a few things." It may as well have been an intervention.

"What do you mean she showed up?"

"I mean the *ghost of Jane Austen* made an appearance in the ladies' mezzanine bathroom at the Driskill—*twice*. Words disappeared off my clipboard—seriously, it was like a supernatural magic show, and Court and I were the audience volunteers. And you can just wipe that disbelieving smirk off your face, because I have proof *and* a witness. At least for the first time."

"She did two shows?"

I glared at him. "Can you be adult about this?"

"I'll try to keep my eyebrow under control," he promised.

I rolled my eyes. "*Thank* you," I condescended. "She basically confirmed that you were my Knightley—if I wanted you."

Ethan smiled to himself. "And you figured I was your best chance to get in on the action of life as a fictional character?"

"Something like that." I nodded, unable to keep a smile from splitting my face. "And now that I've bagged you, I need to give someone else a shot at Gypsy Jane's matchmaking prowess. I wrote my last entry earlier this evening."

"I wondered if that's where you went." His hand slid up my calf, and even a buffer of denim couldn't keep the goose bumps from cropping up in tingly wonder. "And did she offer you one last piece of advice?"

"I haven't checked yet," I said. He raised his brows, making a silent suggestion.

Resigned to the reality that this was my last hurrah with a magical journal—and with Jane herself—I edged my fingers over the little book's binding, the raw edges of its pages, and its pretty little curlicued hardware. Then I slowly turned back the cover and paged once more through my days as Cat Kennedy, my stint as a secret agent, my misguided attempts at matchmaking, and my uncertainties about Ethan. Till the very last page, which read:

every love story is different. yours happened to have a ghost. au revoir.

My lower lip came out, and my eyes felt hot and itchy with tears. I looked up at Ethan, whose face had softened at the reaction. Without a word, I handed him the book and sat up, clinging to his arm and laying my head on his shoulder.

Ethan read the words on the page and then tilted his head so that his face was only inches from mine. "For a high school English teacher, you've had an interesting couple of weeks." He tipped the journal closed and set it gently back on the table.

I straightened up a little without letting go of his arm. "How do you know that's not just a cover?" I asked him matter-of-factly.

"I don't," he admitted. "But I can find out . . . and I plan to be very thorough in my investigation."

"Knock yourself out," I said smugly.

The smugness fell away when he shifted suddenly, pushing me back on the couch under the weight of his very solid body. His breath was hot on my neck, and his hands were already skimming up under my sweater. And I smiled to myself as I murmured, *"My* Mr. Knightley."

Luckily, Ethan didn't call me on the quote, which had come directly from the movie.

"I can't tell if the awesome outweighs the lame, or vice versa," I said from the passenger seat of Ethan's parked car. A car that reeked of garlic and fried beef. En route to our "off-book" sting operation, we'd darted into the parking lot at the corner of Second Street and Congress when we'd seen the Chi'Lantro food cart flip open its serving window. We figured lunch would help us kill time during the surveillance lull. Rookie mistake. After eating two bulgogi tacos and dousing the fire with a medium-sized Coke and half of Ethan's medium tea, and then sitting, inactive but for the Words with Friends game raging between us on our iPhones, I was bored and desperate to pee.

Ethan had called in "backup" about fifteen minutes ago, reporting that the subjects were both on the premises. His actual words were "They're both here; whenever you're ready."

When he hung up, I verbally flayed him. "Whenever you're ready?! Call them back and tell them we're ready now, and *we have to pee!*"

His head was already bent over the word game, but with a sidelong glance in my direction, he said, "They are so psyched for this that they've probably already peeled out of the parking lot. I'd go odds that one of them even tried sliding across the hood of the car, feeling a little Bo Duke. And I don't really have to pee."

I gritted my teeth. "They" were fellow "Language Officers" Ethan had solicited to play along with this little Black Friday payback. I'd already spent a good five minutes teasing Ethan over his badass job title, but my mood had darkened slightly under the pressure, and I was willing to go for round two.

"So are you guys like real-life, legitimate grammar police?"

His gaze slid in my direction, but his expression didn't shift.

"We step in if the occasion warrants," he deadpanned.

I couldn't help it; I started laughing, and immediately pinched my legs together to prevent an unfortunate accident.

"Real-life agents aren't nearly as cool as they're written for TV," he said a little defensively, shooting me a sidelong glance. "We get the job done without resorting to MacGyver tactics."

"Maybe it's the MacGyver tactics that keep the agents from dozing off. Come to think of it, the way Hollywood writes 'em, the agents don't bother to wait for backup. They just go in guns blazing, tie things up, and then go out for a drink. And maybe a bathroom break."

"Jack Bauer never had to go to the bathroom," Ethan said. "In twenty-four hours."

"It was the adrenaline," I snapped. "And I'm stuck on empty, sitting in a parked car playing virtual Scrabble. When is the damn backup going to get here?" I asked, trying to keep the urgency out of my voice, glancing in my side mirror, hoping I could make backup appear by sheer force of will. "How about we detour to the nearest convenience store while we're waiting? It'll take me two minutes, tops."

Ethan reached behind him and produced an empty water bottle from the floor of the backseat. He offered it to me without even glancing in my direction.

I stared at it belligerently. "You planned this, didn't you? You ply me with spicy foods so that I gulp down a jumbo drink, then tell the backup to come whenever the hell they're ready, keep me sitting here for an hour, so I'm desperate to pee, and then hand me a freakin' water bottle?!"

Ethan chuckled. "If you recall, it was your idea to get tacos. And you ordered a *medium* drink and then decided to drink half of mine."

"Dammit, Ethan!" I swung my gaze around to seethe out the window, wondering if I dared go squat behind one of the giant inflatable Santas already decorating a handful of lawns on this street. Clearly these people were proponents of the "decorate for Christmas to kill time before Thanksgiving dinner" way of thinking. My only defense for even considering such tacky behavior was that it was a freakin' emergency.

"I'm sorry, but I can't let this opportunity pass me by," he prefaced, before saying. "Badly done, Emma. Badly done."

I was poised to start pummeling him with the empty water bottle when a black sedan appeared at the end of the street. If this was backup, I'd gladly put my revenge on hold.

The sedan rolled up to the mailbox at the target residence, and two guys got out wearing suit jackets and white button-up shirts with no ties. And aviator sunglasses. Their slicked-back hair glinted in the sunlight. As the driver walked around the hood of the car, he glanced casually in our direction, smirked, and then gave Ethan a thumbs-up.

"So much for keeping a low profile," Ethan muttered, glancing at me with a similarly snarky expression. I was wearing my hair tucked up into a red beret and face-swallowing sunglasses. Not to mention a scarf wrapped high on my neck. But from the neck down I was totally generic.

"What?! I don't want to be recognized!"

We both trained our eyes on the ivy-wrapped, redbrick house and its crisp black door as Ethan's fellow agents, clearly thrilled at the opportunity for a little fieldwork, knocked and waited. Piper's mom answered and then turned, calling back into the house. Shortly, Bad Manners was filling the doorway, his hand resting comfortingly on his wife's shoulder. Ethan had brought me up to speed on the plan over lunch, but when the agents knocked, he handed me an earbud, tucking a second into his own ear.

"Sir, I'm Agent Prescott and this is Agent Aberly. We're here because you are a person of interest in an ongoing investigation centering around the Driskill Hotel in downtown Austin."

It was difficult to tell from a distance, but it seemed as if Bad Manners blanched and adjusted his attitude from dismissive to fidgety with a side of bluster.

"That's ridiculous," he said, turning to his wife. "Mer, if you want to just let me handle this, it's obviously some sort of mis-understanding." Bad Manners looked past the agents, out over his yard and into the street, probably wondering if any of his neigh-bors were spying on him. As his gaze skimmed over Ethan's car, I fumbled for the seat adjustment, pulling it hard and going down with a jolt. Ethan stared down at me. I smiled, showing teeth, pre-tending it had been intentional.

"No, James, I think I want to hear this," I heard Mer say. Good for her!

Agent Prescott went on. "We've had the Driskill under surveil-lance for weeks, sir. We suspect a couple of major players are using it as a headquarters for a high-end drug ring supplying politicians and corporate executives. We have footage of you entering the hotel on several different occasions with a woman we've long sus-pected to be both a courier and a call girl."

I heard a gasp through the earbud and inched myself carefully back up, peeking over the dash.

"What are you doing?" Ethan asked calmly.

"Trying to be inconspicuous." I felt the beret slump slightly.

"I don't think he'll come after you again after this is all over," Ethan surmised. "If he's smart, he won't want the trouble."

"He's not smart—he's an idiot."

"True, but I'd wager he's an idiot with excellent self-preservation instincts."

"Still, their daughter is a student of mine. I can't help but worry about how all this is going to affect her."

"Do you seriously think she and her mom would be better off not knowing the kind of man he is?"

"No," I muttered. "But that doesn't mean I want her hearing it from me."

"She's not hearing it from you," he said, clearly striving for patience.

"No. I'm just a spectator, gawking over some invisible crime scene tape stretched around her lawn."

"Right." Satisfied, Ethan turned back to get a little perspective on the snatches of conversation we were getting. I rolled my eyes, but paid attention.

"I have nothing to do with any of that," Bad Manners blustered. "This is all one huge misunderstanding."

"Perhaps you could help us understand, sir." From the sound of things, Agent Aberly had been cast in the role of Good Cop.

Silence. My lips curled up in vengeful anticipation. I wasn't proud of that.

Bad Manners stared hard at the agents, probably wondering if he could threaten them with counter-investigation. He glanced at his wife, wiped a big hand down over his face, forehead to chin, and finally looked out over the lawn again, staring in our direction, with a clear view of Ethan in the driver's seat and the top three inches of my head just cresting the passenger side dash.

"I was . . . having an affair. For Christ's sake, I met her at a school board conference. I can't believe she was moonlighting as a courier for drugs and sex for hire. I never paid her anything!" The bluster fell away as quickly as it came on. "Just the occasional dinner . . ." He turned to his wife with a hangdog expression. "I'm sorry, Mer. It didn't mean anything. I've already broken it off."

Mer did not respond. With two sidesteps to the left, Mer distanced herself from the whole proceedings.

"Okay then," Agent Aberly said jauntily. "I think that about covers things. You're *not* a drug lord or a courier, but you *are* a cheating bastard. Definitely not a person of interest. Good to know."

Ethan grinned. "I told them to tack that onto the end."

"We'll let you know if we need any further assistance with this investigation," Prescott said warningly. "But I'll have to insist that you not discuss this with anyone. Otherwise you could be charged with interfering with a federal investigation. And if that happens . . ." Agent Prescott let the warning hang in the chilly air between them. "The U.S. government will be all up in your ass. We'll know if you cheat on your taxes, if you accept illegal kickbacks, and if you don't pay your parking tickets. In short, you'll be our bitch."

A laugh escaped before Mer could stop it. With her fingers covering her mouth, she settled her chin in her palm and shook her head slightly, no doubt in disbelief. Bad Manners had chosen not to respond and instead seemed to be grinding his teeth down to the nerves. He glanced again at the car, squinting in the winter sun. He'd obviously made us, and I was tempted to toss him a cheerful wave, but I didn't. For Piper, I didn't.

Then the agents nodded briskly to Piper's parents, turned, and started down the driveway, Aberly stripping off his jacket before he'd even reached the car.

The house door slammed, bringing an end to the sting operation. The status of the marriage remained to be seen. I would have to keep an eye on Piper and make sure she knew my door was always open. As long as her father didn't wander in. The black sedan pulled away from the curb and sailed down the street past us.

I flipped my seat back up as Ethan started the engine. He glanced at me assessingly. "Sorry you came?"

"Yes and no," I admitted. "Take Piper out of the equation . . . and maybe the wife, and I would have been all over this. But with them involved, it just seems cruel. Although he totally had it coming," I said quickly, hoping to derail Ethan's exasperated defense.

"Well, with any luck, he's done with us."

I looked over at him. "You're a pretty handy guy to have around. Is that the sort of thing you do for the CIA?"

"What? Knock on doors, concocting stories about imaginary drug lords while confronting real-life adulterers? No. I'm just a computer geek, intercepting messages, then decoding and translating them."

"But you're still considered a spy," I pressed, turning to look at him.

Even in profile I could tell his grin was huge. "Technically, yes."

"I don't suppose your fluency in French and German is why they hired you."

"No. The German is sometimes useful, but I only learned the French to get girls."

"Naturally. Well, it's clear you have all sorts of secrets up your sleeve. We'll see how long you can hold on to them," I said, smiling. "At least we didn't have to resort to bringing Gemma in. I shudder to think how that would have gone down."

Ethan laughed. "I hadn't thought of that. I'll have to remember her unique qualifications in the event I'm asked to assist in any future takedown operations." I'd filled him in on Gemma's quirky little side job, which until now I'd figured was better kept in the family, during our night in The Castle. He'd said only that he'd had "suspicions." Don't we all. . . .

"I have unique qualifications too," I reminded him. "I could be involved."

"I'll keep that in mind," he said, no doubt remembering my little bladder issue.

Clenching my legs together, I leaned down, reached into my bag, and pulled out the journal.

"Want to go with me to drop this off?" I suggested, my heart tensing just slightly at the finality of it all.

Ethan pulled up to a stoplight and turned to look at me, and my hands clutching the journal. "Do you have somewhere in mind?"

"Yes, I do. And it just happens to have a nice bathroom," I said. "Corner of Sixth and Lamar."

After a couple beats of silence, the corner of Ethan's mouth quirked with amusement. "Needle in a haystack strategy, huh?"

"No," I corrected him, fingering the binding, the pages, and the hardware one final time, saying good-bye, "This is me making one final match."

Indulging myself in one last look, I paged to Gypsy Jane's latest little bit of wisdom:

every love story is different. yours happened to have a ghost. au revoir.

So much had happened. The biggest and best development was the shift in my relationship with Ethan, but not to be dismissed was the fact that I was no longer jealous of literary characters. I had my own story, with the stellar potential for a perfectly lovely happily-ever-after. And like it or not, it would very likely be read by the journal's next owner . . . and the next. I tipped the book up and peeked down into the narrow darkness along the spine, checking to make sure the journal's key was wedged inside. It was. All that was left was to leave it for someone else to find.

Pulling into the BookPeople parking lot on the busiest shopping day of the year, we were lucky to get a parking space. But otherwise, it may as well have been any other day, a melting pot of students and hippies, yuppies and musicians—typical Austin. I felt like the world was streaming past me while I held tight to the journal. Like a fast-forward sequence in a movie, time was spinning out, and I was only catching snatches. I imagined this was how it was for Gypsy Jane too. . . . When Ethan's hand touched my shoulder, everything righted itself and time slid back to normal.

"I thought it was an emergency," he said.

"It is," I admitted, "it is! Hold this for me?"

I was back in two minutes, tugging the journal from Ethan's hands, selfishly wanting this last minute. I led the way up to the second floor and wove through shoppers in the literature section until we reached the selection of Jane Austen's novels. Thankfully we had this section of shelves to ourselves for the moment. I brushed my fingers over all the pretty versions of her six wondrous novels until Ethan's hand brushed my waist and I was forced to get on with things. With one last look at the journal, I slid it discreetly into the narrow space between the tops of the books and the shelf above, wondering how long it would take to be found, and whether the person who was lucky enough to find it would rise to the challenge.

Ethan grabbed my hand, and after allowing myself a single look back, we walked down the stairs and out into the late November afternoon. Now it was just he and I, going it alone, no Gypsy Jane to intercede. I took a deep breath of crisp, chilly air and let it out. Then I glanced up at him.

"You in the mood for a movie? A little Jane Austen gone Bollywood . . . ?" I waggled my brows suggestively.

"How can I resist?"

"Why would you even want to?" I said, giving his hand a squeeze. "We can stop at Sonic on the way and get one of those giant Route 44 drinks to share."

"I think I might like to get my own."

"Okay. But we can still share, right?" I said, only half-teasing, linking my arm through his.

"I guess I had two years to have my own drink," he conceded. "While I was waiting for you to make your move."

I looked up at him. "While you were crushin' on me and keeping your hands to yourself?"

"Hey, I'm a gentleman," Ethan said, blushing adorably.

He was. And for two years he'd hung on, and waited, and we'd become inseparable. There had been secrets, yes, but they'd been kept in the interest of national security. Whether or not that was technically true was irrelevant—that was what I was telling myself. He'd been steady, faithful, and utterly unshakeable, and I didn't doubt that he was a keeper.

"The perfect gentleman," I concurred. "And I am going to take full advantage of that fact," I said grinning, already making plans.

Did You Miss *Austentatious*?

In this quirky, sexy novel set against the lively, music-filled backdrop of Austin, Texas, a young woman learns that romance can wreak havoc with even the best-laid plans. . . .

It started innocently enough. While browsing in one of Austin's funky little shops, Nicola James is intrigued by a blank vintage journal she finds hidden among a set of Jane Austen novels. Even though Nic is a straitlaced engineer, she's still a sucker for anything Austenesque. But her enthusiasm quickly turns to disbelief once she starts writing in the journal—because somehow, it's writing her back . . .

Miss Nicola James will be sensible and indulge in a little romance. Those twelve tiny words hit Nic like a thunderbolt, as if her diary was channeling Austen herself! Itching for a bit of excitement, Nic decides to follow her "Fairy Jane's" advice. The result: a red-hot romance with a sexy Scottish musician who charms his way into Nic's heart in about five seconds flat.

Sean MacInnes is warm, funny, and happens to think Nic is the most desirable woman he's ever met. But a guy like Sean doesn't exactly fit into her Life Plan. With no one but Fairy Jane to guide her, Nic must choose between the life she thought she wanted— and the kind of happy ending she never saw coming. . . .

"Goodnight's breezy style with a believable heroine, lively conflicts and lots of best-friend confidences elevates this above the usual chick lit fare."—*Publishers Weekly*

"*Austentatious* is a fresh romantic adventure with a cast of characters who kept me turning pages way past my bedtime."
—Cindy Jones, *My Jane Austen Summer*

"This humorous romance will appeal to all Austen fans while bringing a fresh twist with its magic journal." —*Booklist*

"Janeites and chick lit fans alike will enjoy this wonderful romp into modern day romance with the ideal Miss Matchmaker from the past leading the way."
—Courtney Webb, *New York Journal of Books*

"Magnetic, compelling, and comedic—*Austentatious* is a novel you should not miss! This romantic and magical adventure is sure to entertain and delight fans of Jane Austen and the Austenesque genre!" —*Austenesque Reviews*